In Satan We Trust

TABLE

CHAPTER 1	SATAN SAYS
CHAPTER 2	THE BIRTH
CHAPTER 3	MEETING GOD ALMIGHTY
CHAPTER 4	CHRISTMAS ON EARTH
CHAPTER 5	THE FUTURE
CHAPTER 6	MOTHER NATURE
CHAPTER 7	THE DARE
CHAPTER 8	TOO MUCH INFORMATION
CHAPTER 9	LAST CALL
CHAPTER 10	LUCIFER & SALIENE
CHAPTER 11	IT'S SHOWTIME
CHAPTER 12	REINDEER GAMES
CHAPTER 13	THE LIGHTHOUSE
CHAPTER 14	VISIONS
CHAPTER 15	IT'S NOT ALWAYS AS IT SEEMS

IN SATAN WE TRUST

It's Not Always As It Seems

BY: SEAN KIERNAN

In Satan We Trust

Chapter One – Satan Says

Is this how it ends? Or, is this just the beginning? Does your life really flash before your eyes? Is it always as it seems? I asked myself these questions many times in the past, but, now that the end or the new beginning is so near it is literally a matter of life or death for me to know sooner than later the answers to these questions. Is there merely black and white in Heaven? I'll bet there's a fine gray area in Hell. And a lot of people have difficulty discovering that gray area. Do gray areas cause overcrowding in Hell like most of the country's prisons? Is there a "get out of Hell free" card or "Head straight to Heaven, do not collect $200, do not pass Go" ticket? If that's the case, what happens when Heaven is at maximum capacity? Do angels go to Hell? Does Satan ever discuss overpopulation with God? The answers to my questions will be answered shortly – good or bad! It's not always what it seems.

The shiny, silver mortuary slab was as cold as a witch's tit, as high school aged boys refer to girls not yet ready to 'give it up'! I couldn't move or even open my eyes and I certainly wasn't able to call out, "I'm here!"

As they cut me open, the blood seeped out like a maple tree's sap being harvested for syrup. My blood slowly made its way to the large, rusty drain via a thick, plastic tube. Steam emitted, like a broken radiator, as the warm blood hit the extremely cold sink drain – the drain that could surely use a thorough cleaning.

My organs and veins began to collapse, like a house of cards. The doctor and nurse were speaking. "I don't feel right; he was so young. We could have saved him," Nurse Lynch exclaimed to Dr. Kiernan.

"Quiet, don't be so damn nervous," replied the evil doctor. "He has a lot of useful organs and we have orders to fill, damn it! You knew this all along, so don't act like you don't know what's going on. If you're having second thoughts; well, it's just too late. Thank Satan, not God, for organ donor cards. It makes things so easy when deciding which poor slobs will be *helped on their way*", Dr. Kiernan continued.

As he surgically opened my chest, like a nutcracker cracks nuts, and began to remove my enlarged heart, I was helpless to do anything as my body no longer responded to my mind, like a bored student.

As I headed to the gates of Heaven; well, that's where I *assumed* I was going, I saw souls worshipping what I guessed was God. How pathetic, I reasoned to myself, and this is my reward for living a good life? Suddenly I noticed another figure sitting on a heavenly bed. Could it be St. Peter welcoming me? As I got closer, I realized it was the devil himself! Did he get a weekend furlough? Do they even have those in Heaven and Hell?

With that, Satan whispered to me, "Not what you thought it would be, huh?"

"Not even close," I replied to Satan. At least I *think* it's Satan.

"Well, then, I have a proposition for you. How would you like to be given a second chance to live again," he asked me while grinning like the Joker from 'BatMan.'

"That would interest me, but what's the catch? You ARE Satan, right," I asked.

"Yes, I'm Satan; you were expecting God Almighty," he answered my question with another question.

While chuckling like a hyena, Satan said, "I couldn't help but notice your reaction when you saw what Heaven had in store for you and I've been observing you for years and you make me laugh. Hell is Party Central, and I could use a guy like you. I've been waiting a long time for you to die for my chance to recruit you. Actually, your organ donor card, the one you signed when you were in high school, is the reason we are meeting. Satan Rocks! Now let me sweeten the deal. There must be something you would like to have," he finally concluded.

After careful consideration, I said, "I think we may just have a deal!"

In Satan We Trust

"Now I don't understand how you can give me another shot at life; I'm being cut up on a table as we speak," was my answer to Satan.

SATAN responded, "well I'm not talking about the body you're in now; I'm going to give you a new body, an upgrade if you please. You'll be physically fit, able to eat anything you want, drink as much as you please, abuse it all you want, and it will maintain its condition. Remember, it's not always what it seems."

"That sounds great," I replied, "but I'm still worried about making a deal with the devil, a devil I don't even know," I admitted.

"Listen to me," SATAN answered. "There's no pressure - you can continue walking and spend eternity groveling at God's feet stroking his ego and I'll wait another 1,000 years for someone of your character but believe me, it's your loss. You have a quality I need, so I'm asking you one last time. Do you want another shot at living," he asked me once more.

I thought about his offer, looked through the gates of Heaven and all the pitiful souls kissing God's feet and said, "I'm in, but I need to know just a bit more."

"I expected nothing less from you and that's why I chose you. I need a warrior with a free will. Come with me, and we'll hash out the details," he finished. It sounded like a sleazy attorney or a realtor only interested in a commission.

In Satan We Trust

Instantly we were transported to the depths of Hell. Now as you can well figure, Hell is a bit warm but some of us prefer it hot and there are a lot of tormented souls all around, but it's not much different than being on Earth. Eventually we came to an agreement and I carved out, like a Thanksgiving turkey, a pretty sweet deal with SATAN.

"Now I need you to return to your old, dying body for a few minor rules. For the next six days you need to remain in your original body and, of course, I need one favor from you as a gesture of good faith. I may be powerful, but even I can't take away a mortal's life, nor can your beloved God; but you can use your death to get me that evil doctor and hot-looking nurse, who both sadly sent you on your way much before your time. They have been getting away with murder for too long. I will find a way to end their pathetic lives," Satan giggled.

"I'm dead, how am I supposed to kill two people," I questioned.

 SATAN laughed, "You don't think I have a plan? I have powers that you're about to find out for yourself shortly. You will be reborn in six days, but before your rebirth you need to get me those two souls! Fail me and the deal is off, but your soul is still mine. That will NEVER change at this point."

"So how exactly does this work," I asked.

SATAN burst out laughing "that's for you to figure out, smart ass!"

In Satan We Trust

I found myself back inside my old body, my corpse actually; but unlike before where I didn't feel anything. I now felt nothing except intense pain, but I still couldn't move. What the fuck have I done? I made a deal with the devil and I'm screwed, like a hooker. Then I remembered his words 'I have powers that you're about to find out for yourself'. It's a test and it's time to get to work, I told myself.

The pain shot through every inch of my body as they have removed my eyes, my heart and my kidneys. If there was any blood left in my body, it would be boiling over, like overcooked spaghetti, by now. I told myself it's not murder I'm committing, rather justice I'm going to instill. I tried my hardest to move, but nothing. By now, they were sewing me up and I felt the needle piercing my skin, like a taxidermist prepping his catch. Every minor stitch created more and more pain.

What's this? I then saw a person on the operating table and they were putting my heart inside the patient. As the heart was strategically and precisely placed, they began pumping blood into it via an intravenous bag. I could feel the patient's pain, but the more intense pain I had been feeling in my original body slowly but surely subsided.

In a different hospital, a Catholic one as I noticed crucifixion crosses all over the place and nuns everywhere, I sensed my kidneys being transplanted into someone else's body. I was drawn back to my body as they loaded it into a funeral car and began moving me to the funeral home. I attempted moving again and my leg twitched like a death row inmate about to meet his maker. A feeling of hope unexpectedly returned to me as

In Satan We Trust

I decided perhaps this was only the outcome of anesthesia and would eventually wear its way out of my body. I may yet figure out SATANS plan! The doctor who stole my organs is talking to the funeral director and he handed him an envelope full of cash and convinced him everything went off without a hitch. Well, maybe for them, but no so much for me!

I returned to the patient who was now the lucky one who possessed my heart and I started to make my heart beat stronger and stronger until he opened his eyes with some difficulty. Don't ask me exactly how I did it, but I did it, nonetheless. Inside the funeral car, I felt my confused body writhing. It finally hit me – I was starting to figure out SATAN'S plan. I found myself in, yet another operating room in yet another hospital and my eyes were being placed inside another man. My mind was still confused, like the rest of my body, with all that was happening; but I had more important things to do and I must finish my tasks somehow.

The funeral director backed his hearse up to the funeral home and nonchalantly unloaded my body. It was late at night and very dark, so the director locked up, like someone was really going to steal a corpse, and went home. As I laid there, I tried with all my will moving again, and to my delight I raised my right arm! An evil smile suddenly appeared on my face.

Morning showed itself and with it, the funeral director arrived. He fired up the oven, first things first, for a cremation and then he went into his office to do some paperwork while the oven reached its target temperature. With all my will, I sat up and swung both of my legs over the side of the gurney and then I dropped to the floor. With anger inside me, it seemed to fuel my strength, I stood quietly behind the door. As the funeral director, Mr. Whitham, entered the room, walked over to the cremation device and opened the ghastly door. While turning to get my body, he saw me; at least it looked like me, standing in front of him. Sheer terror showed on his face when I grabbed him and shoved him into the oven, HIS oven. Eventually, his screams filled the air. Oh, sweet mystery of life, at last I've found you. Music to my fucking ears!

Suddenly I was back in Hell! SATAN looked at me and asked, "Did you not understand my orders?"

"I did," I replied, "but that asshole deserved what I did; besides you said you wanted a warrior with free will. So, just consider this piece of shit a gift, no charge".

SATAN burst out laughing and said, "I knew you were going to make me proud, but you need to finish my task before the deadline I gave you arrives."

"Not to worry," I assured him. "I think I have a knack for this."

I was now back in a hospital inside a small child's body, not sure if it was a boy or a girl. It didn't really matter, so I wasn't even sure why this came to mind. Anyway, this is where my kidneys went; I guess something good came out of my death, I convinced myself. It's all good, as the saying goes.

An angel then appeared. You could tell she was trying to

In Satan We Trust

look the part of a human, whatever that look may be. However, bell bottoms? Weren't those the fad in the 70's? Obviously, she was not aware that here on Earth clothing is marked by the era. Evidently, she was misinformed by God of our attire here on Earth.

"Feels good to know that you are helping a child live, doesn't it," asked the angel.

"Well, duh; of course, it does. A child is innocent. Why would I not feel good about that? Don't make me rip those Heavenly wings off and shove them down your godly throat," was my reply.

"Easy, Big Guy - I have a message from God. He's willing to forgive you and let you come to Heaven. All is forgiven", the heavenly body, the angel, told me.

"Listen to me, you oversized gnat; I'm going to swat you if you don't fly away now! SATAN gave me a good job. I get to reap the evil souls on Earth. I'm not a boot licking piss ant in my mind. Eliminating evil souls is an honorable thing, like serving in the military, and if serving SATAN is the only way to do that, then I'm going to choose Hell. Now piss off and tell glory boy he did a lousy job when he created humans and I don't work for anyone who does such shabby work," I screamed.

I heard a familiar laugh from the annoying angel and with that the angel transformed into SATAN. "Sorry, but I just wanted to see if you were all I had you pegged to be and I'm happy to say you're all that and more," he told me.

"Man, are you going to be a dick for eternity," I asked.

In Satan We Trust

He laughed and said, "What did you expect? I'm the devil but I think you're going to do just fine. You've already done better than all my other prospective demons! Now get back to work. I just wanted you to see one of the evil souls that you're going to take. *This child* is going to kill 17 young girls one day. Ironic, isn't it," he informed me.

I found myself back inside the lucky man who had my harvested heart and he was doing fine. The surgeon was there and he was talking to him," I can't believe how fast you're recovering from the operation. It's a miracle," the doctor exclaimed.

I started laughing, but it came out of the patient's mouth, not mine. I thought to myself how odd it was, so I cleared my throat and sure enough the patient cleared his throat. So, I raised my arm and he did the same. Well, what do you know? I think I can use this to my advantage, I told myself.

Suddenly I channeled myself back into my corpse and I was dressed and made up, like a whore on Saturday night, laying in my cheap, wooden casket. What the fuck, my next of kin wouldn't even splurge for a non-weathering casket. Really, wood? It was time for my viewing, a wake as the Irish folk call it, and people were paying their respects. I heard SATAN'S voice, "I just wanted to give you a treat for doing so well this far," he informed me.

As people passed by, they looked so sad, like they just watched a tear-jerker movie – the kind of movie you'd see on the Lifetime channel. I wished I could just sit up and see how many idiots I could give heart attacks to, but that could interfere with my schedule; so, I just continued lying there and listened to the same old same old:

'He died so young. Doesn't he look good, I wish I could have seen him one last time before he died, I should have told him I loved him,' I thought quietly to myself.

Aarrghhhh, reward my ass; if I wasn't dead already, I'd kill myself. Now this is Hell with a capital "H". There were relatives there whom I hadn't seen in years and years. Cousin, aunts, uncles and grandparents.

The best part was that no one attending the wake really knew the manner and cause of my death and the rumors were flying, like the birds from Alfred Hitchcock's famous movie, *The Birds*. I had to assume either my death certificate had not yet been issued to the family or the attendees had the good sense to avoid asking for the details of my demise.

My great aunts on my father's side; however, were babbling in their Irish accents, which by the way were difficult to understand mostly because in addition to their dialect, they speak so fucking fast as if they don't want anyone but themselves to hear what they are saying.

Well, dear Aunt Rose, she told the best rumor of all. Because of our estrangement, the "aunts" as dear Dad referred to them, knew nothing about us. She fabricated the following to her other dear sisters, whom were estranged from us also:

In Satan We Trust

"From what I understand," said Auntie Rose, "He was robbed for $300 that he kept hidden under a rug which was under his bed. The female who robbed him, she actually cozied up to him in an attempt to rob him, was finally caught. And one of her phone calls from prison to her mother went like this:

"Mother, I don't know why you're angry with me. That guy was stingy. My *real* mother told me so. Hey, it wasn't so bad; when I glued his head back on, it almost looked like he was sleeping. Even the undertaker was surprised at what a great job I did. It saved him a little work. Why did he have a machete in his closet anyway? He was asking for it. The only thing I regret was wasting my own turtle neck sweater to hide the machete damage, so he could be viewed. That was an expensive sweater. I bought it in Belfast and it was a pain in the neck, no pun intended, to squeeze it into the bulging luggage coming home to the U.S.," the prisoner told her adoptive mother.

The prisoner's adoptive mother replied just prior to the prison telephone pre-recording stating 'one more minute remaining', "*I am* your real mother. I'm not your biological mother, but I am your real mother so stop referring to *her* as your *real Mom*. Do you think she would accept your collect calls from prison like I do," she finished right before the 'click' disconnecting them from their conversation. That's how the prison calls go.

After the call was disconnected, Mom simply scratched her head, which was a great mess of gray. After all, she was more of a back to nature kind of woman and would never consider using imitation color or anything like that. Flower power was more her speed.

In Satan We Trust

Glancing toward the piano in the living room, she merely stared intensely at the only two pictures in frames. She lovingly looked at the first one, of her and her boyfriend at the time who eventually became her husband and the father of her now imprisoned daughter. The two lovers were standing with arms around each other, they both donned bellbottoms and her hair was long and held in place with a mess of flowers. What a bunch of flower children and why not – the picture was taken while they were in the great outdoors during Woodstock, a wild music festival during the 70's.

Next, she viewed the second picture frame on the piano, for it was her daughter, who was the mirror image of her, and her son. It was no surprise that her daughter was a tow head; both parents were, too. And her son, well, he didn't look like either parent. The parents' genes were definitely dominant for their daughter, but they weren't sure how far down the lineage would bring them to the son's dark coloring and copper-top colored hair. If one were to look at the siblings, you would never associate the two as brother and sister.

Now that was the best one yet; I couldn't even believe this bullshit! And why did they even come to my viewing? They never knew me, unless they wanted to find out if there was more stash hidden elsewhere in my room. The interesting concept about hearing their conversation was since I was a young child, I always had this surreal feeling that I had another "Mother" out there somewhere. When I approached my parents back then, they always denied an adoption. They even showed me documents, my birth certificate, to prove I was their biological child. So, I figured don't cry over spilled milk because it's not always as it seems.

But before I dropped the 'adoption thing' from my mind, I envisioned my other mother, not that I had anything against my Mom, looking rather earthy; like wearing a long white gown, scalloped edges, long flowing sleeves and a crown of daisies on her head. I guess the look would be of a hippy or beatnik. But very down to earth, very in touch with the environment, maybe even a marijuana smoker. She would be running through a large field of poppies, her hair flowing behind her and her dress would be blowing in the wind. If she existed and looked as I pictured her, I would probably ask her if I could call her something stupid like Nature Mom.

It's morning now and I've returned to the man who got my heart. Lucky for him he's getting stronger and stronger, like the morphing Hulk. Eventually the exhausted-looking surgeon came in and gave the sore patient something for pain. "Tell you what, Doc, I feel great and don't need it," he told the doctor.

"Humor me," he said. "it will make me feel better knowing that I've given it to you; but to be honest, today we're releasing a small child who got a kidney transplant from the same donor as your heart so I kinda believe you're not in pain," the doctor said. I had no clue what he meant by that. When the doctor left, I started laughing, "Donor, my ass; just wait till I get that thieving doctor's hide. A donation is made voluntarily!"

I found myself in the dark, but I could hear voices. "I

want these bandages off. I'm telling you I can see light," one of the voices said.

"It's too soon; trust me," the other voice replied. So, I decided to take matters into my own hands because I realized this was the person who got my baby blue eyes.

I started to remove the bandages myself and suddenly I heard a woman's voice, "Honey, please stop - you have no idea what we went through to get you those eyes. That voice, I know that voice, it's the nurse. 'SATAN,' I said to myself, 'you, wonderful bastard!' My task just got so much easier. I decided to bide my time as this one should be easy.

Back to my heart and what do you know - the doctor who scavenged my organs was there taking vitals. He heard about all the patients and how well they were all doing. So, he decided to check it out for himself. Curiosity killed the cat, how appropriate.

After a while, the doctor said, "You seem to be doing just fine. Is there anything I can do for you?"

"I'm dying in here, no pun intended. It's so hot. Could you open the window," I asked politely. He walked slowly over to the window and started to open it. Just then, I got off the bed and rushed toward him. The IV ripped out of his arm, which was actually my arm, and in an instant, I struck him like a linebacker and we crashed through the window and plummeted seven stories, like stunt men during filming of action movies. With my hands on his throat, we fell like skydivers and my face appeared on the patient's face. The look of terror on the doctor's face was priceless, like New Jersey...perfect together, and I announced, "I'll see you in Hell." As we hit the ground, the sound of shattering bones filled the air. Oh, the sweet smell of success!

A curious crowd gathered around the two lifeless, mangled broken bodies. The man's hand was still clutching the doctor's throat. His fingers were piercing the flesh - no doubt the doctor was dead. Before he reached the ground, glass shards stuck into each of the bodies. It's called justified collateral damage. It appears the "patient" was a prick. And that, my friend, is what happens to a rich asshole and a 'doctor' who puts a kid in desperate need of an organ from the top of the harvest list all the way down to the bottom of that same list. He deserved to die, and I made sure it happened! A jerk like that, whomever could do that to a poor, ill young child has no value to society and especially to Satan. You see, once again, it's not always as it seems.

Again, I returned to my corpse and we were at the cemetery now. As they lowered my body into the grave, the mourners slowly departed, like defeated football fans, and I heard the dirt and rocks cascading down upon the casket. The sounds of the living world became muffled with every shovel the gravedigger tossed on top of me. As the hole filled and the Earth swallowed me up, the ghoulish sounds of the underworld filled my resting place. I heard the tormented souls crying out as I did nothing but simply lie there.

As night approached, we all emerged from our graves slowly and cautiously. We took over the night, like a successful prison break, and then I came face to face with my allies of the darkness. SATAN appeared and started speaking, "My children, I'd like you to meet our newest warrior - not only has he, pardon the pun, hit the ground running and has taken to his role with the same zeal as he did in the real world; but unlike most of you pathetic wretches, he is going to receive a new body because he's ahead of schedule. Not only does he have only one more evil soul to kill but his first victim wasn't even part of our deal. That's pure dedication, people."

SATAN motioned me to come forward, "I'd like you all to welcome him. No, I *command* you to welcome him because most of you will be answering to him when he returns to the fold," he finished.

As I stood there, I saw the hate they had for me; but I found comfort in their anger because I knew I would rise to the top like a dead floating fish. I'm developing a real sense of freedom avenging the victims of those who I kill and best of all, there is no punishment - rather more praise for a job well done. Daybreak had approached, and I must return to where my eyes were. Only one more to go and, baby, I'm back, I told myself.

Back at the hospital, the doctor was preparing to remove the bandages from my eyes. I came to the realization that the nurse was actually the patient's wife. Awkward moment, for sure. "I'm worried about this," she admitted. Strange things have been happening around here and I'm thinking that maybe we should take it slowly."

"Are you kidding me? I've been waiting for this day for quite some time," I finished. She was obviously not aware of just how right she was to be apprehensive about the situation.

"I'm sorry," she replied. "I'm just being silly, I guess", she completed her thought.

The doctor removed the surgical bandages and I blinked a few times and then I actually smiled. Much to my surprise, I was able to see everything clearly. I stood up to gather myself to make sure I had control of this body. Surprisingly, I felt I had control, so I put my right foot in the doctor's chest slamming him against the wall. I grabbed the nurse and threw her to the floor and sat on her chest. Then I told her, "You should have saved my life instead of just scavenging parts from me." I clearly discovered that she was totally aware of what I was referring to.

"Now let's see how you'd feel if the shoe was on the other foot," I explained as I took my dirty fingers and jammed them into her bedroom brown eyes and ripped them from her fucking face.

She shrieked out just as her eyes began to bleed in my filthy, greedy hands. Then I grabbed a scalpel off the metal hospital tray and cut her chest open, just like the Thanksgiving turkey stunt they pulled on me. I plunged my hand inside her and tore out her heart, as easily as flossing my teeth every day. My task was now complete, as far as I was concerned anyway!

Suddenly I was back in Hell and SATAN glared at me and said, "Congratulations; you're the first one in centuries to

In Satan We Trust

complete such a task and now you get your second chance! Hooray!

Chapter 2 - The Birth

It was now September 10, 1960 and Hurricane Hanna hit the east coast with no mercy. Destruction was everywhere - trees were torn out of the ground and crushed cars and houses were abundant. People got tossed around by her wrath like the munchkins in *The Wizard of Oz*. But, in the maternity ward at St. Clare's Hospital, a very pregnant woman, who was two weeks overdue, gave birth to a ten-pound son. She announced to the doctors and nurses, hell, she told anyone who would listen, " I'll call him Sean", and my second chance at life had been granted!

Because of the chaos from the hurricane, forceps had to be used to 'extract' this bruiser. I mean, he was so huge that it looked like his cheek was in another county. The only after effect of the forceps was it left what looked like cysts on his forehead but in the hairline. Too bad he was bold, though. Now these 'cysts' looked like what occurs when a deer starts growing antlers. They were easy to hide when he started growing hair and when he was old enough for haircuts, the cysts dictated where the cuts were made. Kids used to laugh at him and call him a

In Satan We Trust

devil and as he grew older, he would be called a *horny* devil. Not to worry, they'll get theirs one day for sure!

Now, because it was close to Halloween at the time of Sean's birth, volunteers dressed in Halloween outfits and spread themselves out so that each floor was covered. They were handing out Halloween treats. Nancy, the head nurse of the labor and delivery ward entered Sean's mother's room and announced to her visitors that they could expect to see Satan soon. Another nurse, in the room taking vitals, said to Nancy,
"Nancy, you mean Santa, not Satan, right?"

Nancy replied, "I said Santa, not Satan. This is a Catholic hospital and there are no abortions performed at St. Clare's nor any representation of something as ungodly as the devil would be allowed to be displayed."

The nurse taking the vitals said, "Well, it's just interesting that someone is dressed like Santa for Halloween. You would think that costume would be saved to Christmas visitors in December. And come to think of it, all the other volunteers are handing out typical Halloween candy, like chocolates. Santa is only handing out candy canes. But, hey, what do I know? I just take vitals, retrieve bed pans and take blood."

NOW THE REAL HORROR STORY BEGAN, but it wasn't realized by most people until many, many years later!

All dressed up in my Seanta Clause outfit, going about my day passing out candy canes and singing carols just pissing off people. On one particular day, I handed a candy cane to a man on the street and as I was wishing

In Satan We Trust

him a Merry Christmas, I watched the candy slowly start to melt in his hand, so I looked at him and right at that time it hit me. So, I held nothing back and came right out and said to him, "Damn it, Lucifer, can't you just show up in a person without the fucking games?"

The man chuckled, and his fake face changed into his real face and replied. "You can't expect Satan to do the expected. Where's the fun in that? But you're getting much better at catching me doing it, I have to admit."

"Fine, to what do I owe this honor? I haven't seen you in over fifty years and we have a deal that, if I do say so myself, I've been doing an exemplary job at," I retorted.

"That you are, my man, but I have missed chatting with you because you're my favorite demon so I just thought it's Christmas - my favorite time of the year, as the song goes, and I just wanted you to say 'Merry Christmas' to me; after all Christmas is my creation," he retorted.

I lost it and burst out laughing. Fire began to shoot out of his nostrils, like a fire-breathing dragon, and he exclaimed, "DON'T EVER DOUBT WHAT I SAY."
Well in the countless lives I've had to endure, never has Satan raised his voice to me and I must tell you it was unnerving.

"Forgive me, Lord, but isn't Christmas a Jeebus deal - you know birth of Jeebus and all, I asked.

Satan laughed and said, "I love the way you call him Jeebus but he wouldn't appreciate it."

In Satan We Trust

"Well, I work for you so, you know, fuck him," I told him.

"HEY! JEEBUS, as you call him, is my friend and one of your fellow demons," was his reply.

"I beg your pardon," I said. You're telling me that Jeebus is on our team," I asked.

Surprised Satan responded, "Yes, yes he is; why do you think I haven't stepped in to stop you from doing your Seanta Clause thing and why do you do it in each of your lives? It's because inside you know evil better than anyone in the creation of mankind which is why you're my favorite demon. Shit, you haven't needed any training or guidance at all. But now I'm going to tell you exactly what Christmas is really about but first...." he said before getting cut off.

Suddenly we're in Hell again and Satan said, "I want you to meet my friend, JESUS. Come in here, please. A bearded man around 35 years of age entered, and Satan stated, "Jesus, meet Sean; Sean, Jesus," he finished.

I looked at him and said, "So you're the son of God."

"I have no father; just some asshole who turned his back on me when I needed him most," Jesus huffed.

"Wow, I think I owe you an apology. I always thought you were some kind of pussy," was my reply.

"I can understand that, but Satan tells me you keep calling me Jeebus; don't do that. I don't like that. I've earned my name - you get nailed to a fucking cross with your father watching and not raising his hand to save you and tell me you would let someone diss your name," Jesus replied.

"It's all good. I said we have a common enemy." Then, to lighten the subject, I sang out 'JESUS HE'S MY BROTHER, JESUS HE'S MY FRIEND'.

Jesus busted out laughing and said to me, "You're funny I can see why Satan speaks so highly of you. You are definitely quick with your comebacks and that makes for a real talent.

"Well if Satan likes you, I will use your name correctly," I told him. Then I reached out my hand as if to shake his and as he reached to shake it, I pulled it away and said," Yeah, not without a glove. that's one nasty hole you've got there. No glove no love," I finished my thought.

Jesus laughed and looked at Satan and said, "He's all you said he was. Well, I've got to go; I've got the religious souls that fucked up and I need to keep the pain going. It's nice to get to meet you" and off he went.

Satan said, "Now let's get back to earth and I'll tell you the story of Christmas." Just what I needed – another story!

Back on Earth with Satan, sitting on a park bench, like two conspiring spies, snow was falling all around us. And I mean around us – there was not a flake within a ten-foot radius. I announced, "I love the snow; it muffles the sounds of man, it's so damn peaceful."

In Satan We Trust

"Don't forget why you're here - I've given you hearing better than anything on earth so that you can hear the evil in man and better serve me," Satan replied.

"Yeah, yeah; I know, but it's nice to get a break every now and then. So, let's hear the true meaning of Christmas" I demanded.

"Very well," replied Satan. "You must first understand that everything you have heard about Christmas is wrong! Christmas is about the murder of Jesus and the completion of mankind's evil ways. Did you know the first ones to celebrate Christmas were my pagan followers - those sick fucks worshiped blood rituals and never truly understood how the crucifixion of Jesus brought him into the fold. Don't get me wrong; I can appreciate the twisted fucks, but they shall pay dearly for their sins especially since Jesus himself doles out their punishment for eternity and, believe me, I think He enjoys it a bit too much. But he's my friend and I give him free reign to decide how to punish the souls in his section of Hell," Satan finished his thought.

I interrupted him and asked, "What about the fight they talk about between you and Jesus when he walked upon the earth?"

"Good question - that was my first face-to-face meeting with him. I knew just what his Dad had planned for him and I was trying to help him. As you can imagine, that didn't go well. He still believed that his father loved him and he couldn't see just what a self-indulgent vicious prick he was and just how much more evil he was capable of being. So, we got in a fight and that's when I knew that my newfound friend had the qualities that I look for. Man, that fight went on for days; a little advice - watch out for his left hook as he'll ring your bell with that bad boy, and that bell does not result in an angel receiving his wings like in *It's a Wonderful Life*," Satan confessed.

Needless to say, I was pissed and saddened at the same time for it was at that moment I knew that his father's vicious plan would be fulfilled, and I'd have to wait for the hand he was dealt to be played out before I could see him again. God is a horrible dictator who gets off on torturing his followers.

Just then a man snatched a woman's purse, a Michael Kors no less, and ran off with the expensive ware. She worked hard for that purchase. Satan simply snapped his fingers and a half-dead branch fell off a tree impaling the thief, pinning him to the cold, wet ground. "I never get tired of seeing you at work - nicely done," I told him.
"Aww, that was nothing; I just hate being interrupted because you're one of the very few who gets away with it, he replied.

Momentarily, Satan got up, walked over to the thief who was still twitching and choking on his blood, like a gagging denture wearer. As he stepped out of the grass onto the freshly fallen snow, I distinctly heard the snow sizzling under his feet. He gently touched the thief's forehead with his long, thin finger and carved the number 4 into it, picked up the woman's purse and returned the large, heavy piece of attire to the woman.

In Satan We Trust

Being curious about the significance of the number, I asked, "May I inquire about the number you put on his head?"

"Ahh, that's just so they put him in the right section when his soul gets to Hell. They are lost without me when I leave, and I found this way they can do their job without any mistakes when I visit you. And if they do fuck up, well, let's just say they don't want to fuck up. I'm hungry", Satan said. "Let's get a bite to eat," he suggested.

As we walked to a diner, just a tiny greasy spoon type thing, I noticed after entering that there was no one else there. We had our choice of booths, so I chose one close to the exit just in case. Satan asked, "Now, where were we? Ah yes, now as the idea of Christmas was gathering more and more followers. The church found that people were celebrating the death of Jesus, who; by the way, was just a man like you and I. So, the Pope at the time decided to embrace the idea, too. They saw people feasting, giving each other gifts and just coming together in harmony. Deep down, they knew they could milk the followers of the church out of more of their money and they tried to change the date to celebrate the birth of Jesus. I found out about this conspiracy and decided that it was time to draw a line in the sand, if you will. I appeared to Pope Julius the second and told him to back off on changing the date of my holiday, but in the arrogant way that church officials act, he tried to tell me that I had no power in the house of God. I remember laughing as I scorched his insides, like a piece of very burnt toast, and set his blood aflame, which is why to this day the church still holds fast to the claim that He died of fever. I have to give them credit; they didn't lie, it was heat that took that fat bastard's life. I turned to Julius the first and said, 'I know that you're going to take his place and I warn you now - don't fuck with me or your reign will be short lived.' He must have taken heed of my words because the date has been the same since that incident," he explained to me.

The waitress walked up to our table and took our order, and something just didn't seem right about her. I couldn't explain it, but I just felt uneasy about her. She bought us coffee, her hands shaking slightly, then she promptly returned to the kitchen. Shortly thereafter, I heard sounds coming from the back, but they certainly didn't sound like someone cooking.

Satan resumed his conversation, "I find it funny how God's Heavenly flock is drained of their money by the church, the same men who took a vow of poverty and celibacy; yet they live like kings in their monasteries and continue to rape and perform perverted sexual acts against their congregation!"

The waitress returned with our food, sweat beads covering her forehead. While approaching the table, in her right hand was Satan's meal and in her left was mine. I recognized this tactic instantly and noticed the grease on the plate was coagulating already - a clear sign that the food is cold! She took Satan's meal, crossed over and placed it in front of him then she started to pass mine over. As she did this, her right hand slid behind her to her apron string. As the plate landed in front of me, she whipped her right hand around, but I was already instinctively moving my hands and reaching out blocking

In Satan We Trust

her strike. A blade nicked my forearm; the pain was unbearable, but I locked both of my hands onto her skinny, little wrist and drove the blade with all my might into her ribcage. Then, I rose out if my chair and forced her against the counter. Giant white wings burst out from the uniform and feathers flew everywhere as she exploded into nothingness. I now held the blade in my hand as a few feathers waft to the floor, like a chicken coop in chaos.

I became confused about what just happened just as anyone would have been. Satan, clearly shaken sat back and said, "Cain's blade, I can't believe you saved me. I don't know what to say; I'm grateful for your quick response and saving my life. I can't believe I didn't sense it. We need to leave this place now," he exclaimed.

Again, as we returned to Hell, Satan shouted, "Gather all souls, I have an announcement."

I looked out at a sea of tortured souls all waiting for Satan to speak. I thought to myself, 'he must be getting ready to proclaim war on Heaven. Now that I have Cain's blade and I have mixed feelings about it, I've been enjoying my duties for centuries gathering the souls who I deem evil. I have no fear of war because I know the souls we gathered are strong and have what it takes to remove God and his army from existence.'

Satan rose just at the moment I completed the thoughts in my head. It became silent, like church worshippers praying for peace, and he spoke, "You, worthless bunch have the honor of standing in the presence of greatness! Before you, stands my number one demon and today he has defeated God's dearest angel. In doing so, he also saved me from what God has been trying to do for eons, but better yet, he has gained possession of Cain's blade - the deadliest weapon ever created. Now to show my gratitude you're about to witness something never seen before. I release your soul, Sean, your contract with me is null and void and you're free to do anything you wish from here on out. Would you like to say a few words before you leave and start your life over," he asked me.

I approached Satan cautiously and replied, "You call this a reward? I've been doing your work for all these many years and achieved what no one has been able to do and I'm fired, oh wait - free," I asked quizzically.

As I attempted to hand him the blade, he shied away as a collective gasp came from the sea of souls.

Satan said to me, "I can't touch this blade - it will destroy me!"

"So, you're just going to let me leave with it," I threw it back into his court.

Satan looked into my eyes and replied to me, "If you didn't let that prick in the diner kill me, I don't think I have to worry about you coming after me, do I?"

"Why do you want me to leave then," I continued my questioning.
"I don't, but I want to show you how much I appreciate your help. What would you like then, he asked.

In Satan We Trust

I started stroking my long, red beard - I looked like a red-headed Santa, and I replied, "Well you know why you were cast out - I want you to share your followers with me.

The laughing Satan retorted, "Well, I can't refuse your request - that would make me a hypocrite. Very well then, but you realize that you're going to be hated by all," he finished.

"Oooooh, like I'm not already," I chuckled.

"Very well then, it shall be done. So, tell me, what do you plan to do now that you have all the power that I do, plus the blade that makes you a force to be reckoned with," he asked.

"First, we're going to go get that meal. I'm still hungry and I think we're safe for a while," was my reply.

Satan asked me, "So, where do you want to eat?"

I thought about my favorite steak house and instantly we were outside of the building, but Jesus is standing with us this time.

"What are you doing? You can't bring Jesus with us. It's not safe for him to be outside of Hell," Satan snapped.

"*I* did this," I questioned.

"Yes, you did; you now have the same powers as me as you requested. you need to be more careful about how you use them," he informed me.

In Satan We Trust

I laughed and said, "Well, you should have told me that I already have them. Besides, we're talking about the true story of Christmas and having Jesus here can only assure that the whole story comes out".

"You have a reputation for twisting the truth. I've never lied to you in all the centuries of our friendship," he said.

"Well, he's here and between the three of us, I think we can handle it. Let's go inside and get this feast going, I suggested.

As we entered, the building was full of patrons, not like the last diner we went to, and I thought to myself 'I was hoping it wouldn't be busy' and suddenly the place was empty. Jesus started laughing, looked at me and said "Cool, isn't it?"

Confused, I said, "Yes, very; but I think I'm going to enjoy these powers." We grabbed an ordinary table and I announced, "I would like to hear the rest of the story. I believe you stopped at Christmas being about Jesus's death."

Satan, slightly irritated by me using my newfound powers so freely, began with a warning to me, "I need you to think about what you're doing from now on. You can do so much damage that cannot be undone."

Then he laughed and said, "Like a fish to water. Ok, now as I said I tried to warn Jesus about what was going to happen to him and we fought when his trial was over and Pilot condemned him to the cross. I walked the route along with him and the entire time he stood fast to the belief that his father would intervene and save him from the ridicule and whippings. Even as they put a nail into his wrist after they stood the cross up, Jesus felt the weight of his body pulling on the spikes that held him to the crucifix. He looked at me and said, "I'm sorry I didn't believe you. Please help me. I had a tear in my eye as I told him that the only way to help him now was to end his life because the cross had now become bonded with his powers. Jesus, seeing that his friend, Satan, was full of sorrow telling this part of the story overtook him."

"That's when Jesus said, "I understand, and I want you to do what you have to in order to end this pain." Now Satan was there as one of the soldiers and took the spear and drove it up and into me."

Sadly, I looked at Satan and his expression was that of one who was full of remorse over the act he performed.

Jesus put his holy hand on Satan's shoulder and told him, "Don't feel badly, my friend, you did all you could to prevent my death. I'm grateful for you ending my pain! I love you, my brother, besides you don't want your nephew over there to see you like this."

"I beg your pardon," I said. "NEPHEW," I asked.

"Yes, I guess it's time I told you - I'm your father and Satan is my brother," he told me his secret.

My body went limp quickly, like a buzz kill during sex, in my chair my jaw dropped, and I started rubbing my forehead. I felt a migraine coming on fast and furious.

In Satan We Trust

"Well, I understand the story of Christmas; but now I have more questions than ever," I confessed.

"Your questions will have to wait. We're not finished with the story just yet. You don't want to know where Santa Claus came from," Satan said wiping a tear from his eye, clearly still moved from the story thus far. Just then the waitress arrived at the table and took our order.

After we ordered our food, she simply asked, "Would you like a drink while you're waiting?"

Jesus asked for three waters, obviously embarrassed that we forgot to order drinks. I piped up and exclaimed, "I don't drink water."

Raising his brow, he told her to just bring us the waters. So, she left without allowing me to order a real drink. "I could really use a drink, you know being told that I'm the son of Jesus has me shaken up a bit. Perhaps a cocktail would calm my nerves," I suggested.

Satan laughed and replied, "You know all the stories about your Dad. You will have your drink."

Jesus chuckled, and Satan smirked. The waitress returned to the table and placed the three waters in front of us and left without a word. I pushed mine away and Satan demanded, "Drink it!" So, of course, I grabbed it and took a deep swallow. And don't you know that I had the rum and coke that I planned to order. I guzzled the thing down and slammed the glass down on the table.

In Satan We Trust

A quick glimpse at the glass revealed it was full again. I smiled at that sight and asked, "Why didn't we just order a loaf of bread and a fish?"

At that, we all started laughing. "It's time for full disclosure," Satan said. "You know that you've had to endure many lives, but what you don't know is each time you're reborn your memories are hidden from you to avoid you starting your work at an early age. But we do this for your own protection. Your grandfather has been hunting for you in an effort to end your life, but by the time he can discover your true identity, you have become the warrior that your destined to be," he completed his thought.

"Wait, your telling me that God has been hunting for me, to kill me," I asked in disbelief.

Jesus replied calmly, "You have a destiny and the only way he can keep up his reign of terror is to kill you. Fear is how he keeps his followers!"

Satan assured me, "I found out about his plan to kill *me* in the beginning, so I hid away until I was strong enough to defend myself. I only wish I could have defeated him because I could have saved my brother and you, too."

"Are you telling me that I'm slated to die like my father," I asked?

Jesus responded, "Honestly, we don't know now. You've changed the outcome since you hold Cain's blade. None of us saw that coming. Dad surely fucked up good this time. From here on out, you are writing the story - you seem to be in charge of your destiny now."

"Can we get back to the Santa part of the story now," Satan asked sarcastically.

"Ok, but you can't blame me for jumping around. You two are overwhelming me with all this," I exclaimed. Our food finally arrived and asked, "Shall we say grace?" And we all burst out laughing together.

"We're glad to see you still maintain your sense of humor. It has always brought us a certain amount of pleasure knowing that you can laugh through almost anything. Actually, it shows that you can keep fighting from whatever comes your way. Now let's continue," Satan said.

Satan, Jesus and I were having our meal when Satan asks, "Have you ever wondered why you always dress up as Santa in all your lives or why you make your own outfit and not just buy one?"

I can now remember all my past lives and I replied, "I don't know because I like making people smile, I guess."

"No, not even close," he said. "How about why you love singing Christmas carols but not the religious ones, he asked.

"That's easy, because I work for you, I replied.

Now Jesus took over, "Wrong, my son, Satan and I created Santa Claus just for you. You see the Christians found they could use it to their advantage to get their followers to give the church more money, but Satan and I figured if those idiots want to give their money to those crooks, no biggie, we could care less how badly they want Hell to treat them in the afterlife. And, believe me, Hell is full of greedy clergymen and I punish them harsher than else anyone else in Hell. They enjoy raping little boys. You don't really want to see how they are treated by me.

Satan's turn now by saying, "Excuse your father, he likes his work too much sometimes. We knew you had a long journey ahead of you and we knew how hard it was going to be, so we created Santa, so you could relax and have fun now. You've been giving out candy canes for centuries and the reason for this is they represent the shepherds hook and your destiny is to be just that a shepherd - your flock is a hundred times bigger than your grandfather's flock. Even though you take the souls of good men and women at times, we know that you're building an army and everyone in Hell knows to treat your flock with respect at all times. Hell is not what you think - most of the souls you're gathering are enjoying themselves much more than if they went to heaven so I know that there are times that you want to take your life and just quit, but you can't because deep down inside you know that you're going to do wondrous things. About Cain's blade, we need you to be vigilant. Your grandfather is going to want to get it back - stay alert and guard it well."

As we dined, I asked Jesus, "So how come no one ever talked about your missing years?" And he told me, "You need to understand that my father and I were just regular men. Dad ruled with fear and violence slaughtering men, women and children. He staged attempts on his life, so people thought he was immortal in order to thwart real attempts against him. As I got older, he wanted me to be just like him; but I could never understand why he had to be so cruel. So, he hid me away and tried to have me trained in a way that he could be proud of. You never heard that Mary was a peasant that he raped and got pregnant, so he created a story about a virgin giving birth to a son to which he would call his son because his Queen was barren and could not bear children. Therefore; with a wave of his hand, this woman would give birth and all those who doubted his word were found murdered in a most gruesome manner until the people dared not speak otherwise. To ensure that a legend was in the making, he concocted a plan that King Herod, a rival of his, was going to kill the baby upon its birth. Then he had his guard hide the mother away. Upon my birth, he dressed his soldiers in King Herod's men's clothes from slain battles and carried out his evil plan, knowing full well that I was safe, and Herod would be hated by his people. How I wish I could have done more for man, but I only learned of the things that transpired because of my birth late into my life - your grandfather is ruthless," I explained.

Satan, hanging his head, stated that he was the one who told his brother about their father's endeavors.

"Ok, now," I interrupted. "What about 'the one and only begotten son of god' shit that I heard," I finished.

Satan replied, "Well, Pops had a woman before he became a ruler; you could say that I was God's dirty little secret; but unlike Jesus, I wanted his respect and did everything he asked of me. I quickly became his number one warrior working night and day until we became the most powerful army in the land. As I became a man, I figured that it was time I was rewarded. Well, standing up for what was rightfully mine, Dad cast me out. This is when I decided to find my brother, Jesus, and try to save from Daddy's wrath thus the 10 commandments were born! No one but you, my nephew, knows the whole story. Everyone was told that I was a traitor to God and hence, I became an outcast and all who joined me would be put to death. Dad heard about me trying to find my brother and knowing where he was, instructed his men to deceive Jesus with trickery and by the time I found my brother, his mind was engrained with his plan. It took me years to find him and when I did; well, I told you about the fight we had." The meal was finished, and Satan said we should go.

"Whoa, I don't know about you; but I want desert. It's the best part of a meal and I have more questions," I informed him, being the sweet lover that I am.

Shortly thereafter, the waitress found her way over to us and asked politely if everything was ok, as waitresses typically do.

"Why, yes; it was," I replied. "Now we'd like to order desert and just because of the occasion I'll have the devil's food cake," I completed.

Satan laughed and chimed in, "So it's like that and in that case, I'll have the lava cake," he told her.

I laughed softly and said, "Good one; how about you, Dad?"

In Satan We Trust

Jesus smiled and retorted, "Ok, you guys took the easy ones, but I've got this." Then he said to her, "I'll have the hot cross buns." BADABING! Good, no one ordered angel food cake. That would be very bad luck.

I just about fell out of my chair and on to the floor laughing.

"I have another question for you. After this mortal shell is done, am I done with all the reincarnation shit?"

Jesus answered, "Yes, my son; my brother and I are tired and we were hoping that you will take over. we simply would like to relax; maybe get a front seat for Armageddon."

"Armageddon, you mean it's really going to happen," I questioned.

"Well; yes," Satan said. "You should know; you're the one who will be leading the way to man's destruction. Now that you're done with your time on earth, you can end mankind's suffering."

"Wow, I'm going to destroy the earth. That's a bit unsettling. I like the planet - I really don't want to destroy the earth," I confessed.

Jesus replied, "Now, now, let me set your mind at ease; the planet is going to be fine. It's the people who are going to be destroyed."

"Well I feel better about that but there are some decent

humans that I don't want to harm; maybe not a lot, but some. Why must they suffer," I asked.

Satan looked quizzically at me and told me, "They don't have to suffer; you have the ability to take them into the fold; however, you want the war that you will be leading to take place on earth. It has been the battle ground for as long as it has existed. Those in Hell and Heaven cannot cross into each other's domain, so earth is the arena for both sides. Your destiny is to bring the war to its conclusion if God somehow ends your life before you die naturally! This all is a moot conversation. Unfortunately, the body you're in now is a fine vessel - the natural order must be as it should be suicide and the hand of God is the only thing that would stop you from filling your destiny; but we will have some of your warriors by you all the time."

"So, if I don't die of natural causes, my essence will cease to be," I asked.

"No. We're not saying that - you can be shot because you're an asshole which is the way I figure you will go," Satan laughed.

To that Jesus says, "I'm hoping that you, my Son, live a long happy life for your last round. You have a zest for life. Even though your trials and tribulations push you to the brink, you have always bounced back and have fun. I think that's a wonderful thing! The winds of change are blowing and when you take over, you will bring peace and harmony to Hell. In your heart is the answer to all the problems. You will create a new and wondrous Hell. Yeah,

In Satan We Trust

all I have to do is destroy Heaven in the biggest war mankind will ever see, just great!"

After that, Satan looked at me and said, "You're not going to cause this war, you're going to end it! Just remember that your grandfather has done this. We are the ones who truly believe that man should be *freed* from his tyranny."

Jesus said, "My son, show me your arm - the one that was cut by Cain's blade," I held out my arm and he looked at the cut. It's a neat scar now and he continued, "That blade would have wiped me or Satan out of existence; but you, you have endured so much pain and suffering that it has no power over you."

"Have you hidden it well," Satan asked.

"Yeah," I replied as I reached inside my Santa jacket and pulled it out.

Satan says to me, "Do you think that's wise carrying it with you?"

"Well, I have always had a blade with me and I find it to be very handy. Having this, the most powerful knife ever made, has given me a sense of security and you know that I know how to use a knife," I answered.

"Be careful with it - if you're grandfather gets it, it could change the outcome of the upcoming war," Satan implored.

Chapter 3 - Meeting God Almighty

As we finished our food and I asked for the check, the waitress, who looked like a hippy, went to her station to get our bill, as requested. Suddenly we were surrounded by God's angels and God himself was standing in front of us!

"You foolish children. Did you not realize that I would not let you get away with being on earth and not take advantage of your stupidity," God asked.

He looked at me and stated, "Well, grandson, we finally meet. I thought that at one time you were going to walk right through the gates of Heaven, but you met your uncle first and he pulled you away from me, like a protective parent shielding his child. I'd like to tell you that this is going to be a long and heartwarming experience, but this is the end for you. I'll take my blade back now!" Then he held his arms up, like a fake faith healer, and I looked at him thinking to myself 'what an ignorant prick'.

God looked confused as he snapped his arms forward like something should happen. Satan and Jesus looked at each other and smiled a very evil smile. No sibling rivalry apparent there.

God, in a stern voice demanded, "Give me the blade and I'll let you sit by my side and not let you suffer the same fate as your father and uncle."

I slowly and carefully removed the blade from my jacket while remembering that Satan gave me my reward for saving him and I told myself I want to be behind God instantly, trying to use the same powers when I forced the patient and doctor out of that death causing hospital room window! Eureka, I ended up behind God, so I proceed to thrust Cain's blade against God's throat. After my sly move, Satan and Jesus instantly attacked the angels and made short work of them, so to speak.

I felt God's body shaking, like a convulsing epileptic, and Satan ordered, "Kill him now end the war!"

Thoughtfully, I removed the blade from his throat and pushed him away. "Listen up, Gramps, I could have wiped you out of existence, but I've never started a fight and I'm not going to begin now. I'm going to let you get your army ready. You want a war? You're going to get one, but as you can see you have no hold on me. You've become convinced with your own lies and it will be your downfall," I told him.

Satan said, "You could have ended it today! what do you think you're doing"?

"Well, I figured you guys have been hating each other for so long; where's the fun in ending it so soon? You said that I can end man's suffering with a war and if that's what I have to do, I will; but I'm going to do it in my style and when I want," I finished.

God says, "You've made the biggest mistake you could. I will kill you in a manner that will prove that I'm the true God. I think of all of us in Heaven, using my powers once again, and sure enough we all appeared in Heaven adjacent to the Pearly Gates, to be exact.

Satan and Jesus, looking startled, both ask, "How is this possible," they wonder.

Once again as I placed the blade to God, I saw the confusion and fear in his eyes. Witnessing this, his angels began whispering among themselves. "I'm the new ruler of Hell and as you can see my boundaries are endless, so if any of you dare to try anything against me or my followers, there is no safe place for you," I warned them.

While removing the blade from God's throat, I also place my father, uncle, and me back to Hell. Jesus and Satan were smiling like the cat who swallowed the canary. Jesus came over and hugged me, "My son, you did something just now that I wish I could have done. I'm proud of you," he said with a heavy chest.

Satan; however, seemed somewhat disappointed. "Uncle, I'm sorry; but, you've trusted me to do your bidding all these years but just like you, I'm my own boss and if war is the only way out of this, trust that you've given your kingdom to one worthy of the honor. I will not disappoint you as I do have a plan," I promised.

In Satan We Trust

"I'd like to take a tour of our army if that's ok, Uncle," I requested.

Satan looked at me like I had two heads and replied, "Well, aren't you a real go getter but isn't it a bit soon for you to be preparing for the war," he replied.

I responded to him, "Well, I just embarrassed Grandfather like no one ever has and from the way you talk about him I'd say time is not on my side. The way I see it I'm sure that God is already planning his revenge and I damn sure won't make it easy on him."

Jesus begins, "My Son, we intend to have our best demons around you from now on. I promise you my father is not going to take you without a fight."

"Thank you, father, but I still need to rely on myself to feel secure. I am grateful for your concern of my wellbeing but as I stated, I have a plan and without proper preparation it could all fall apart, like the Great Wall of China," I retorted.

"Well then," Satan says, "let's take a tour of our army."

As we paraded to the kingdom of Hell, I told father, "If you don't mind I'd like to see your souls first. They are my first wave and I need to prepare them."

We entered his level and it's just what I thought it would be - hundreds of thousands of worthless scumbags, but the centuries of torture hardened them, truly the worse bunch of people who ever roamed the earth. I stood in the middle of those wretched souls and spoke, "My fellow demons, I will be taking over as your leader and I intend to be merciful and relinquish the torture being instilled on you all. But, I know that many of you will only think this is just a sad, cruel joke so,"......

Once again with my powers, I thought of a lush green field and instantly we were all standing in a beautiful meadow and a large lake in the middle of it. Satan pulled me aside and said, "I know I've given you the same powers as I, but you cannot just relinquish their sentences."

"Uncle, you must believe that I know what I'm doing. Believe me, you have prepared these souls exactly how I needed them. I will tell you my plan when we're not within earshot of them; just know that they are crucial to my plan," I begged for his patience.

Returning to the souls gathered there, I continued my pitch. "Now this is just a beginning, but it can all return to the way it was if you don't do as I ask and know this - I can make it ten times worse if you fuck up. Hell is going to be a paradise for all when I take over. Your suffering has gone on long enough. God cast you out and I said, "It's time that we fight back and show him we didn't deserve his wrath! War is coming and we shall bring down the kingdom of God. Who was the last soul to arrive here?"

A soul came before me and I said, "Well, you really came here at the right time, my man." I gingerly placed my hand on his shoulder and I saw, in my mind, all the horrible things he has done to be sent to this section of Hell. It was so hard to keep the smile on my face, like

In Satan We Trust

trying to ignore a fart in church, for this horrid soul. I mercilessly turned him to the sea of souls gathered before me and told him, "This is how we shall take down God's army!"

Reaching into my jacket and once again and pulling out Cain's blade, I plunged it into his back fast and furiously. He exploded into nothingness and the smiles on the souls faces vanished immediately as I resumed my speech.

"I will be fashioning one of these for each of you," pointing to his bloodied blade, "and we will attack Heaven and bring about change so we can live out eternity in the manner that they have lived. But first you need to train. Are you with me," I finally finished.

They began cheering, like an intense football game, and I encouraged them, "Now relax and clean yourselves in the lake tomorrow as we begin training."

Satan transported us back to his home right after we left that section.

"You have no right to come into my kingdom and attempt change without discussing it with me," Uncle snapped.

"I'm sorry, Uncle, but they needed to see your reaction to my actions - it's all part of my plan, a well-oiled machine operates best," I tried to convince him.

Jesus said to me, "You can't make a blade like Cain's blade - it's impossible."

In Satan We Trust

To that I laughed and said, "I know that, but they don't, and what they don't know can only hurt them."

Satan chuckled and replied, "you lied to them?

"To what end if I may inquire? Despite their hatred for you, they will trust me as you said I'm their shepherd and my lambs will be led to their slaughter. All I ask is that they remain in that section and are kept away from all the other souls in Hell because each step of my plan depends on no one else in Hell knowing what I'm doing," I stated.

Jesus told Satan, "Well, brother, he seems to be doing everything we expected, and might I say give my boy some space and let's see how things play out."

Laughing, Satan replied, "I was thinking that same thing; looks like we may get to retire without worry. Just one last thing" Satan asks, "Are you going to extinguish all the souls in Hell?"

"Not at all," I exclaimed, "but those worthless fucks don't deserve a second chance. I'm just using them to deplete God's army. Oh, sure they're going to lose, but they will take out a large number of God's army. Remember, it's not always what it seems. I've been trying to adhere to that philosophy," I informed him.

"Now if you don't mind, it's getting close to Christmas and I need to get back to earth. Remember, you made me Santa Claus, so I could relax and enjoy myself and I'd like to get back to just that, rest and relaxation," I reminded him.

In Satan We Trust

Jesus retorted, "Please, my Son, be careful. Dad is going to be after you on earth and I would like to get to spend a lot more time with you. I'm counting on him coming after me. I can hardly wait and I, too, would like to get to know you better. Well, I'm off."

Back on earth and despite the fact that I have learned about my destiny and a man with more common sense would be constantly looking over his shoulder for the danger that is imminent; but to be honest, I feel relieved and somewhat anxious for my life to end so I can get down to business. As I walked around passing out candy canes to everyone I met, I could almost feel the misery and pain in the eyes of man - all the cruelty and hate that we all see daily has taken its toll on the populous; but, as a strange little man in a Santa Claus outfit handed them a tiny gift of candy, a slight glimmer of hope was sparked in their souls. The whole 'ending man's suffering' thing weighs heavily on my heart. I wracked my brain trying to figure out how to end the upcoming war. But God's need for man to bow down and worship him isn't something that he was willing to relinquish. Perhaps I should have killed him when I had the chance, then who knows, maybe just maybe man could change for the better.

A homeless woman ran up to me yelling, "Santa, Santa,". I stopped dead in my tracks and as she reached me. I had a peppermint candy cane ready for her.

"Please Santa, may I ask you for something for Christmas," she begged.

"Of course," I told her. "That's why I'm here," I finished my thought.

In Satan We Trust

"Things have been so very hard for me this year and all I want to ask you is will I have a hot meal for Christmas," she inquired pitifully.

While looking her straight in the eyes, I told her, "Christmas is a very busy day for me, but it's all up to you. I will grant you your request, but I can't be there for Christmas."

While reaching deeply into my right pocket and pulling out $20, I handed it over to her and said, "Merry Christmas, Child, be sure to get a hot meal for yourself."

Tears running down her face, like a soft rain shower in Ireland, she hugged me and whimpered, "I can't believe you're doing this for me. Thank you so much".

Softy and gently wiping the tears from her face, I whispered, "You've been a good girl. If you get exactly what you said you wanted, a nice hot meal, I promise you that this time next year your life will be better."

After hugging me once again, I saw a noticeable bounce back in her step as she turned and walked away. I continued on my merry way and decided that I'm going to do my best to not to wipe mankind from the earth. I have hope that they can change, but if they don't; then I will remove them from earth and let the planet heal itself.

It was getting dark and as I headed home, a man was walking toward me, and I got an uneasy feeling that something isn't right. Remembering, 'it's not always as it seems' kept me on alert. As he got nearer, he dropped to his knees, like a genuflecting Catholic, and showed himself to be an angel.

Expecting trouble, I pulled out Cain's blade as quickly as I could, and the angel begged, "Please spare me. I have no intention of harming you. God sent me to end your life, but I don't want to do it. Can you help me?"

Looking directly into both of his eyes, I sensed his sincerity. "Why would you not do as God instructed you to do," I inquired.

The angel explained, "I was there when you had the blade to God's throat and you could have killed him, but you showed him mercy. Now I find myself full of doubt. I've seen the hand of God do some very cruel things to his followers and I can't help but wonder why. If you're as evil as he's telling everyone, why didn't you end his rule?"

"First, please get off your knees. I never want anyone to feel as a lesser being than I," I demanded.

As the angel stood up, he took the form of the man who was walking down the street. While walking abreast of each other, I said to him, "Now, if I killed him and took control of his kingdom all of his followers would think of me as cruel as he is. This is not how I want to be seen. We're all different, but at the same time, we're all the same. Things are going to change, or the world is doomed. God wants to destroy mankind by having his war on earth and to me that's the most insane thing. Why hurt man who has no chance of defending himself in a holy war between the two kingdoms? if you ask me, that just shows he really doesn't love mankind. I have a question for you, what do you think he's going to do to you for disobeying his will?"

He said, "I guess I'll be cast out and then be tormented in Hell."

"Set your mind at rest, my friend, I won't let that happen. You have my word. Are you ready to take a place in the kingdom of Hell," I asked.

Sighing relief, he answered, "Please."

I placed my hand on his shoulder and we were both now standing in Hell.

As soon as we arrived in Hell, Satan's demons were on the angel. They restrained him, and Satan said," KILL HIM!"

"Easy everyone, I brought him; he wants to join us," I explained.

Satan looked at me and then at his demons and demanded, "Take him outside. I need to tell him how we do things around here."

Upon their departure, Satan asked, "Are you crazy? Angels can't be trusted."

"I know you told me countless times and I have heard you. I'm counting on the fact he cannot be trusted, but I'm going to be leaving soon and I'm going to need you to welcome him to Hell. Just don't kill him as I have an idea and he's going to help me whether he knows it or not," was my reply.

Satan replied, "I've always enjoyed watching you work. It's never dull."

"I've got to visit Dad. Time to start my second phase of the operation," I informed him.

Satan replied, "I'd like to know more, but you like to surprise us all the time. You're my favorite soap opera."

"Hey, Pops," I yelled, as I interrupted Jesus training the scumbags. "I knew I could count on you but, get someone else to train them because I need your expertise elsewhere," I completed my thought.

As we walked through Hell, I said, "Pops, I need some good workers to make weapons and I know just the section - those souls we think should have gone to Heaven but didn't because they made a few minor mistakes."

Upon our arrival, they seemed to be in good spirits, so I informed them their sentences would be eased, but I need them to fashion some weapons for my army. "My father will guide you," I instructed.

After that, I transformed the section into a work area and informed them, "A few weeks of work and I'll never make you work again." They are instructed by me that they may spend eternity lounging around and enjoying themselves.

In Satan We Trust

Taking Jesus to a safe place to talk, I pulled out a box from my Santa jacket and Jesus asked, "What is this? it's Cain's blade."

This making him uneasy, he said, "I can't touch this."

"I know," I said. "That's why it's in the box. I need you to make another one out of the jawbone of an ass because they need to be identical," I added.

"My son, you understand that it will just be a knife and that it will have no power," was his answer.

"I know; I just need one. Trust me. This could save millions. I've got to go I must get back to earth, I informed him.

Back on earth, I spent days just strolling around passing out candy canes and even though God sent a few angels to end my life, I managed to tear them apart, like a bear mauling a hunter. Even though I can now die anytime I feel like it, I wanted to get one last Christmas in and make it my final curtain call - one last hooray, so to speak. After all, I won't be around to see the people of earth become nice to each other ever again around the holiday and knowing that Satan and Jesus did this, just so I could have fun made me want to make this one special!

As I walked around, I pondered how the end of this life was going to be over very soon. I, in my wildest dreams, could never have figured out that this was going to be the way it would end. And I do realize that it's not always what it seems. But, it's dusk by now and the sky has a familiar reddish orange tint which reminds me of Hell and

In Satan We Trust

I feel, oddly enough, homesick. Suddenly, I recalled the conversations with Satan and how if I took my own life that I'd have to live another life on earth. Perhaps I could put extend mankind's time on earth by enduring another mortal life or two. After all, I can't be sure that I can pull off what I have planned. I hung my head and for the first time ever I felt like giving up.

"My son, I've finished the task you set before me and just in time I'd say," Jesus said while putting his arm on my shoulder. "Satan knows what you're thinking, and he sent me to see you, my Son. After all we both have had a moment of doubt granted for two completely different reasons. But you, my Son, you have me to help you; unlike my father. I will give my very essence for you. Set all your doubts aside and know that I am here for you," he told me.

"Father, I can't be sure that I can win," I told him honestly.

"Probably not, but the difference this time is unlike me and my fate. You, my Son, are not alone; you have your uncle and me to watch your back," he told me.

I hugged him immediately after he finished his thought and a tear rolled down my cheek while doing so. "Thank you, Father; but I don't want anything to happen to you as you've endured so much pain already. I can't ask you to do this for me," I said.

"My son, the best part of being a father is taking care of your children no matter what. I wish *my* father understood that. Now if you don't mind, I'd like to see my confident fighting son back in your eyes. Here's the case and the duplicate blade," he asked of me.

I took Cain's blade and put it in my jacket and the duplicate one in my sleeve. "Come with me, my Son, and we'll return to Hell," he told me.

Before we transported back, a band of angels appeared and attacked Jesus, like pissed off mothers to pedophiles. We started kicking ass and while doing so, I took out Cain's blade and began exterminating them one by one, like Hitler did to the Jews. After wiping them out, we finally returned to Hell. I was enraged and wanted revenge. So, I brought the souls who had been training and the weapons that were made and told them the time has come to begin the war. I implored them to get a weapon and finally prepare. I looked for the angel who came to me with the desire to join me. When I saw him, I noticed he had been stripped of his wings and he told me that Satan ripped them off because no one in Hell is allowed to have wings. Clearly, he's in severe pain. I apologized to him and assured him that I didn't know he would do something like that. I explained that I had asked Satan to watch out for him. He would have to continue suffering the pain as there are no controlled substances in Hell.

The angel in pain said to me, "It's fine as long as you allow me to stay and be your follower."

I took him to a lavish room and said, "You've shown your dedication to me, so I need you to do something of the utmost importance. I'm bringing my warriors to Heaven and I'm going to wipe them out, but I can't take this with me," I explained.

Carefully and slowly removing the blade from my jacket, I told him, "I need you to guard this for me and place it on the table."

"You can count on me; it will be safe until you return," he promised.

I asked him to clean up and make himself at home and I'll be back soon. I returned to the warriors and they were chomping at the bit for some payback. After resolving that dispute with them, I transported my faithful demons to Heaven where they went crazy on the angels.

God sent the ensuing battle to earth - California to be exact. I didn't agree with God, but if you have to pick a place to burn you can't pick a better place on earth than California. This battle went on for weeks and I was impressed by how my demons performed. The state was burning all around and this fire only inspired the demons. Heaven's casualties are greater than I expected when the battle finally ended. With the remaining demons who survived, I returned to Hell, home sweet home.

With a definite look of disapproval, Satan greeted me. "You told me that you have been listening to me and you trusted an angel and now you lost the most powerful weapon we ever possessed. He's gone and the blade with is him also," he said.

In Satan We Trust

Jesus was in the corner by this time, and he burst out laughing. "You think this is funny, brother, we're in jeopardy and your son fucked up royally," Jesus said.

Looking Satin in the eye, I answered, "Uncle, I have listened and all the times you tested me to see if I was loyal taught me that you must test those who you come in contact with." I reached into my jacket and pulled out the true blade and spoke, "I kept this little gem a secret from you to get even with you for doubting me," I finished.

Satan laugh at that and said, "Well, is my face red? **Congratulations,** you little prick, no one has ever put one over on me."

"Enough of the cloak and dagger shit. I think it's time to let you and your uncle in on the battle plan. Quite honestly, I don't like being kept in the dark," Satan informed us.

Jesus replied, "Brother, my son has told me of his plan and I think we've put too much pressure on him with our talk about wanting to relax and have him take over. His plan borders on a suicide mission. He plans on allowing Pops to stab him with the fake blade and then using Cain's blade he will take him out before he actually dies. It's a risky move and there's no guarantee that he can pull it off."

Looking directly at Jesus, Satan stated, "Brother, I know that you're thinking that you're doing just what Dad did to you, but it seems like he came up with this idea all by himself and you've been watching out for him all along.

In Satan We Trust

He has proven himself to be a noble warrior and endured all the shit Dad has thrown at him. I say let him decide for himself, but I agree with you that it's a risky maneuver, but I believe that if anyone can pull it off, our little Santa is the one. Either way, he'll be with us after the battle the moment he dies. He will appear in Hell so it's a win-win!"

Walking over to Jesus and then hugging him, I said, "Dad, I've had a good life overall or shall I say lives. Now that it is all out in the open, I see things more clearly and I am ready to take the reigns, so to speak. You and Uncle, here, deserve to enjoy the afterlife because you've both sacrificed so much and I'm ready to do my part!"

Chapter 4 - Christmas On Earth

Well, back on earth I start preparing for Christmas getting trinkets ready to leave under the tree since this could very well be my last Christmas at which time. I decided to issue a world-wide test of sorts. I intended to see if mankind had forgotten what Christmas was all about; it's not what the Christians turned it into. It has never been about greed - it was and always will be about love of family, the kind that Satan and Jesus have towards each other. Let me put it this way - the song 'Do you hear what I hear'. A child shivers in the night; we must bring him silver and gold - greedy fucking priest! How about some blankets and a warm place to stay, but no; they think only of getting silver and gold, so they can live high and mighty. It' sad that's how mankind operates, but I will find out this year if mankind has any hope left. If you fail my test, as much as it pains me, I will bring about Armageddon. So, this year be happy for the small insignificant gifts. Don't be the ungrateful souls the church has programmed you to be.

As I strolled through the woods in the freshly fallen snow, it's so peaceful and I heard a familiar sound. It was the sound of footsteps and I could see the reindeer coming. My heart was full of joy as it has been a long year and the thing I enjoyed the most is the feeling of speeding above the clouds with my team working as one. It didn't take long before all the reindeer were there with me. Upon the last arrival, I broke out carrots from my stash and started talking to them ever so softly. They seemed to have been looking forward to this as much as I was, so we walked a few miles. Up ahead in a clearing was the sleigh. The proud reindeer lined up without any help as they were evidently anxious to go on a flight and they are not the only ones. I hooked them up to their harnesses, like a Mom places her child in a car seat, and I took my seat right up front.

"Alright, team, let's do this," I announced and away we flew! The first flight is always the best because we all know that it's just for fun and the playful reindeer like to turn it into a thrill ride. They seem to always come up with a new stunt to see if they can scare me, but we're a team and I know that they would never put me in danger. But I did like to pretend that they had me scared because it makes them feel good and they snicker at that.

Suddenly they bolted downwards, and their explosive grunts let me know that danger was approaching. We struck something, and feathers were everywhere! Those fucking angels were after me yet again, but my team was the fastest thing in the sky.

"I yelled out to them, "Ok, guys, let's have some fun!" I guided my sleigh towards the woods and lead the angles through the thick unforgiving forest. Unlike the angels, my strong, healthy reindeer practice flying every day and I know that I have the advantage here and now. As we twisted and turned through the familiar forest, I heard the 'thwack' of the pitiful angels crashing into trees with each one, like flies to shit. I gave out my traditional 'HO, HO, HO'. Suddenly an angel came in from the side and the team turned a hard left and just before the angel reached us, he raised up his wings for one last burst of speed to grab me. But an unseen branch sheared off his wings and he tumbled forever through the trees and finally crashed to the ground. It appeared that was the last one, so I took the team to the ground to check on them.

In the clearing, the playful reindeer appeared somewhat anxious as the flight was supposed to be a fun time - not a death run, but my team performed like world champions. Despite a few minor cuts and scratches, they were none the less for wear. I reached into my bag and pulled out some stick candy canes for the reindeer team. They love candy and as they enjoyed their treat, I slowly made my way down the line brushing them all the while and making sure that they were not too badly hurt. They were slightly spooked, but in overall good condition. After I cleared them for take- off, we ascend to the sky and headed to the North Pole. During our descent and landing, I noticed the elves were armed and in excellent shape as always. As they surrounded the sleigh, they mysteriously hurried me inside.

Noticing my father standing there, I said, "Dad, it's not safe for you to be here."

Jesus replied to me, "Son, we're thinking this year you should let someone else deliver the gifts because of our concern that your grandfather has concentrated all of his efforts on killing you."

In Satan We Trust

"Yeah, I kinda noticed that, but with each attempt he loses more and more of his warriors and I'm loving the challenge. Besides, the reindeer are faster than anyone God can send and what's up with my elves," I answered.

A laughing Jesus replied, "You should know that these elves are your elite demons and they will be with you from now on."

"Well, that's not going to happen Christmas is my time for fun and relaxing. Believe me, nothing is more fun and relaxing to me than killing Gramps' pussy squad," I boasted.

"Be that as it may, my Son, your uncle and I feel that you're not taking the threat seriously," he answered.

"Wow, Dad, I understand exactly what is transpiring but it's OK. I'm ready to leave this mortal shell and take my place in Hell. As long as you're here I'd like to give you your gift now," I stated.

Walking briskly to the sleigh and opening the back compartment, I dragged out a freshly collected soul. Jesus' eyes widened like a child on Christmas morning opening gifts when he saw that.

"You shouldn't have, my Son, especially now; but, thank you so much," he thanked me as I tossed Cardinal Bernard Law, the newly acquired soul, to the floor.

"I will admit this fuck was hard to get my hands on, but I know that it would make you happy and I got to do it and take out some of God's finest warriors," I told Dad.

"So now Dad knows that he has a fake blade and you possess Cain's blade," Dad asked me.

"HELL, NO," I replied. "I took them out without the need of it. You and Uncle should know that I'm not going to be that easy to kill; God's angels are soft. They don't train those fucking idiots and they still think their beloved God will protect them. They just don't get that they're just lambs being led to slaughter," I retorted.

"I'm impressed, my Son. I know that Dad wanted this fucker's soul, but now he's going to want to kill you even more," Jesus told me.

"That's why I chose to take him. The more I can enrage him, the less clear he thinks. Now take this piece of shit to Hell and make him pay for his sins and MERRY CHRISTMAS, DAD," I finished.

Leaving the North Pole, I was now less than happy to have a band of little demons wearing elfish garb trailing along with me. This is definitely not my idea of fun. From my right side, I heard one of the silly looking things say, "Don't sweat it, you see demons following you, but trust me, mere mortals cannot see angels and such, so don't worry about it interfering with your celebration. Just do what you always do."

Glancing to my right, I began chuckling when I saw the most convincing elf-looking demon and asked, "So your serious about this? And by the way, that's an amazing disguise, who might you be?"

In Satan We Trust

While smiling a stupid smile, he answered, "I'm Louie, your #1 elf and bodyguard. Over there is Mac."

To my left, I saw yet another most convincing little dude with a bag of candy canes. "Huh, you guys got me fooled. You look just like fucking elves," I told them.

They all laughed exaggeratively and I said, "So, Louie, no offense but you guys don't seem like much protection. I may as well be alone."

"Jesus said you were going to give us a hard time," replied Louie, "but and I mean this with no disrespect. We're a lot tougher than you can imagine. And please don't think I wish to prove it. We've been able to watch you throughout a few of your lives. Many of us are here because you personally chose us and we're loyal and ready to fight for and by you," Louie finished.

"I apologize for my remarks then, my little friend. It's a pleasure to meet you," Jesus admitted.

As we walked, he detailed his mischievous adventures and even made me laugh. Along with Mac's color commentary, I busted a nut laughing. Arriving at a small village, the demons fanned out; but not so far as to leave an opening for trouble. Going about my business handing out candy canes, I noticed people truly couldn't see the demons. While handing a goopy candy cane to a small child, she said to me, "Thank you, Santa and I like the elves." Looking directly at Louie and Mac, I turned to Louie and told him, "We need to talk." After that, I worked my way out of town and turned once again to

Louie and said, "So no one can see you, huh," referring to the little girl who said she liked the elves.

"Easy, big guy. I think what I said was no one can see the demons. You obviously see me and Mac. We're actually elves, but we're kinda like you, not nearly as big a deal as what you have going on but we're filling out contracts for Satan. Also, we just haven't crossed into HELL yet, but have no doubt about our abilities and we are more than worthy of the positions your father bestowed upon us," he explained defensively.

I laughed and replied, "I'm going to call you Lokie Louie."

With a puzzled look on his stupid face, he replied, "Come again."

"Well, you're a mischievous trickster like Lokie from Greek mythology. But don't test me, little man, or I'll cease your existence. I need to be sure I can trust you. If I doubt that for even an instant, your gone," I informed him.

"I apologize for any misunderstanding," he said. "It will never happen again," he assured me.

Studying the raging snow while walking into another small town, I looked at Louie and Mac and said, "Nice, I feel like playing in the snow like I did when I was a kid."

Louie replied, "Santa, you should really take into consideration the danger you're in."

While laughing, I told them, "First of all, call me Seanta Clause. This life is his and each one of the lives I've lived deserves its recognition; each one has been different and has given me a look into all aspects of the human mind. Second, I know exactly what is facing me and I more than welcome God to try something. Besides, aren't you here to protect me? Now let's get down to some fun."

I convinced a snow plow driver to let me use his rig and hit the road. Louie and Mac were riding shotgun and the demons were appropriating alternative methods of travel. Some chose to snag snowmobiles, others took horses and many of them just followed by leaping and bounding through the snow. As we traveled, I gazed at the faces of the demons and they genuinely seemed to be happy. I guess being outside of Hell agreed with them.

Mac says, "Seanta Clause, I really don't think we should be taking time out to help the humans."

I said, "LISTEN, DO YOU HEAR WHAT I HEAR? It's mankind's pain and suffering, this is what God gave man. It's his legacy and if Armageddon is coming, I'm going to win this war and I'll be dammed if I'll allow it to become mine. I'm going to change the world for the better if I can save it at all, just know that I'm going to try my hardest to not destroy everything."

As we rounded the bend in the road, an army of angels stood waiting for us. In an instant, my demons were on them - ripping and tearing them to shreds like lions to sheep. Louie was out of the truck and going full force. I was extremely impressed with what I was viewing. I started for my door handle and Mac grabbed my arm and said, "Relax, this isn't even a challenge for them. It will all be over soon."

In Satan We Trust

The battle lasted less than 15 minutes and the snow was covered with the remains of God's feeble attempt to get me. Getting out of the truck, the demons gathered around me. A very sorry-looking angel lying on the ground, who was assumed dead, lunged at me. Watching this, Mac is out of the passenger side and tackled the vicious angel, pulling and grabbing his stupid little wings. He twisted and snapped them, folding them like a Thanksgiving turkey.

As his screams filled the air, my demons advanced on him. I yelled, "STOP, LEAVE HIM ALONE." Then I grabbed the furry little faggot by the throat and lifted him in the air and informed him, "You're going to live to deliver this message to God. I've been patient with him because he's my grandfather and I was hopeful that he may see that things can be better, but now I can see he's too full of himself to ever change. So, the gloves are off and after Christmas we will meet; so, get ready for me!"

The feathery winged angel spat at me and replied, "I'm not your messenger boy."

Grinning from ear to ear at him, I jammed his puny wings under the arm of the truck tarp system. Then I told Mac, "Mac, nice job stopping this piece of shit. I'm going to let you roll back the tarp."

Mac had an even larger grin on his face, it was an evil smile. While rolling it back, the angels wings cracked and snapped, getting tangled up in his scrawny arm. His screams filled the air once again. Now that he was well twisted like a ball of yarn, I said to him, "Well, from what

In Satan We Trust

I know of my grandfather he's not very forgiving with failure. And when you see him, I'm sure that you're going to wish I killed you. Ok, everyone, one last ride and then back to the Pole."

While walking back to the truck, I made the suggestion that Mac drive as I wanted to have a talk with the angel for a bit longer. As we drove along, I hung out the window taunting him. His legs were bouncing off the snowbanks getting beaten all to pieces. Then I said, "Louie, wind back the tarp." While doing so, the angel's wings untangled, and the angel fell off and rolled into a deep, dark ditch. Proceeding to a valley, we saw a herd of reindeer.

I told Mac to stop and we all gathered around the road. Then I told them, "I just want to say that I'm proud of the way you all performed today. Now relax and I'll be back." With that, I strolled out into the herd and spoke to the reindeer. They all walked up next to a demon and I said, "Hop on, my friends, we're going back to the North Pole." As we took to the sky, I yelled, "The last one back goes to Heaven, the race is on."

As we all dashed to the finish line at the North Pole, Louie was bringing up the rear. I pulled back on my ride and he whipped past me and my plan began now. We landed, and all the demons pointed at Louie and said, "You've got to go to Heaven and begin razzing him."

I landed my reindeer and said, "Hello, I believe that I'm lost so who wants to try busting my balls?" Unexpected silence filled the air. I busted out laughing and said,

In Satan We Trust

"Gotcha!" They all burst out laughing and Satan and Jesus appeared which caused the demon to go silent again.

"WHY IS EVERYONE LAUGHING," Jesus asked.

Stepping forward, I tell Uncle, "These fine demons performed flawlessly and we're just celebrating."

"MAY I REMIND YOU ALL THIS IS HELL AND YOU DO WHAT WE SAY OR ELSE YOU SUFFER," Satan replied to all.

"Whoa, Uncle, you knew that change was coming with me and it may be drastic to you, but I promise you that any disobedience will be met with a severe punishment worse than anything you could think of. Now as far as them enjoying the assignment before them, that's my call and I believe that if my warriors work as hard and efficiently as these ones did, I say enjoy, Boys," I explained.

Looking at the demons and detecting a glimmer of hope in their eyes, I whispered to Satan, "Come on, Uncle, they won't be any good to me if they don't think you're behind me on this." I specifically called him 'Uncle' to let him know I knew by a slight difference in looks when he was 'Satan' and when he was simply 'Uncle Lucifer'.

Satan glared at me and for the first time I thought we may have been at an impasse, but to my delight Satan spouted, "You heard my nephew - ENJOY BOYS!"

The demons went wild with laughter. Satan looked at me and said, "Let's get inside and talk. Louie, Mac come with us."

In Satan We Trust

Entering through the stables and before we got to the main house, I stopped suddenly and told Louie and Mac, "Now I need you two to look over my travel plans and work out a system to have me protected at each house. Let them relax a few minutes and then remind them that if I don't succeed then Satan will remain in power and things will return to normal only worse for those who fail. I'll be out soon to fill in the details. Take them all back to hell except the ones that need to stay here for protection and find more demons for the battle tonight." I entered the main house where Satan and Jesus were waiting.

Jesus said, "Son, you need to respect the work your uncle's done here."

"I do, father; I truly do," I tried to convince him.

Satan disagreed, "You're telling them that it's going to be better when you take over."

"So, what you think is that I'm wrong in how I've been doing things. I'm so sorry that you think that, Uncle, but I think you did everything right. You molded me the finest army ever created, but now I need them to believe in me if I'm to pull off the greatest defeat ever! You are my hero and I've learned about love from you and my father and I want the two of you to enjoy the rest of your days together," I said.

Looking confused and slightly relieved, he answered, "Nephew, it's just that I've been watching you for millenniums and I'm worried about you, nothing more."

"This is my destiny, Uncle, and unlike your father, my father and uncle are behind me. That's the most powerful weapon I could have," I replied.

Jesus told me, "Brother, this is not going to be like my fate. My son is ready and if you think that *you're* worried think how I feel."

"I hate to cut this short but, I've got the biggest night of all my lives and I need to get busy. We'll go back to Hell and handle things there," suggested Satan.

"Thank you, Uncle; but, please lighten up on them. Let hope build in them. It will help me to win," I scowled and then grinned.

"OK, nephew, give 'em hell tonight, Satan said.

Heading out to the toy factory and remembering all the Christmases before this one, a tear involuntarily ran down my tired face. Just as that happened, Louie came up from behind me and said, "I've been watching you a very long time and I just want to say I believe that you can win. You definitely have a certain something that I haven't seen in anyone in all my life. I'll be there for you till I get wiped out of existence.

As I began to thank him, he demanded, "Go out and put on the suit. I'll be sure to see that everything is loaded onto the sleigh."

After my wardrobe change, I pranced out all decked out in my official suit and the sleigh is ready to go. Mac and

Louie are waiting for me and I heard Louie say, "Everything is ready for us to begin."

So, I gathered the reigns and off we went, just like the typical Santa and Rudolph story. However, as we were flying house to house, I noticed my demons were watching out for an attack. They bolted from here to there checking to ensure the way was clear. The night went so smoothly that I almost forgot about the final delivery. My heart was full of joy once again. After finishing the last home, I jumped happily into the sleigh and call out to my demons, "Merry Christmas, my friends. Now you can return to Hell and partake in the celebration that I've set up for you."

I took to the sky and informed Louie and Mac that they could go join the party. Louie replied, "We appreciate that, but my place is by your side," and Mac just smiled a nervous smile. While pointing my sleigh to the heavens and bee line it straight for the gates of Heaven, a hoard of angry-looking angels were waiting for us.

Just as they attacked the sleigh, Mac grabbed Louie and threw him out of the chariot. watching Louie plummet towards earth while the angels continued attacking him on the way down, I grabbed Mac by his fat throat and ripped it wide open, like a bashed watermelon. He gurgled, "You lose."

Pissed off about his betrayal, I tore his head off and threw it mercilessly at the gates of Heaven. Angels were everywhere, and they ultimately overwhelmed me. I recovered enough to find myself in front of my grandfather and the angels had me by the arms and legs, better than my balls, I supposed. I couldn't move for the life or death of me and God laughed his evil laugh and said, "Ahh, Grandson, your cocky attitude is your downfall. As I said, pride cometh before the fall and now your time is over."

With the blade in his hand, I said to him, "Well, at least before I die, I can take comfort in knowing that my father loved me despite how his own father betrayed him."

Enraged by my defiance, God lunged the blade at me. At that very instant, demons were everywhere led by Jesus and Satan. Twisting my body and forcing one of the angels who was holding me into the path of the blade caused it to pierce his back. With that strategic maneuver, he loosened his grip on me and I was able to break my arm free and retrieved the true blade of Cain. With my trusty weapon in hand, I slashed the hell or heaven out of the remaining angels holding me.

The anger in God's eyes revealed that he finally realized that he had been duped and I could tell that my death was the best he was going to be able to do. The demons and angels were cast to earth to face each other. Could this be the end of mankind? Is Armageddon upon mankind? Remember, it's not always what it seems!

Jesus and Satan were still there but, they weren't able to reach me in time. God again struck toward me and I put my arms out to the side awaiting the death blow, so I could finally take my place as the new ruler of Hell and then wipe God out of existence. The blade pierced me, and a giant white flash and an explosion occurred. Standing there, and to my surprise, still very much alive the explosion sent God into a wall and he lied on the ground motionless.

Satan galloped over and pulled him to his feet. By now, God looked like a rag doll just hanging in Satan's hand. I asked, "What in Hell's name just happened?"

Satan demanded, "Finish him, Nephew, and fill your destiny."

Jesus looked sadly at me and I said, "Father, you said the blade that you made had no power, so what happened?"

Jesus hugged me and answered, "I don't understand myself. All I know is the entire time I was making the blade I was sad and crying knowing that I, too, was about to sacrifice my son and I never wanted to do to you what my father did to me."

I held Jesus tightly in my arms and kissed his cheek. Then I proudly said, "You saved me, Father. Your tears shielded me from harm. You are not your father, you are the Savior of man!"

Jesus smiled sheepishly while Satan glimpsed my way and demanded, "Now finish him off."

Walking over slowly and grabbing God by his holy neck, I peered into his eyes. There was life there, but not much else left inside him. Looking toward the earth, I saw a black dot in the universe. It's no longer the beautiful blue jewel in the sky like it used to be.

In Satan We Trust

"Sorry, Uncle, but I'm my father's son," I explained to him.

Flashing to earth with God still held securely in my grasp, I appeared on top of a glorious mountain and a brilliant white light shone on us. "STOP FIGHTING NOW," I echoed loudly and clearly. Angels and demons all stopped what they were doing and noticed God just dangling from my hand, almost lifeless by now. "Return to where you belong before I get mad," I finished.

Simultaneously, the earth returned to the beautiful blue jewel in the sky and everything was as it used to be. Man will see this as an eclipse and go on still unaware of how close they came to being extinct.

Returning to Heaven, still clutching God's limp body, Jesus and Satan accompanied me. At one point along the way, Jesus asked, "So, my Son, what do you plan to do now?"

Satan returned with, "I still say kill him!"

"Uncle, your sentence is over. You're free to be who you truly want to be, and I know that way down inside, you just want a family who loves you. It's time to put away your hate."

Turning to the angels, who were now waiting to hear their fate, I placed God on a slab of stone and told the angels, "I know that you're not to blame for the way things were, but none of you had the strength to stand up to him and now you have to face the consequences. So, from this day forward all the souls deemed unworthy will

In Satan We Trust

be cast to Heaven and you will have to deal with them from now on. Do a good job and one day I may allow you to enter HELL!"

Satan, Jesus and I returned to Hell; I should have been very happy but all I did was sit on the ground with my head in my hands staring at the fires of Hell. Jesus looked sympathetically at me and said, "My Son, what's wrong? You've accomplished your goal and you've done it without destroying mankind. You should be happy; I'm so proud of you."

"I know father; it's just that I failed Louie. I should have been able to save him, but I was focused on taking down God," I answered embarrassingly.

Satan asked, "Is that all that's bothering you? How do you think that we knew that you were in trouble and who told us about it? Louie get in here."

Louie walked in like an MVP, puffing his chest out like a rooster, and I asked, "How did you survive the fall? You're not a demon!"

While holding back his laugh, Louie explained, "When the Angels flew down to finish me off, on the way down I grabbed one, killed him and jumped to another one and so on and so on till I rode the last one safely to the ground."

"Now I'm happy; this is the best," I announced to all.

Enjoying a walk in the rain is extremely peaceful! People run for cover when it rains, so it's almost like I'm the only one on earth. Suddenly during my brisk stroll, a circle of blue sky opened up around me. "Lucifer, is that you again," I asked anyone who was listening.

To my surprise, Jesus appeared out of nowhere and replied, "No, son; it's me."

"Dad, what the Hell are you doing out of Hell, I asked rather startled.

"Relax, my Son. Ever since you took possession of Cain's blade from your grandfather, it has been safe for me to walk the earth. And your uncle has actually taken a shine to the changes you made in Hell. So, I just thought that you might like to take a little break from earth," Jesus said.

"Isn't Satan upset with the change? Come on, Dad, what's really going on," I implored him to answer.

"Trust me, Santa, you're going to be pleasantly surprised with the changes in Hell. You've made me proud and things are changing just as I knew they would," Dad replied.

Once again, I was transported to Hell and Lucifer smiled at me, which gave me an uneasy feeling. Then he told me, "Good to see you, Nephew. Sorry I didn't come to get you myself, but my brother has been itching to get out of here for a while and now that it's safe for Jesus to leave. Who am I to stand in his way?"

In Satan We Trust

"Well, you're Satan and your word is law here," I reminded him making sure he knew that I knew the minor difference in the looks of Satan verses Uncle Lucifer.

Hideous laughter filled the air as Lucifer put his arm around me and he whispered, "You've given me a new outlook and I look forward to handing over control to you."

"You mean its time? I need to say goodbye to my family first; you owe me that much, I stated.

Once again, more laughter filled the air. "Now-now, Nephew, I may have done something so cruel a year ago; but you have reminded me of why I was cast out of father's kingdom. I thought just as you did back then. Now with father incapacitated, we are changing the world," he said.

"You're freaking me out, Uncle. I'm not comfortable with you acting like this," I admitted.

"Believe me, Santa, mankind has a battle coming and it's not going to be pretty! what religion has done to those who have twisted the original ideology of it has brought serious doubt as to whether or not they will survive," Satan said.

Chapter 5 - The Future

Jesus interrupted, "My son, we brought you here to discuss the future."

Looking out across Hell and sighing, Satan announced, "For far too long I've been holding a grudge against Father; but, now it's as if a great weight has been lifted from my chest. However, my intentions were pure in the beginning, but Father had no room for love in his heart. He was and always will be a self-centered egotistical bully just like many dictators throughout man's history."

"Uncle, I know you wish that things worked out differently, but you were just a child when you chose to challenge your father and you paid dearly for it. But, it's not too late. As I understand, all you really have to do is be genuinely sorry and all is forgiven. As I see it, you just need to forgive yourself," I justified.

Stepping forward, Jesus asked me, "My son, you say your uncle was a child. what makes you say such a thing when yourself are quite young in the grand scheme of things?"

"Well, Father, I have been given many lives to live and have been sheltered by you and Uncle, untouched by

In Satan We Trust

Grandfather's influence and since you and Uncle have told me of my destiny all those memories from past lives are coming together. I can't begin to say I know all the answers, but I have seen the mistakes of Grandfather. I believe man was created in his image because man is every bit as judgmental as Grandfather and three times as cruel," I told him.

"So, Nephew, you think you can fix things do you," Jesus asked.

"Sadly, no, Uncle. I fear man has condemned himself, but in my lives I've witnessed some very compassionate and loving humans, so I guess God didn't count on that. In the darkness there is a slight glimmer of hope for some," I corrected him.

"My son, would you care to tell us of your plans? The reason I ask is that Mother Nature is now doing your bidding. The hate in your heart causes her pain. She loves you for all you do for her and she's determined to make him pay," Satan answered.

"Father, I'm confused. What are you talking about," I inquired.

"Haven't you noticed, my son, all the disasters going on around the world? It's your pain that is actually making her tear the world apart. It's kinda the whole woman scorned thing," he suggested.

"I guess I take after Uncle in some aspects of punishment. I'm not as easy to forgive as I tell you to be," was my answer.

In Satan We Trust

To that, Satan chuckled while slapping me on the back. "That's good, Nephew some people don't deserve to be forgiven. I'm glad you've learned that valuable lesson," Satan mumbled.

"I need time to think, Father. Uncle, do you mind if I go for a walk to compose myself," I asked.

Walking through the fire and brimstone, I couldn't help but think about what Uncle said about turning over control of Hell to me. Will I become like Lucifer over time or worse yet, like Grandfather? As I passed the different stages of Hell and listened to the screams of tortured souls, I thought about saying goodbye to my loved ones on earth. After all, why would Lucifer tell me of his plans to put me in charge? I knew he said it was not going to be now, but he is Satan, despite being my uncle also.

Out of nowhere, my thoughts were rudely interrupted by an unfamiliar smell, no longer did it smell like rot and decay but of lilacs and roses. As I rounded the corner, I came to the place I had changed just before Christmas and I heard laughter and talking - not screams of despair and pain. Noting me, the souls become eerily silent. I continued walking out into the lush green field and ask, "Do I smell funny or something?"

Nervous laughter was heard from the crowd and someone asked, "Santa, how may we serve you?"

I responded to this certain someone, "I'm just taking a stroll. Please go about your business."

Looking puzzled and confused they surprisingly did as I said. As I walked along, I saw a small group who was harassing some soul. As I neared, I become enraged by who I saw them bullying.

"ENOUGH," I yelled. They start cowering and then they took off leaving the poor soul all alone. As I approached the soul, in a sad voice, implored, "Santa, please forgive me."

Startled at first, I put my hand on his shoulder and told him, "There's nothing for me to forgive, my friend. It is I who should ask you to forgive me, Louie."

Looking up at me, he confided, "I don't understand. You're not mad at me for not discovering Max was working for god?"

Through my laughter I admitted, "I didn't figure it out either and it almost cost me your life, my friend. Why are they giving you such a hard time and more importantly why is my elfish warrior taking their shit? I've seen you in action and they wouldn't stand a snowballs chance in, well, here."

"Because they know as well as I how I failed you," Louie cried.

"Ahhh; Louie, my good friend. I'm going to fix this right now," I advised him.

"EVERYONE SHUT THE FUCK UP RIGHT NOW! Louie come here, now I'm very displeased with you right now.

In Satan We Trust

Louie saved me in battle and killed more angels than any other warrior and from this moment on, he's top demon in Hell and anyone who even looks at him wrong will suffer more than any soul in Hell has ever experienced. Believe me, I'm not going to make this speech a second time. You've enjoyed the change I've made, haven't you? Now you wouldn't want me to return this section to what it was when I first saw it, would you? Never let me see this again. You're all acting like Catholics and I won't stand for that. Now get back to what you were doing. Care to join me on my walk Louie," I said to all.

"Thank you, Santa," he replied with a tear in his eye.

"You're my friend and I'll always have your back. Just don't let it go to your head. I trust you to set a good example," I finished.

"You can count on me, Santa," Louie proudly exclaimed.

As we strolled along the lake, we came across a woman crying. So, we stopped and I inquired, "What's wrong, Miss?"

While sobbing and looking up at me, the woman, whomever she was, explained, "It's not fair. I lived a good life; I did my best to treat people kindly and be respectful to everyone I met. My mistake was falling in love with a monster. I wish I could have seen it before we got married and had children. Now I'll never see my children again because I killed him in his sleep to save me and my children. The only thing that gives me any comfort is knowing my children are safe and that's all that matters to me."

In Satan We Trust

"I understand why you did what you did, but you could have left, right? Personally, I would have killed him, too, but I didn't make the rules," I mediated.

Louie defended her asking, "Santa, doesn't it seem strange to you that in an effort to protect her children and herself that now she has to spend eternity in the same place as the one who rightfully deserves to be here?"

"An astute observation, my little friend; but I promise both of you she shall not be here forever," I promised.

Drying her eyes while still looking at me in obvious shock, I told her, "If you want, I can move you to where your husband is being held prisoner and you can actually dole out his punishment yourself."

With a quizzical expression on her face, she explained, "Every day I must relive what I've done and even that's too much for me to endure; so, thank you for the offer; but I don't have it in me to do that."

Forcing myself to I smile at her, I suggested, "See now, the way I look at it, I don't believe that you deserve to be here. So, from this day forward that memory will be removed from your mind."

As I'm talking to her, two swans glided down and landed in the lake. "From now on, your punishment is to feed my two friends here," I compromised.

In Satan We Trust

She smiled as the memory she's been forced to live with disappeared and she told me, "I love swans!" Music to my ears.

I responded, "I know they don't call me Santa for nothing. Please consider this an early Christmas present."

"Come on, Louie, let's leave her to face her punishment," I facetiously demanded.

While walking away she started humming a little tune to which Louie continued, "Satan isn't gonna like this."

"Louie, my man, soon there's going to be a new sheriff in town. My uncle isn't aware of this little twist of fate, but very soon his punishment is coming to an end," I speculated.

Before we reached my Dad and uncle, I wanted to make one more stop. Once again, the stench of rot and decay filled my nostrils upon our arrival. Its uncanny how I knew exactly who I was looking for but, I guess it comes with the territory.

Approaching a couple of demons beating this one guy mercilessly, I took it upon myself to suggest, "Take five, boys, I need to speak with this one."

As he raised his head up to look at me, I yanked him to his filthy, little feet. Watching in awe as the stubby fingernails on my right hand grew an inch as I grabbed him by the throat, they pierced his fucking neck. Blood started spouting out like a released fire hydrant on a brutally humid summer day. With my other hand, I shredded his flesh and poured salt in the fresh wounds. His screams permeated the air as I tossed him aside. Then I told him, "Your wife sends you her love." BADABING!

"Now, my little minions, I want you to continue beating him and as an added bonus, do what I just did to him three times a day, just like a doctor prescribes medication," I said.

"Ok, Louie, I feel much better now. Let's go back to Uncle's office," I ordered.

Louie, looking somewhat puzzled at me replied, "I thought maybe you were going soft after your conversation with his wife...... Guess not."

"Please, Louie, call me Sean. Now let's go see my uncle," I retorted.

As Louie and I approached Uncle Lucifer's area a plummeting body crashed through an ancient stone wall, landing with an awful 'thud' on the ground smack in front of us. Jumping back quickly and seeing Louie ready to fight, I busted out laughing. As the crumpled pile of flesh gazed up at us, I said, "So, did the meeting with Lucifer go as well as you thought?"

The half-dead demon, at least he looked that way, jumped up and hobbled back into the bowels of Hell. "Santa; I'm sorry, Sean, maybe this isn't a good time to go in there," Louie suggested.

In Satan We Trust

"Ah, Louie, I appreciate your concern, but I'll be fine. Tell you what, though, why don't you go back to where you were and get some payback on those assholes? Remind those guys they're still in Hell, then go around and learn everyone's story. I'm going to need an advisor in that section when I take up residence here," I mumbled.

"Anything you want, Sean, I'm your man," he whispered.

With a bounce in his stride and a shit-eating grin on his face, Louie sauntered away. But, before reaching his destination, he stopped in his tracks, turned back and said, "You know, Sean, in thousands of years I can't ever recall anyone ever wanting to come to Hell; but, I'm glad you are here and not wishing you an early death but I'm looking forward to seeing you again."

"Back at you, little man, now get to work," I demanded.

Smiling back at me and waving, he bounced off into Hell. Likewise, I jumped through the fresh hole in the wall into Lucifer's chamber still chuckling to myself about my conversation with Louie.

In a stern voice, Lucifer asked, "Nephew, can't you come to Hell just one time and not change something? Did you actually change some punishments? Feeding swans, are you fucking serious!"

"Uncle, on my first visit here, I passed a small but beautiful area. You must have been the one who created that, am I wrong," I questioned.

In Satan We Trust

With a somber face and a melancholy voice, Satan explained, "You have to understand, Nephew, when Father cast me out. I had great expectations and was going to create a paradise unlike anything Father was willing to give his followers. But the souls he sent in the beginning were so horrid that I couldn't find it in my heart to forgive them and after a couple hundred years, well you can see how my kingdom took shape, and when he allowed my brother to be crucified, all the love and kindness in me was gone forever."

"Ohhh, Uncle, that's not true. Just the way you spoke now shows me that that love is still in you. Jesus and you are reunited. Isn't that a good thing? you kept him here safe all this time which proves you still care about others," I demanded he listen to reason.

Clearly angered and grabbing me by the face, Satan picked me off the ground and threw me, like a discus, at the wall.

"DON'T TELL ME I CARE; I'M SATAN," he was pissed.

Attempting to stand, I stumbled and started to fall, like a shit load of dominoes.

Catching me and holding me in his arms, Lucifer told me, "I'm sorry, Nephew, I didn't mean to hurt you."

Still reeling, I told him, "So, you don't have any love and compassion left, aye?"

Expecting once again to feel my body slam off the wall, I was surprised when Satan hugged me and stated, "Your father told me you weren't going to make it easy on me and I've never known him to be wrong when it comes to you."

"Believe me, Uncle, I don't mean to anger you. I just want your vision to come true," I admitted to him.

Entering apprehensively and seeing my battered body, or what was left of it, Jesus declared, "Brother, what did you do to my son? I'd expect this from Father, but not you. Jesus gingerly lifted me into his arms, like what happens on Ascension Thursday, and instantly I was healed.

"Father, Don't be mad. I pushed him into this and I knew what I was getting into," I begged of him.

"This is between me and my brother. I'll handle him," Jesus ordered.

"Dad, stop! You're both to blame for the way things turned out. It's bound to be difficult at times and I can take a beating as well as you so, too, can I forgive," I told both of them.

"Now come with me," I suggested. Leading them to the beautiful place I saw on my first visit, I offered, "I'd like both of you to look at this place and remember the dream of a better place. With that, Lucifer peered over at Jesus and told him, "Well, brother, you're right - he's good," And then he giggled like a school girl.

Surrounded by the most beautiful landscape I've ever seen, we sat silently and merely listened. The songbirds were in complete harmony and all the other wildlife chimed along in unison. Actually, hearing the lyrics was the most amazing thing I had ever experienced. At a certain point, I couldn't stand it anymore and I blurted out, "I swear I know that smell, but I just can't place it."

While Lucifer and Jesus both burst out in a laughter, Lucifer nudged his brother and replied, "See, Jesus, I told you he'd notice."

"Why is this so funny? It's so familiar and so sweet that I can taste it; it's like........," I said.

As a smile stretched across my face, Lucifer also grinned and announced, "Mmmmmmm Candy," and now the three of us were in tears laughing our evil asses off. My jaw ached as Lucifer continued, "Nephew, you and I have a fondness for candy; as a matter of fact, this is your nursery, and when the time comes it will be your office."

At this thought, my face lit up like winning the lottery. Jesus vocalized, "The three of us worked tirelessly on this place and it is essential to who you are."

"Hold up the three of you. Am I missing something here? Who's the third one," I demanded an answer.

Chapter 6 - Mother Nature

"Your mother. Who else would have come up with the idea of feeding you through the air knowing she couldn't be with you after you were born, or Father would have been able to follow you here. It's bad enough we had to move you to the mortal world when we did. Without you man would have never been given candy. You need it to survive and the only way we could keep Father from finding you was to give it to billions of people," Lucifer uttered.

"So, mother is still around," I queried.

"Of course, you know that you've been talking to her all your lives," Lucifer spoke.

"Wait, what do you mean I don't know what you're talking about," I inquired.

Jesus smiled that evil smile of his and voiced, "Take a minute and think about a woman that you don't know and I'm pretty sure it will come to you. Think about when you're at peace. Where are you and whom do you always talk to?"

Rolling my eyes, I inquired of them, "Are you kidding? Why has she never come to me?"

Looking sadder than any person I've ever seen, Jesus answered, "After giving birth to you, Father became outraged and took her beauty away, but I only loved her more."

"Father, I have to see her. Will you please try to convince her to see me," I begged of him.

"Well, my son, today is your lucky day. It just so happens that no matter what she's doing, as long as you're in your chambers, all you have to do is call her and she has no choice but to appear," Jesus admitted to him.

"Mother, I need you," I screamed at the top of my lungs.

"So how long does it take for her to appear," I asked excitedly.

"You must call her by her name, my Son, just as you did when you were talking to her before," he explained.

"Mother Nature, I need to see you," I spoke gently.

The giant tree behind us started to sway and as I looked closely at the bark on the tree, a shape began to form and out stepped Mother Nature. I trembled with nervousness, but I saw by the way she was standing with her face turned away that she was even more nervous than I was.

Walking over to her and hugging her, I admitted, "Mother, I've missed you so much." Just as I rested my head on her chest, her hands softly cupped my face and she raised my head. Her eyes were the most mesmerizing green I've ever seen, just like I remembered them. That was it – her white, flowing dress, her hair enveloped in daisies. That was the mother I remembered; not the one constantly trying to convince me I wasn't adopted. I held her in my memory all these years and throughout all my lives. For she was my real mother!

Stepping backwards, she told me, "Let me get a good look at my little boy."

The farther back she stepped, I saw just how much more beautiful she was. But then I noticed that her skin was like bark on a pine tree. "Mother, I'm so sorry what Grandfather did to you because of me," I cried.

Jesus said, "My love, you are still a natural beauty to me."

While wrapping my arms around her and staring to cry, she held me tightly, like a found missing person, and whispered, "Do not be sad; there's nothing I wouldn't do for my baby." As she continued holding me, my tears soaked into her and her face began to smooth. Reaching up, she touched the smooth complexion that once looked and felt like bark, and she started to cry.

Placing his arm around Jesus, like a proud parent, Lucifer blabbed, "That's quite a boy you have there, and I forgot just how beautiful Mother Nature was."

In Satan We Trust

Jesus uttered, "I have never seen her any different all this time. "My love," he whispered to her, "Lucifer and I have some things to do, so I hope you don't mind if we meet up a little later. Besides, I think our son needs some alone time with his mother."

"I understand, my husband, and I want to spend some time with my baby, too. It has been far too long and my heart has been longing for this day," she spoke softly. She hugged me and I've never felt so much love before.

"Do I have to call you Mother Nature all the time, or is 'mom' ok," I asked.

Squeezing me even tighter, with a tear in her eye, she told me, "Mom is just fine, Baby."

"Mom, you can keep calling me 'Baby' if you want. I would never take that away from you especially after all these years, but I'm almost 60 earth years old now. You can call me Sean," I corrected her.

"Sean isn't your name, Baby. Trust me I should know; I named you," she informed me.

"I know," I said, "but Santa just doesn't feel right until December," I blurted out to her.

"Baby, your name isn't Santa; its Satan," she surprised me. So, that was it; I would be taking Lucifer's place as Satan one day. It's not always as it seems.

"You mean I was named after Uncle Lucifer," I queried.

Placing a hand on her forehead and rubbing it, as if she had a severe migraine, she asked, "Baby what have those men been doing with you all this time? I guess I should start at the beginning. When your father and I were living in Eden your grandfather disapproved of us for not living in his kingdom, so he conspired to turn all of the others against us so they, too, would not venture out on their own."

"I'm sorry, Mom; but you and Dad are Adam and Eve," I asked sheepishly.

"Baby, Listen to me. Forget everything about the Bible that man taught you. That garbage is nothing more than a war manual," she explained.

Touching the side of my face, she informed me, "I call you 'Baby' because you really are a baby; every one of the human lives you have lived were just stages leading up to your true creation. You, my Son, will be born very soon."

"Mom, I'm confused," I confessed.

She laughed at me and said, "My sweet little baby, I guess it's not fair to laugh; you've done so much and I'm so proud of you; but you are destined to do so much more. I wish I could tell you more, but you've done way more than I thought already. Defeating your grandfather in a human vessel was never predicted."

In Satan We Trust

"Mom, I didn't defeat him. Nothing went the way I planned, and Grandfather isn't dead; I just couldn't bring myself to finish him off," I admitted to her.

"Don't you worry, Baby, your uncle has Grandfather under control," she promised me.

Raising her hands, motioning me to slow down, she demanded, "Easy, Baby, all in good time. You've got abilities that you don't even know about. You've used some already, but it's a natural part of your growth.

When others moved away from God, his faithful raided them and the things they created in a way that made it look as if we had something to do with it. By the time you were created, they were upon us. We could have chosen any living thing, but humans were unpredictable, so we put you in one of them and created babies of all forms. So, when they attacked, and battle broke out, thousands of babies took off spreading out across the planet. Your father fought bravely and gave me a chance to hide you away, but by the time I returned, your father was captured, and I was busy mourning him. Meanwhile, back in Eden, your grandfather ambushed me and did what you saw when I appeared. He intended to cage me for eternity, but Lucifer, who had already felt his father's wrath, saved me. Your grandfather kept him busy with hundreds of souls he had murdered and by the time your uncle figured out his father's plan, it was too late. Your uncle vowed to me that he would protect us, and he has never broken that vow to this day."

"Mother, I'm confused again. Dad's dead? But I've been talking with him - am I just dreaming," I asked.

Mother laughed and replied, "Oh, Baby, you have to stop thinking like a human. How can I explain this to you so you'll understand? Ah, I know. The others call those of us on earth CAT's like the little fuzzy animal, but it stands for Crystal Autonomous Terrestrials and I'm sure living with humans for so long you've heard that cats have nine lives. We're kinda like that. Your true form is far from here on a place that humans call the sun. That's also what your grandfather uses to put himself on that pedestal the humans placed him on - the whole 'I AM THE LIGHT' bullshit!"

With my head spinning, mother must have seen that I was getting confused. She comforted me, "Baby, come here." Once again, she enveloped me in her arms and continued, "That's enough for now, Baby. How about we all get together and have a meal?"

"Now you're speaking my language," I exclaimed with excitement in my voice.

Motioning with her hands, like a magician, the roots of the trees rose up out of the ground and began taking the shape of a table and a few small chairs followed. "This is going to take a few minutes, Baby. Do Mommy a favor and get your father and uncle for me, but don't walk. I want you to think about finding them and you will get there but before you do...." She appeared before me and hugged me once again and kissed me softly on my forehead. "I've been wanting to do that for hundreds of years. Now go," she finished.

In Satan We Trust

Concentrating on finding Father and Uncle, I thought of not being seen by them, and the next thing I realized was that I heard Jesus, "Lucifer, I know my son's not going to like what he's got to do when he's born. I'm not looking forward to this discussion."

"Brother, Don't worry about Satan. He's going to do the right thing just as soon as he is able to," said Lucifer.

Suddenly, he stopped and said, "Nephew, it's not polite to eavesdrop on private conversations," said Lucifer.

Coming out from around the corner, which is where I thought I was hidden, I asked Jesus, "Damn, Uncle, how did you know that I was there?"

"While I commend you on using your gifts, there are still some things you don't understand and concealing yourself after you materialize is one of the things you need to work on," he chuckled. "Why would you feel the need to hide in the shadows and spy on us? It's just wrong," he finished.

"Yeah. What are you going to do - put me in Hell," I asked while laughing my evil ass off.

Jesus answered, "You don't want to piss off your uncle. As you know, he's got quite a temper."

"It's ok, Brother, he's just testing out his gifts. It was probably an accident," Lucifer stated while winking at me.

"He knows exactly what I was doing and so, too, does my father; but I'll take the free pass on this one and with

In Satan We Trust

Uncle's advice I know now that I need to think a bit harder if I don't want to get caught next time," I replied. "So, what exactly am I not going to like," I finished with a question.

"In due time, my Son, all in due time. Is there something you wanted," Lucifer asked.

"Oh yeah, Mom wants us to sit down to a meal," I told them.

I saw a gleam in Jesus's eyes about the meal. Uncle Lucifer didn't seem to car one way or the other, but simply nodded.

"You want to try taking us all back or would you like me to do it, Nephew," Lucifer asked.

"You two go; I'll be right along. Dad, tell mom I'm bringing a friend to dinner," I requested and then I swiftly vanished.

Lucifer said, "That boy of yours is going to be a handful."

Upon hearing that, Jesus replied "That's probably a good thing considering the upcoming task he has. Now, Brother, if you don't mind. I would love to see my wife before the boy returns."

I reappeared near my friend, Louie. He was still going ballistic on those souls who were tormenting him. Watching my little friend kick ass was like witnessing poetry in motion! He moved so swiftly and smoothly that I almost hated to interrupt him, but I had to.

In Satan We Trust

"Louie," I called just as he landed on one of the tormenting soul's shoulders. Grabbing a handful of hair, he sucker-punched him in the face knocking him backwards, like a mallet hitting a croquet ball, and landed softly on his feet.

"Sean, sorry, I didn't see you coming. How may I serve you," he asked.

I looked at the souls he had been pummeling and suggest, "This is your lucky day; I need him. Now away with your sorry asses."

"I'd like you to join us for dinner," I announced.

Looking worried, he replied, "I hope I didn't do something wrong, Sean. I was just doing as you instructed me to do."

As I laughed, I told him, "You're my friend and I just want to introduce you to my mother."

Now the look of confusion is unmistakable on his face. "I know you said things were going to change, but I don't know if I'll ever get used to it. You could say it has been Hell around here," he confessed.

I slapped him on the back and told him a stupid joke. "You're already changing," I said with laughter in my voice. "Ready? Check this out," I finished.

Instantly as we appeared in front of dear Mother, she smiled that motherly smile of hers, and I looked at Louie.

In Satan We Trust

Everything about him seemed relaxed and peaceful - Mother had that effect on people.

"And just who might you be, my little man," she inquired.

"I'm called Louie, Ma'am, he replied.

Patting him on the shoulder, she asked, "And how are you feeling?"

With a nervous smile, he replied, "I feel…….. Good! Whoa, what's happening to me," he asked.

We all laughed except Lucifer, who asked, "What's this assassin doing here?"

"LUCIFER, THAT WILL BE ENOUGH OF THAT," Mother exclaimed. "He's Satan's guest," she finished.

Lucifer's eyes widened, and he leaned back slightly. I'm not sure because I've never seen it before, but he looked scared of her.

Jesus snickered and said, "Now you know why I say, 'it's not nice to mess with Mother Nature'!"

The table Mother set was truly a work of art. Her command of all things natural were awe inspiring - the way the roots twisted and turned to make the table and chairs was beautiful to say the least. I especially liked the heart shape she had woven into the center of the table and backs of the chairs. At each place setting, the plates had a spiral pedestal base and they held food unlike anything I had ever seen.

"Everyone, sit," Mother announced in her usual motherly way, motioning to the table.

Picking up a golden orb and biting into it, the exquisite flavor filled my mouth. It was so sweet and juicy which made me feel so rejuvenated like I just experienced sex for the first time. Looking around the table, I realized that no one else had one of these on their plates.

"Mother, this is the most delicious thing I have ever tasted. Why does no one else have one," I asked shyly. Something just didn't seem right to me.

"Baby, that's mother's milk. No one else would be able to ingest it without dying. It will give you strength to break free from your mortal shell when the time is right," she embarrassingly informed me. That was definitely too much information. I didn't really need to hear that, but I guess that's what I get for asking a question even though I was apprehensive.

Lucifer had not taken his eyes off Louie and finally he spoke, "Nephew, why do you feel the need to anger me by having this assassin sit at our table? He's in Hell because he murdered over 100 men."

"I understand that, Uncle, but all those men were, by their own right, simply and purely evil," I justified.

"Now, just how do you know that, Nephew? You've only known him since Christmas time," he reminded me.

In Satan We Trust

Rubbing my chin, I blurted, "Hmmmm, honestly, Uncle, I don't know how I know that; but, as you were telling me he *was* an assassin. I saw his life clear as day and I've always followed my visions," I tried to convince him. Mother smiled at that and told me, "Well said, my Son, you've accepted another one of your gifts - the ability to see into a man's heart and know the true person. Now, Lucifer, I think you should lay off his little friend and remember what Satan's role is."

Louie, who all this time hadn't looked up from the floor, finally glanced over to me and added, "I appreciate your standing up for me, Sean; but perhaps I should go. I have no desire to cause a rift between family."

Lucifer, now in an unprecedented move, revealed a side of himself long hidden away and replied, "Louie, my nephew finds you worthy of his friendship and trust. I hope you can forgive me for all I've done to you I was forced, nay deceived, into believing that I had to punish all who came to me. It was fear that drove me. I didn't really want to go to war. As a matter of fact, every time I went against Father, I should have been stronger. After thousands of years being given horrid souls, I stopped looking for the truth and I'm sorry."

Louie, still fearful of Uncle and his rule over him, was unsure of how to respond.

"Well," I said. "Louie, I hope you're not going to disappoint me, and you accept Uncle's apology because I know he's telling you the truth," I finished.

In Satan We Trust

Louie, with tears in his eyes, replied, "I do accept your apology and I thank you, Sean, for your befriending me.

At this point in time, Mother piped up, "Louie, would you please stop calling my son by that mortal name and call him Satan event though he's not actually Satan yet?" It was a simple request, to her anyway. It was a mother thing. Things just always aren't what they may seem.

"Hey Dad, this calls for a celebration. How about you do that 'water into wine thing'," I asked.

With Mother waving her hand, the vines reached down slowly from the trees and filled our cups. She said, "My Son, I have been away from your father too long and I enjoy making a feast and seeing your father enjoy my feast makes me so very happy. My faithful husband, I love you, and I'm looking forward to finally being together again." Now that was surely something to celebrate!

Getting up from the table, Jesus swaggered over to her and held her petite body in his massive arms. The love they had for each other filled the area and such a calming feeling overtook us all.

Nudging me and pointing toward Lucifer, Louie whispered to me that his face looked so differently now. The crusty mean surly appearance was fading away. This look was neither the face of Lucifer nor was it the look of Satan. Simultaneously, both Mother and father gazed at him also and proceeded toward him and then hugged him.

"Welcome back, Lucifer," Dad simply stated.

In Satan We Trust

Puzzled by the event, Lucifer asked, "What in Hell is wrong with all of you? Are we flashing back to the sixties? Love, peace, sex and rock and roll," he finished his questioning.

Mother laughed and again she waved her hand mysteriously like a band conductor. With that, the nearby river rose up in front of Lucifer's face, like a mirror, and became still. Lucifer stared at his face and wept. "Nephew, right now no one is more grateful than I that you've arrived," Lucifer ended.

"Uncle, you're a very handsome man. I think it's time we find you a true love," I suggested.

Louie added, "Damn straight; if I were a woman, I'd be all over you."

Suddenly Louie realized who he said that to and his eyes widened, and a look of fear took over his face, but Lucifer saw it and told him, "You're cute, but I prefer my women a little taller."

Jesus grimaced and added, "Yes, Brother, you have returned!"

Shuttering, I interrupted my mother by saying, "I have to go, please excuse me." Without another word, I vanished. Now I was seated on a rock. It seemed so familiar, like a **dejavu** moment, but I didn't know why. Out of the corner of my eye, I saw walking up the hill which made me curious as to why I was even there. As the man neared, I realized who he was. "Hey, you, miserable old fuck, what the fuck are you doing," I finally spoke.

In Satan We Trust

Stopping and rolling his eyes at the same time, I heard, "Jesus Christ, Red, what do I have to do to get away from you?"

"Listen to me, you, crazy fuck. I've come to give you a chance to enjoy the afterlife. How would you like to meet Jesus," I laughed.

Laughing right along with me, he replied, "Red, if you can introduce me to Jesus, I'll follow you to Hell."

"Well, old man, hang on," I demanded of him.

As we appeared at the table and the four of them saw us, Lucifer yelled, "THIS IS NOT HOW WE DO THINGS IN HELL, NEPHEW!"

Mother added, "Lucifer, you saw that he had no choice. He had to go; this is the first soul he chose. I think this is important to him. Why don't we see what he's going to be like?"

"Dad, I'd like to introduce you to one crazy prick, but also someone who has helped me to be the man I am," I said proudly.

Shaking his hand, Jesus told him, "Nice to have you here with us.

The man, whomever he actually was, pulled his hand back slightly and said, "Ah, you really should warn people about those holes in your hand. It kind of freaks a person out."

Lucifer cracked up laughing and barely audible, muttered, "Well, now you know where the smart-ass answers come from."

He placed his hand on his shoulder and said, "My son, this is Louie. He's going to take you to the best fishing hole you've ever seen. Enjoy yourself, you've earned it."

Lucifer announced, "Nephew, I hope you're going to make more of an effort to scare the new inductees; you didn't do a very good job on your first one just now."

"Uncle, you seem to forget that we're not going to operate like that anymore, remember? The shitbags are being sent to Grandfather now. You're just going to have to get used to it," I corrected him.

Smirking, Jesus replied, "Son, you need to be born before you can do that. Just because you plan on changing things when you become ruler of Hell doesn't mean that it is happening now."

"Sorry, Father, but you're wrong. It has already started," I informed him.

Looking quizzically, Father and Uncle that is, watched as Mother stroked my fine, red hair. "What an imagination you have," Father finished.

"I'm telling you I've already started doing it. Grandfather can't do a damn thing about it in his condition," I retorted.

Lucifer, annoyed by my statement, snapped, "You didn't kill my father yet and it is said that change can't come about until you kill him."

"Uncle, things aren't always foretold. Change has come," I reminded him.

"Nature," meaning Mother Nature, "Would you talk some sense into your son," asked Lucifer.

Mother glanced at me and almost whispered, "My baby, you are starting to irritate your uncle. Please just try to wait until you are really in charge and stop talking like you're doing the things that you have planned."

"Ok, enough," I announced. "I guess it's time to show you all just what I've done," I finished.

Instantaneously, four of us were in Heaven. Mother, father and Uncle look frightened, like they had seen a bear mauling a small, innocent child or something of that nature. A band of angles approached and looked ready to fight, like the 'fighting Irish' mascot, both fists in the air.

Maneuvering Cain's blade from my waist and plunging it into one of the horrid angels, he exploded into dust. The others ceased upon seeing that and the fear in their eyes was apparent. "Get the fuck back, you, maxi pads with wings, or suffer my wrath," I ordered.

They disbanded as quickly as they appeared. Father said to me, "Son, get us out of here now especially your mother. Father would *love* to get his hands on her. Please don't worry; I promise *you're* safe."

Mother, with tearful eyes, was trembling, so I returned them all back to Hell. Perusing the area, I saw some of the souls I had sent there. They're all packed into a tiny spot much like sardines in a can. Being the nice guy that I am, I released them and instructed them to go wild for the angels had gone against my orders. Upon seeing what I had done; the angels, once again started towards me.

Momentarily, Lucifer and a group of Hell's finest warriors appeared, and Louie was first to spring into action pouncing on one after another of the winged warriors. "STOP NOW, LOUIE," I commanded. Like a well-trained attack dog, he retreated to my side.

Lucifer scowled, "Nephew, you've taken an unnecessary chance coming here. We should leave this place now."

"With all due respect, Uncle, I have to see Grandfather and set him straight," I informed him.

With a nervousness about him, Lucifer said, "Nephew, I think it unwise for you to see Grandfather. After all, he'd like nothing more than to remove the only threat to his complete dominance over all life. Your mother, father and I are just an inconvenience to his rule but we are so close to ending it, so why push it?"

Vanishing, I heard Lucifer ask, "Damn it, where did that boy go?"

Out of nowhere a voice was heard saying, "I'm right here, Uncle!" With that, I reappeared. "As you can see, Uncle, I've been keeping secrets, too. I want you to know that

In Satan We Trust

I'm not as defenseless as you think, and Grandfather will find out just how powerful I am," the voice was none other than my own.

A snickering Lucifer replied, "Well, well, well, aren't you just a little trickster? Like I've told your father, you're going to be a handful. I guess my trying to talk you out of this will just be a waste of time, wont it?"

"Now you're getting it, Uncle, but don't worry. I've got more tricks up my sleeve," I said.

"Before we see him, I should tell you that you're not going to view him as he was when you last left him," Uncle chuckled a sinister giggle.

"Uncle, what have you done," I demanded to know.

"It was your parents' idea. I just helped them, and I agree with why they did it. You see, now that Father knows who you are, he will launch an out-and-out war to get to you," Lucifer said.

"Fine, let's just go," he demanded.

Approaching the alter, where I laid his body, I saw a glowing chain wrapped around Gandfather's entire body. "Uncle, this seems kind of like overkill. Do you think God is that big of a threat," I asked.

"You don't know him like we do, Nephew. He's never without his own bag of tricks. Standing right beside him, Lucifer said to me, "You have the means to kill him now, Nephew. Why put it off any longer?"

"I'm going to let you in on a little secret I've been keeping, Uncle. I just happen to know that unlike me, God is trapped in that form of his and he made a serious error in doing that. So, killing him would only allow him to free his essence allowing it to flow freely. So being as I'm the only able to free him, he's fucked," I whispered.

"And just what makes you think that, Nephew," he asked.

"It would seem that certain things pass on to the offspring and some of the gifts I've been given are most helpful.," I finished.

Smirking, Lucifer admitted, "I'm impressed, Nephew. It takes C.A.T.s centuries to unlock many of their gifts. You've grown faster than any of us. Are you sure you're not just dreaming these things," he inquired.

"They're not dreams. Just like now, your father has you fooled into thinking that he's still unconscious when, in fact, he's listening to every word. Isn't that right, Gramps," I queried. God remained totally motionless while Lucifer simply shrugged.

"Guess that gift needs work," Lucifer laughed.

"Hmmmm, maybe I'm wrong," I announced as I reached over placing a finger against Grandfather's forehead and sticking my fingernail into his skull at the same time.

God screamed and thrashed, like a rolling fire victim, in his chains. Now I was giggling inside and said, "Old man, next time I ask you a question, you'd better answer me.

In Satan We Trust

You're new to pain and I'm not afraid to show you plenty of it!"

"My baby, I know you've seen all the disasters going on in the world lately and it is going to get worse. It's time to put mankind in its place. Baby, the horrible things you're going to see make me sad for you but it's once again time to cleanse our home and try again to get man to change for the better," Mother informed me.

Holding me ever so gently in her arms, I asked Mother, "Am I going to have to kill man too? I've become fond of some of them."

Cupping my face while a tear ran down *her* face, she explained, "Awe, Baby it's not likely you're going see them too much longer. You, my love, won't have to harm any of them."

Lucifer snarled, "Your father, mother and I will get them to kill each other. They are, by nature cruel and violent!"

"So, what is it I'm supposed to do while you're taking away something I've grown to love? Mankind certainly has some wonderful attributes. It's a shame to wipe them out," I confided.

Jesus, while slamming a fist on the table declared, "This is our home and they must learn humility, compassion and caring. We allowed them in our home and they trashed It. Their time to learn is now!"

"Son, you are going to see what hate is, so gruesome and ugly. I'll bet in your heart you know this already; you have to witness this, so you can remember why you must teach those survivors how to start over and try to be more humane to each other and the planet. Your mother is hurting; she doesn't show it, but I know her pain. The man stopped being respectful and is destroying her. Now I am going to end her pain. Your grandfather dropped mankind on her the same time he tried to make her ugly; but, my love, in my eyes you've always been beautiful," Father said while turning to his wife.

Mother touched her face remembering what God had done to her and showed anger. "When he put man here, he had other C.A.T.s hiding amongst all. At first glance, man seemed harmless, but the others encompassed the planet teaching different beliefs and tales pitting man against himself. We've done this many times before in hopes of getting all God's agents, but they aren't without their abilities. Which brings us to you, my baby. You can battle the C.A.T.s. Find them all and dispose of them. Then we can finally teach man to live a good life, but this is after you relinquish this mortal shell. Baby, you've never asked how you're going to die. You've always just said 'I'm ready you know when' but how could you not care," Mother asked me.

"Mother, it can't be much worse than the other lives I've endured, so as I told dad, I write my own destiny from here on out," I, Satan to be, said.

Gritting his teeth, Lucifer divulged, "You're a hot shit, Nephew. The life you lived before this one, when I met you outside Dad's kingdom, you already started messing with the plan and I have to admit you have me stymied. I look forward to seeing how things unfold."

Rubbing my jaw, I continued, "And what am I going to be doing for the remainder of this life," I inquired.

With a slight sigh, Jesus replied, "My boy, you are going to try to save these people but to no avail. Sure, you care about them and we understand why you wish to stop the slaughter of man, but you're young and naïve. Your birth just coincides with this cleansing. The Incas, the Mayans, the Egyptians and all the others perished for the same reason. They became, to put it into a context you will understand, like locust killing your mother. Instead of nurturing and loving her, they raped her and tried to destroy her beauty. We have hope with you arriving that you will discover Father's allies and kill them. Then, you can teach the few souls left and hopefully we can finally stop the hate Father feeds on."

"As I see it the, problem is and has always been God. I believe it's time to put Grandfather on trial or as he himself calls it, it's God's judgment day. What do you say we all go see him and judge his actions? I can pop us all up to him and we can pass judgment on him," I said.

Jesus grabbed me, like a would-be kidnapper, and exclaimed, "Son, never remove your mother from earth again; it could kill her!

Confused, I looked at mother, but she was looking down at the ground with a sad expression. "Mother, I'm sorry if I hurt you. I would never intentionally harm you," I insisted.

In Satan We Trust

"My baby, it's not your fault. I've been hiding something from you," she confessed.
Raising her gown ever so inconspicuous, I understood that she was quite literally rooted to the earth.

Jesus asked, "Why do you think she's called mother earth?"

"My baby, I will go to your grandfather and stand by you. I'd give my life gladly to see you fulfill your destiny," she implored.

"That's not necessary, Mother. I just thought you'd enjoy seeing what I have planned for his actions. I know Dad will appreciate the punishment I have in store for that egomaniac," I proclaimed.

Lucifer, AKA Uncle, chimed in, "Nephew, it's not time. You must be patient and do what is preordained."

"Uncle, I have never stayed inside the lines. I thought you, of all, would know. Perhaps if I stop him now man can be saved," I said.

Encompassing me with his arms, Jesus voiced, "My son, when I walked with man and tried to save him, Father had me put to death in such a cruel way that I don't wish you to go that way. We have seen your future and there's a slight chance that the next time man will learn. You keep changing destiny and we don't know how the future will go."

"Father, the future should be a surprise. If you know how things are going to go, you may as well die now for life holds no surprises and uncertainty makes getting up in the morning a new adventure. You say you've seen the future and man may stand a chance, but if I shuffle the deck, then man's chances may very well get better," I tried to explain.

Scratching his head, a habit that adults do when they don't know how to deal with their child, Lucifer stated, "You could end man's existence altogether too, Nephew."

"Well, Uncle, I've always enjoyed animals as you know. Would it be so bad to give Mother a break from man? As far as I can tell from our conversations, the world would be better without them keeping animals, like the bullshit story of Noah and his wondrous arc."

Shaking her head slowly, Mother retorted, "Baby, you can't lose your compassion, or you will become no better than your grandfather."

"Mother, I'm confused. you're going to kill billions of people. Why leave any if they constantly make the same mistakes," I queried.

"Baby, if you can't hold onto love and hope, then you will be like your grandfather," she begged of me.

"Fine, then let me save them all now and don't slaughter any of them," I argued.

With a sympathetic look on her face, Mother replied, "They've gone too far astray to be saved, but that's how I want you to think."

"I understand, Mother, but Grandfather will be judged. And now, father, Uncle, come if you want, but I'm going without you if you decline. It's time to twist the bowels of fate once again," I snarled.

Standing beside me and looking at Jesus, Lucifer suggested, "Brother, I know the boy is going and I'm going with him. You can stay here with Nature. I know Father still scares you, so if we don't make it back, you need to take over Hell."

Jesus hugged Mother Nature and kissed her. "My love, I have to go and help our son," he explained.

Mother Nature advanced to me and confessed, "I'm coming with you, too. You're my life and I will not let you fight God without me. We're a family and family stands together in tough times."

"I'm sorry, Mother, but I won't let you die for me. However, let me assure you we will all be back - I promise. The only reason I'm taking Father and Uncle is so they can see justice finally being served," I exclaimed.

Beginning to cry, Mother stammered, "Please take me. I can't bear the thought of being alone for eternity."

Gazing at Jesus with a question on my face, I finally asked the unimaginable, "How long can Mother last separated from the planet?"

Not really surprised at the question, He kind of knew it was coming, Jesus apprehensively answered, "It all depends on how much energy she uses. If she has to fight, I fear no more than an hour."

With the sad, puppy-dog eyes only a child makes to his mother, I, soon to be called 'Satan', demanded, "Mother, promise me you will not fight, and I'll bring you."

Turning toward me and pleading, Lucifer begged, "Nephew, leave them here. I will die by your side if need be, but your parents have a love unmatched throughout the cosmos. It would be wrong to let it end."

"I AM SATAN! You keep saying you have seen my destiny, but I've been gathering powers with each moment and none of you has to fight. Grandfather has a surprise coming, believe me," I yelled.

Ok, it's time for a family reunion. Once again, we were standing in Heaven by the altar where God is chained. God, clearly angered that those he had turned out of his kingdom were standing in his kingdom once again proclaimed, "I will kill all of you for daring to think you can rule over me."

Wondering exactly who 'called' this reunion, I began, "Rule over you, old man, we're not going to rule over you, we're here to judge you."

As if pixie dust was just spread throughout the air, angels swarmed around us preparing to do battle. Waving my hand like a magician, it's only fair since pixie dust was released, the little fairy angels fell like raindrops to the ground.

In Satan We Trust

Looking shocked, Lucifer, Jesus, and Mother watched God struggle in his chains trying desperately to free himself. "You want me to remove your chains, Grandfather," I facetiously asked.

Chapter 7 - The Dare

"You don't have the balls to take me on, Satan. You never should have revealed yourself to me. It's only a matter of time before I kill you, so you may as well kill me now," God, answered. Walking up to God, I started slapping his ugly, old face lightly to piss his enslaved body off. "UNCHAIN ME, YOU LITTLE BASTARD AND I'LL KILL YOU," he called out.

"Very well, Grandfather, or do you prefer I call you 'God'. And you can call me Satan-to-be because I'm not quite there yet. Lucifer is still Satan. Have it your way, like Burger King; but, promise to be nice and this will be easier on you," I suggested. I grabbed the rusty chains like a magician pulls a tablecloth from a table, and the chains disappeared. Voila!

God was up in a flash and ready to battle. Let the game begin!

God rushed towards Mother Nature with vengeance in his mind. Waving my hand once again landed all three of them are back in Hell. Turning to me, God attempted to attack me. One punch hit me hard and catapulted me against the alter, which told me we were back in Heaven.

In Satan We Trust

In an instant, he had me by the throat. Throwing a bevy of fists, he then hurls me at the pearly gates. Hitting so hard that the gates sheared off their hinges and crashed down on me, I heard the angels cheering, calling for my blood. God, like a cocky prizefighter, raised his arms in the air as if to confirm his victory over me.

I pled for mercy, like the Brits wanted Braveheart to do. While reaching down throwing the gates to the side and grabbing me, he proceeded to slam me on the ground time after time. Looking into my eyes, he pulled me up, so I said, "Grandfather; please, we're family. Can't we live in peace?"

God, with malice and pure hatred, answered, "I am the one the only, the most powerful being in the entire universe and all of you serve me. You should bend to my will like all these pathetic souls' but now, you little insignificant piss ant, will discover just how vengeful I can be and when I kill you, you can take this final thought to your grave: When I'm done with you, I'm going to raid Hell and nail your father back on the cross and remove Lucifer's head from his body. Then I will rape and have your mother as my sex slave. I'll beat her near death and then wait for her to heal and do it over and over for eternity!" The angels were silent and shocked by what they have heard. It's not always what it seems.

Now this wasn't like a 'Your mother wears combat boots' remark. No, those were fighting words. "Grandfather why is it you preach love thy neighbor, but you act so cruel," I protested.

In Satan We Trust

"You, stupid child. To get people to follow you blindly you must trick and deceive them into seeing the goodness in you and then you can get away with just about anything. Now, you rotten little bastard, It's time to end this," he informed me.

An evil, red glow in my eyes caused the lava that flows in the rivers of Hell to now floated through my veins. God's hands sizzled, like frying bacon, where he was holding me. As he let's go of me, I grabbed him fast and furiously and smashed his Heavenly head on his beloved altar. Dragging him to me, I told him, "I just wanted you to brag in front of your angels. Now they know that you're a piece of shit." With my unheavenly finger, as if I was dipping it into holy water, I carved '333' into his forehead because he's not worthy of '666'.

"I'm being nice giving you this mark. My '666' has bothered me, but now you will carry this mark, so everyone knows you're half the man I am. You're not worthy of '666'. Now it's time for you to face judgment day and, believe me, you're not going to like what I have in store for you," I warned him.

I returned to Hell dragging God behind me like a child's rag doll. Lucifer looked at God's new mark and asked, "Why didn't you kill him? It's part of your destiny!"

"The whole destiny thing is out the window now, Uncle. Let's just consider from here on out a blank slate but right now we are all going back to Heaven and giving God his just desserts. Mother are you well enough to go back," I asked.

"Baby, I'm fine but why are we going back? You have him with you now. Can't we just do it here," she asked her son.

"We could but the angels need to see what's in store for them if they don't change their ways," I answered.

"Lead on, Nephew. I really am curious as to what you have planned," said Lucifer. "Plus, there are a couple of angels I owe a beating to," he finished.

We returned to heaven but when we arrived, the mood of the angels was somber and not one of them moved to help God. It seemed fear had them paralyzed. It was time to see what happens to a wolf in sheep's clothing. It was apparent that if we were defied any longer, you, too, would be punished to this degree.

Again, I waved my hand, Jesus staggered backward, and his saucer-sized eyes widened as he viewed the cross he was nailed to. "My son, that's not what you had planned, is it," he asked me.

"Hell yeah, it is. I'm taking a page out of his book. AN EYE FOR AN EYE. This one's for you, Dad, except if anyone takes him down, they will pay dearly," I declared.

God had a terrified look in his eyes begging, "Please, Grandson, I will change. Just don't do this to me. Kill me, but don't place me on the cross."

Shaking my head, I replied, "You, miserable little bitch! You'll never change, and this is the only punishment that seems fitting. You thought it was good enough for my father so assume the position. I grabbed God by the throat and put him on the cross. I closed my eyes and my body glowed like fire and god was heard letting out a blood-curdling scream. His flesh seared to the cross and the smell; well, it was like that of a pig on a barbeque spit.

"Mother, "Cool it off if you would please," I asked referring to the weather.

Mother opened her arms and it began to snow like a small-town Christmas card creation. As he cooled off from the newly-created weather, I removed my hand from God's throat and he was actually fused to the cross like a nicely welded machining tool. I glanced at him and said, "Just be thankful I don't drive a spear through you now. Then you'd really look like a pig prepping for a block party roast.

"Mother the '333' marking on him is for what he did to you. Uncle, after all you've done for me, I will allow you the honor of choosing your payback," I announced.

Lucifer stared mysteriously at me and shrugged his shoulders replying, "Nephew, I thought I knew how to punish someone, but I'm just an amateur compared to you. Nothing more needs be done."

"Very well, Uncle, now to all your maxi pads with wings. This is the new Hell and I will be sending some of my elite to watch you. Dare not defy them or I will return with a vengeance and you don't want that just now. In a few centuries, I may release you from here but since your all good Christians, consider that time as penance. Well, I'm starving. What do you say we break bread back home," I suggested.

As we gathered around the table, I noticed Jesus staring at me with a concerned look on his face. "Father, what's on your mind? I can see that something is bothering you," I inquired.

Jesus sighed, "My son, I've seen you usher your first soul into Hell. You showed him compassion and mercy, but with your grandfather you couldn't find any for him?"

Responding with contempt, "All along you all told me I was going to kill him, but I didn't. That was compassionate and when Uncle didn't take his revenge, I let it slide. That shows mercy, so yes, I did."

Taking my hand as she walked over, Mother told me, "Baby, it's just that we're worried that you may forget that you need to be kind to others. Once you give in to vengeance, it's easy to be complacent and take out your hatred of people on those who don't really deserve it. Misery loves company and it's not always what it seems."

"Whoa! I did those things to Grandfather because he deserved it and then some. Believe me, I will never be like him," I said.

Jesus replied, "Well, you've advanced so far already and we, ourselves, are confused. You are carving out your own destiny, so if you could help us understand your plan it might ease our minds."

In Satan We Trust

"Believe it or not, Dad, I'm just flying by the seat of my pants. I just do what feels right at that moment, but I promise that I will listen to the three of you going forward. If I ever go astray, I'm counting on you all to guide me in the right direction," I answered.

Suddenly collapsing on the ground, my body didn't respond to anything no matter how hard I tried. Cradling me in her beloved arms, Mother cried, "Baby, what's wrong?"

Sobbing back, I answered her, "I'm not sure, Mother. I can't move my body. Is it time for me to be born?"

With redness in her eyes and a teardrop appearing, she answered, "No, Baby, its way to soon. Husband, please help your son."

Startled himself, Jesus lovingly replied, "I can sense nothing wrong with him, my love; so I don't know what I can do." Not the answer she wanted to hear. But then again, fathers don't protect the way mothers do. It's not nice to piss off Mother Nature.

"Oh, for fucks sake," said Lucifer. "He's been here too long. You've been nursing the baby inside the mortal shell, but the man needs meat to keep up his strength," Lucifer finished.

Summoning a deer, Mother watched as Lucifer strolled over to it and snapped its thick, brown neck. Then he called out for Louie. As Louie entered, he realized that something was wrong with me and asked what he could do to help. Lucifer instructed him to butcher the animal, so I could eat. So, Louie cleaned the carcass and placed the meat aside as Lucifer waved his hand over the freshly cleaned meat. That simple wave made it cook perfectly.

With Mother feeding me gingerly, as if I was a newborn, I slowly began to regain my strength. Standing up and continuing to eat eventually I am once again back to my usual self. With Lucifer's hand on my shoulder he voiced to me, "It's not that we don't want to have you here, Nephew, but you must return to walk among the mortals once again."

"I don't want to return to them. I've found my family and wish to stay here," I resorted to begging.

Jesus sadly replied, "My Son, you have to go back. You must remain in the mortal shell a few more years, but we will be visiting you more now that you're aware of what's going on."

"Mother, will you appear to me when I'm there now that we've met," I asked with those sad, puppy-dog eyes of mine. I'm telling you it got them every time.

"Baby, nothing in the universe will stop me now that your grandfather is imprisoned. So, don't worry; I will be by you from now on and don't sweat the few years you have left. You don't know it yet, but those years are just a blink of an eye to us. I have to warn you though earth is going through a change since you've been with us. Be ready for it when you return.

Louie was standing beside Lucifer by this time and asked "Master, is it possible for me to accompany him on the final leg of his journey? I think I could help him face the destruction that's coming."

Lucifer grinned to Louie and answered," I may have judged you a bit harshly, you little assassin. You've guarded my nephew quite well the last few years and if he would like you to join him, by all means, go with him."

Louie looked at me with a sign of hope in his face and I admitted, "I'd like the company, my friend, and thank you for all you've done for me."

Lucifer asked, "How are you feeling, Nephew?"

"So much better. Thank you, Uncle," I confessed.

Snickering, Lucifer continued, "First time parents are the best. They love so completely that they can't see the obvious when it comes to those so dear to them. I hope you realize just how much your parents love you despite their inability to understand what was wrong just now."

"Uncle, for the first time ever I feel loved. I can die a happy man. You realize I could have died just then and beat the rules, don't you," I inquired.

Looking me square in the eye, Lucifer answered, "My little warrior, trust me. You need to age a bit more. I feel your power already and a full term will make you all you have been foretold to be."

"Uncle, you have my word that all you asked of your father will be granted when I'm born," I conceded.

In Satan We Trust

"Ahhh, Nephew, I have no doubt that times are changing but I don't believe that I can change. It's been so long," Uncle Lucifer answered.

"Uncle, you of all people gave unselfishly making sure Grandfather never got me with your little facade and you did it all to protect me. If anyone deserves to be rewarded it's you," I continued.

Satan, AKA Uncle Lucifer, replied, "You, my king, will be a great ruler and I'm proud of what I've done."

"Uncle, I will always value your opinion. This is your dream and I'm here to serve you just as soon as you reclaim your heart. I know in my heart you desire this more than anything. Also, I will always refer to you as Uncle Lucifer, rather than Satan even when your demeanor changes from Lucifer to Satan," I explained.

With a shit-eating grin on his face, Lucifer exclaimed, "Enough of this serious shit; it's time for some fireball. You've never beaten me yet and since this is our last game for a while, I suggest you put on your game face and give it your all."

All excited, I announced, "Ahhhh, I totally forgot about this game with all the changes lately, so can we really have a game, Uncle?"

"We've never missed a game in all your lives and this one will be the best one yet," Lucifer assured me.

Just then Louie pounced around the corner, like Tigger

In Satan We Trust

from Winnie The Pooh, with a group of miserable souls. Lucifer started pulling aside one after another. Then I interrupted him and said, "Uncle, I'd like those three over there to play."

The three souls must have felt somewhat pleased that I hand-picked them by the look on their faces, little did they know this was by no means an honor. After the teams were picked, Lucifer said, "OK, Louie you can take the rest back."

Looking heartbroken, poor Louie who really wanted to stay but simply couldn't, watched as I waved my arm ushering the souls back instantly. They returned to their section and Louie appeared beside me.

"May I ask you just what you're doing, Nephew? This is our game," Uncle Lucifer asked.

"Why, yes; it is, Uncle, but as I recall the only rule is there are no rules so I'm taking Louie as my teammate," I informed him.

Jesus and Mother Nature entered the arena and Lucifer, grinning from ear to ear once again, said, "Fine, Jesus is on my team."

"Since you two are seasoned veterans at this game, I'm taking Mom, too," I said with an evil smile.

"Fine, but no more players," demanded Lucifer. "Agreed," he asked.

In Satan We Trust

"Agreed," I said, "but we need five minutes to get a game plan together."

Louie looked at me and replied, "Satan, I have no idea what the rules are, but I'll do my best."

"Nothing against you, little man; in fact, do what you can but I just thought you'd enjoy watching. And remember, Louie, I'm not Satan just yet so stopping calling me that," I told him.

"If I remember correctly, Satan, your mother specifically asked me to stop calling you by your mortal name, Sean. She demanded I call you Satan and you know what that means, right," Louie asked.

I replied, "Yep, it's not nice to piss off Mother Nature."

Louie was pulled in both directions, like whose side to take during your parents' divorce. He knew Sean/Satan was right, but then you have the Mother Nature thing. A Catch 22, so to speak.

"Now, Mother, I've been working on a new power. I feel that I can take the souls essence and turn it into a fertilizer for the planet to help heal. I just need you to get Dad and Uncle off their game," I finished.

Mother glanced at me lovingly and said, "Baby, Mommy's got your back!"

I laughed, "This game's all ours."

In Satan We Trust

Lucifer called out his favorite Hellhound, "Koda, come." The massive hound bounded into the arena and plopped itself beside Lucifer.

"Ok, Brother, hope you brought your A game because Junior here seems too confident and after what's transpired around here lately, I think we have our hands full," said Lucifer.
Jesus replied back, "He's just a baby. I think we got this."
Mother sneaked a majestic glance at Jesus and said, "Honey, you know now that your father is detained and unable to harm us. We can rebuild Eden again and pick up where we left off. I'd hate for something like a silly game to ruin that."

Jesus turned slowly to Lucifer and explained, "Brother, sorry; but my A game just dropped to a C game."

Lucifer threw high fives to his brother and boasted, "I'm glad to see my brother is no fool anyway."

Hugging Mother, the way only a child does, I replied, "I see the old saying 'you don't mess with Mother Nature' still holds true."
"Koda, any time you're ready," laughed Lucifer. Raising his gigantic head to the sky, he unleashed a ground shattering howl. Lucifer, being an avid game master, released a fireball at one of the souls in the area striking him which sent body parts in all directions. In the blink of an eye, another shot another kill he fired again. Mother graciously lifted her arm and an enormous stump arose, halting his shot.

In Satan We Trust

"I saw my chance and like a major league baseball pitcher, I let a fastball unleash unlike Uncle's red flame. Mine, however, came out blue like the flame of a glass oven.

My first shot hit its mark, yet the soul didn't explode like they normally do. Rather, it sizzled like the fuse of a firecracker. In the smoke, every horrific act this piece of shit did flashed much like a television show. His final screams filled the air, like fireworks display finales. Lucifer was taken aback and paused his assault. I unleashed a second blue orb of destruction and a soul jumped behind a tree. Mom bumped her hip and the tree mimicked her move shoving the soul back in the fireball's path. Again, the soul sizzled, and another horror story was shown. The first soul's remains were liquified and seeped into the earth and a tiny sprout broke through the soil. Already I was looking at the next target. Louie darted out on the field and grabbed one of the three souls that I had picked earlier and as I fired off another fireball, Louie hurled the soul in front of my intended target. The soul began yet another show. My body went limp as I noticed a familiar face. It was one of the vessels I resided in. Fire raged inside me before his horrific deeds played out, so I fired a yellow reddish fireball at him. Nothing of this soul remained, not even the memory of him by anyone. I spied a second of the three and fired another blue orb hitting him, another show, another of my vessels being murdered. A horrific scream emitted from behind a tree and the third soul had the same blueish glow as his predecessors. "I was just thinking about you," I snapped.

"SHOW ME YOUR SINS," I shouted as his show commenced. I launched another yellow reddish fireball at shithead number two, whipping him out if existence. Mother softly placed her hand on my shoulder as a tear streamed down her cheek. "Baby, Don't give into hate - it will consume you," she implored.

Pulling away, I saw one of my favorite vessels being butchered along with his wife and children. I launched another exterminator, looked at Mother and said, "Everyone hates something."

Turning to Louie, I noticed a look of fear on his face, but also a grin like he's proud of his part in the recent development. Mother also turned her gaze to Louie. He looked down towards the ground as a small sapling rose from the earth behind Louie and cracked him across the ass. In a stern voice, I heard Mother say, "I hope you're pleased with yourself, little man, your life just took a turn for the worse.

Louie straightened up, looking proud as a peacock, and boasted, "Yes, I am I've become very attached to Satan. I've had to stand in the shadows and watch him die over and over even though I know it must happen. It has been harder than anything Hell has done to me, so any punishment you give me will be a welcome change."

I walked over to him, pat him on the shoulder and assured him he was going to be rewarded, not punished. For I, too, was fond of those who helped me along my journey.

This entire time, Jesus just watched his beautiful wife like a love-sick teenager. I thought to myself I've been wrong about this man for most of my life. True love is hard to find, but it's easily found in his eyes.

"Uncle," I said. "I hate to do this to you, but you lose," I completed.

I waved my right arm and a barrage of blue orbs flew out into the arena, each hit its mark. I turned, hung my head and listened even more to the screams of the remaining souls as they are recycled into the planet and announced, "Game Over!"

Mother gazed at Louie while asking, "Can you forgive me, Louie? I've never had much use for humans never having gone through what Satan has and you're not so bad yourself either. Here I am telling my baby not to give into hate and doing just the opposite."
Lucifer replied, "Nature, your glowing its breathtaking." Years seem to fade from her face like ice melting on a hot summer day.

Jesus walked up to her and told her, "That boy of ours just keeps amazing me, did you know he could do that?"
Mother responded, "He said he was working on something, but no I have no idea how he did it."
Not able to take his eyes off his true love, he kissed her passionately, like teenagers on lover's lane.
I don't care how old you get; seeing your parents necking just makes you uneasy. It may not always be what it seems, but it is what it is.

Lucifer apologized, "Satan, or is it Sean, I had no clue that you had the ability to do what you just did and I'm sorry to have ruined our game. I truly did this to make you happy not to depress you."

"Uncle, don't feel like that I'm fine; in fact, I enjoyed it immensely and I might add I kicked your butt. And I noticed you are referring to me as Satan now. May I assume you have unofficially passed the 'torch' to me? Because, I'm beginning to think I'm never going to receive that passage. Or is it that I will not be told when you retire, and I step in," I replied.

All Sean wanted was recognition and notice. That's not asking for so much, was it?

Lucifer snickered, "I think we have to have a rematch. You threw me off when you started recycling souls in the middle of our game."

Then, I started laughing and replied, "As I see it, I didn't break any rules because, as you so avidly stated, the only rule is there are no rules."

We looked out upon the arena. Koda, the mighty Hellhound, was lapping up bits of the souls. "Koda, don't put that nasty stuff in your mouth," we all said at once.
Lucifer conceded, "Good game, Nephew, but it's about time for you to return to the surface. Say your goodbyes and stop by to see me before you return."
"If I knew you were going to send me away, I would have let you win," I pouted.

Lucifer quickly retorted, "It's not like that. The mortal shell you're in is going to deteriorate down here and I'm just watching out for you."

In Satan We Trust

Jesus walked over to me and put his hand on my shoulder. "Son, I hope you know that I love you and you've healed your mother with your love, but I hope you don't mind if I take some alone time with her. You've still got some time to say goodbye before you go back," he suggested.

"EWE, DAD, fine just don't tell me anymore," I repulsed.
Lucifer called out, "Koda, Come On!" He pat his massive head." Let's go home," he ordered.

They strolled across the arena heading home and Koda picked up a severed leg from one of Lucifer's kills and ate it as easily as any household dog eats a biscuit.

"I'd rather face Grandfather's entire army single handed than fuck with the mighty Koda. Luckily that dog likes me I'm hoping Lucifer brings him later for I feel like the angels are getting ready to try and stop me before I gain rule over Hell. What do you say, Louie, you want to come along and get some work done," Sean finished.
"Satan," Louie replied, "you never stop do you?"

Jovially, I answered, "Well, my little friend, it appears that I haven't even begun. I must confess I'm a bit confused. And there you go calling me Satan again. Whatever," I answered.
Louie stated, "You certainly hide your confusion well."
When we reached the lake, I ordered, "Louie, gather the souls In this area. We're going to do some cleaning."

I walked up to the woman I met earlier and she was feeding the swans humming a cheerful tune.

In Satan We Trust

"And how are you today," I asked her happily.

"It's a beautiful day. My children will be here with a picnic basket very soon. You're welcome to join us if you're not so busy. What's your name, sir," she asked.

"Call me, Sean. And thank you, but can I get a rain check? I have a meeting that I can't postpone," I replied.

"You, young people, always so busy. Take my advice, Sean, and spend as much time with your family as you can. Nothing is more important than family," she suggested.

Meandering over to her and giving her hug, I informed her, "I promise you, Ma'am, I will do just that."

As I left, she smiled and said, "I'll be waiting for that raincheck to be used and feel free to bring your family. There's always plenty to eat."

By this time, Louie was standing around the bend with the others. "Satan, why do you care so much about this woman. I didn't mean to eavesdrop on your conversation," said Louie.

"You were there when I first came across her and you, yourself, said it wasn't fair. The winds of change are blowing and you, my friend, are going to be pleased with the change. Now let's get down to business. I'm going around the bend. Send me one soul every five minutes – it's going to be a long day," I answered him.

In Satan We Trust

One after another, Louie brought me a soul and I asked him, "What's this poor soul's story?"

Louie did a fine job getting their stories but every now and again I found a consummate liar. I broke the souls into three groups: true evil, cruel, and the accidental sinner. I instructed the group of accidental sinners to return to the lake and relax. The true evil, I took to a section of Hell. Still unchanged since Lucifer's rein, I spread them out and again used my blue flame to recycle them. Soon, this too, shall be a lush green pasture. The cruel I do likewise, but in another area.

"Louie," began Satan, "I never thought I'd say this, but I think I'm going to like it in Hell!"

Chapter 8 - Too Much Information

As Jesus approached looking like a kid accidently locked in a candy store, he noticed this section was not nearly as crowded as it should be. "I see you've been using your new ability and your mother felt it too. She just about wore me out. Your timing was impeccable! Your mother and I have always been good together but oooh man this time was epic," he boasted to his son.

"Oh; gross, Dad. Why do you tell me this stuff? it gives me the willies. If ever a TMI moment, this is one," I replied back to him. Better it gave him the willies than a woody. Now, that would have been way more gross!

Jesus answered, "Sorry, Son. but it has been so long since I've experienced what your mother felt like. She was as beautiful as I've always seen her to be that....."

"STOP! PLEASE, DAD," I begged of him. "You have a brother; can't you talk about this with him," I asked desperately.
Jesus giggled, "Ok, ok; I forget sometimes. You're just a baby because you've done so much. I feel like you're a man."

In Satan We Trust

Louie bumped me and said, "So, Satan, ironic isn't it? You're making it better here, but your own father is putting you through Hell."
We all enjoyed a well-deserved laugh. "Satan the reason I'm here is your mother wants you to eat and we need to get back," Jesus said while placing his arm around my shoulder as we walked away.
Louie sat on a rock and Jesus turned toward him and announced, "Louie, didn't you hear me? It's dinner time and Mother Nature made it a point to be sure that I brought you too."

Leaping up, I saw that bounce back in Louie's step and it filled my heart with joy.

Arriving at my residence, the sweet smell fueled my true essence; but unlike our first meal. There were meats of plenty on the table. Louie gazed at the end where he sat at our first meal and his eyes widened as his favorite dishes covered that area.

Mother glanced at him and pleaded, "Louie, I hope you can forgive me for my earlier discretions. Please eat up, both of you."
Louie, acting like a starving animal, tore into his food and confessed, "Mother Nature, you can whoop my ass anytime if this is how you apologize."

She smiled a bit and assured him something like that would never happen again.

In Satan We Trust

Looking at Mother, she appeared to be a young woman in her twenties. Finally, I understood why Dad was so happy – it was like he was robbing the cradle. Dirty, old man!
Mother spoke while hugging me, "Baby, I love and appreciate how you've helped me heal, but I'm afraid if you keep recycling souls I'll turn into a child."

I saw the most beautiful woman in front of me and assured Mother, "I can do this and just feed the earth with no side effects. To her, I'm not a pharmaceutical company. My will is side-effect free if I so desire, so please put your worries aside."

Dad was still sitting there like a love-struck schoolboy just gawking at mother and it kinda made me chuckle.

"Pops, do you think you could stop thinking with your pecker long enough to answer a few questions," I inquired.

Jesus snapped back to reality and apologized for being so distant. "You have to realize how much in love we are, my Son; but for so long I've been waiting for her to realize nothing that your grandfather could ever do would change how I feel about her," he confided.

Mother walked, moving her hips like a 17-year old, over to Jesus and pecked his cheek and he was back into lovesick mode. "Louie," I say, "I think I'm ready to go back to earth, so let's go say goodbye to Uncle Lucifer."

As we made our way to Lucifer, Louie shook his head and announced, "Well, let's see how this 'speak your feelings' thing goes. Lay it on, my friend. I want you to be able to

say anything. Well, Satan, I just hope you aren't upset with your father; he's been missing your mother for ages and now that she feels better about herself maybe paradise can be rebuilt once again. I've known your father for more years than I care to think about and in all that time I've only heard about your mother's beauty, but words didn't do her justice and if your father didn't lose it when he saw her again, I'd think him a fool." He called Sean 'Satan again'. How confusing was this going to be? Sean just decided to go with the flow from then on. 'Sean' or 'Satan' what was the difference? He just wanted to know how to act and that was dependent on who he actually was at the time!
Why does everyone want to talk to me about the fire between my parents? Trust me, I understand but I'd prefer not to think about them doing the horizontal bump if you don't mind. At least Uncle is unattached and all business," I reiterated.

Louie smirked and replied, 'It's not like he doesn't wish for the same; in fact, he has a big crush on the siren of the sea, but he can't get her to give him the time of day. Now your Uncle could use a good lay. Maybe then he'd loosen up a bit and not be so gruff.'

"So, Uncle has a love interest; good to know. I'm going to have to look into that and see what I can do to help it along. After all that Uncle has done to protect me, I feel his reward should be equal to or greater than the punishment his father gave him," I explained.

"Louie, I'd like to speak with Uncle alone if you don't mind," I requested.

Louie sighed and answered, "Nothing pleases me more than that request. To be honest, your uncle scares the crap out of me, so I'll just sit out here."

"Now it's my turn," I said sternly. "I don't think you know just how hard Uncle had things. The more I learn, the heavier my heart becomes for him. How he's maintained his sanity speaks volumes of just how strong he is and my uncle, very soon, will be given his due," I finished.

I pointed behind Louie and suggested, "Hey, look- a bar! And I know they have ice cold drinks. Why don't you chill out there while I say goodbye to Uncle."
The words barely left my lips and all I saw was Louie and the bar room door closing behind him. I jokingly said, "I guess it's been a while since he's had a cold one."

As I entered Lucifer's chambers, he had his back to me and he was unaware of my presence. I thought to myself how odd Lucifer is - off his game for the first time ever. He reached up to pat Koda's head and stated, "Well, boy, I guess soon they won't need us anymore. Where do you want to go from here?"

I chimed in from behind him, "I hope you are talking about a vacation because you don't think I'm having Father and Mother help me run things around here, do you?"
Lucifer's head spun around while asking, "Don't you ever knock?"
"Sorry, Uncle. I guess the devil made me do it."

With both of us laughing, Lucifer asked, "Nephew, I guess this means you're leaving us now?"

"Soon, Uncle; but first I have an early Christmas present for you," I told him.

Lucifer said, "Nephew, none of this has been about a reward for me. I vowed to your mother I'd make sure nothing would happen to you and you pull any of that reward shit on me, I'll sick Koda on your ass."

A growling Koda showed me his teeth. "Dog, you uncurl that lip now or I'll turn you into a kitten," I demanded.

Koda put his head down and tried to hide in a corner; but unless there was a bus or better yet a forest for him, the massive beast was hard-pressed to hide anywhere. I told him, I'm just kidding Koda. You're a good boy and I have a job for you."

With his tail wagging away, the puppy came out in him. "I want you to go to the section with the 'holier than thou' fuckwads and bury those pricks up to their necks and use that section as your bathroom from now on," I implored.

Prancing out the door, Koda headed off to deal with the priests, reverends, archbishops and popes.

Lucifer stated, "Your father has been torturing souls and has never thought of a punishment like that."

Smiling I replied, "Well, I think Dad has other things on his mind these days."

Lucifer rolled his eyes and said, "Yeah, he's got it tough. You've made your parents very happy."

In Satan We Trust

"I appreciate your saying that, Uncle, which brings me to you. I think it's time you lost those horns; deep down it's not who you really are, but then again it's not always as it seems," I blabbed.

Reaching up while touching one of his horns, Lucifer queried, "Don't you think I've tried to lose these eyesores? They've made me look ridiculous, but nothing seems to work."

Looking at him as serious as Hell I said, "Uncle, as I was fusing Grandfather to the cross I looked into his mind and I saw how to remove them. It's going to hurt but it's nothing you can't handle."

Lucifer winked at me and stated, "You know what, nephew; I will accept your reward in that case."

I explained, "This isn't your reward; this is because I love you."

Taking a few deep breaths, Lucifer replied, "Ok, let's do this."

I tossed a right hook and then a left and Lucifer was rocked by each punch. Staggering but staying on his feet, like Mohamed Ali, his head finally cleared. He reached up and surprisingly felt the horns still attached to him.

With a look of frustration, he said, "That wasn't very effective."

Bursting out in laughter, I said, "Oh, that had nothing to do with removing the horns. I simply owed you that for that ass kicking you gave me earlier. Remember, Uncle, it's not always as it seems." Snapping my fingers, the horns popped off his head like champagne corks and they stuck into the ceiling. Red, fiery smoke bellowed out of the holes and his once red complexion faded to a nice, soft flesh tone.

Rubbing his jaw, he chuckled back, "Well, nephew, I see you've learned some lessons from me, you little prick."

Hugging Lucifer I told him, "I've learned everything from you, Uncle. However, the one thing I can't fix is your asshole attitude. That you must do on your own. I have one last place to visit here and then I will return to man. Uncle, can I count on you to come to me on earth when I call you? I've got to say, Uncle, you're one handsome some of a bitch."

Lucifer assured me that he would always be at my beck and call. Nothing could ever stop him from coming to my aid and I knew that. I hugged him even tighter and thanked him for all he had done for me and I then headed to join Louie at the bar.

Chapter 9 - Last Call

As I entered the bar, I watched Louie drink a frozen rum runner surrounded by a couple of shapely females on either side of him. After seeing me watch him, he grinned an evil grin and explained, "Satan, you realize people are talking. They are afraid to enjoy the changes you've created, and they think they're going to be punished if they do."

"Good; it's working, "I replied
Louie looking quite confused said, "I don't understand. You mean they're right," he asked in return.

With a devilish grin on my face, I replied, "No, but don't you dare tell them either. You see, some of them have still got to ponder their wrongdoings and until they come to realize what they did was wrong, they are going to torture themselves. It's quite brilliant, if I do say so myself."

Louie cracked up and replied, "A maintenance-free Hell. Impressive, Satan. I was afraid that your goodbye with Lucifer went horribly wrong as I heard two thunderous claps. I thought your uncle got mad at you."

In Satan We Trust

I retorted while giggling, "Believe it or not, he let me pop him twice to make up for the beating he gave me, but I wouldn't say anything about it to anyone. You know his temper."
Just then Lucifer entered the bar and Louie jumped to his feet ready to pounce into action, like a saluting soldier. "I wouldn't that if I were you, Louie, that's Lucifer," I informed him.

With a stupid smirk on his face, Louie replied, "Sure it is."
Lucifer said, "Give it your best shot, my little assassin."

Louie's jaw almost hit the ground at that as he told him, "Satan, you just keep changing things. How about a little 'heads up'?"
At that, I raised an eyebrow at him and asked facetiously, "Now where's the fun in that? And as I hear it, I rule this place, so it's you who should be giving the heads up to me."

Lucifer chuckled, "You beat me at one game of fireball and now you're a regular game master? Bartender, give us a couple of fireballs." The busty wench behind the bar saw the new look that Lucifer's sporting. "Hey, hot stuff; looking sexy. You remind me of a nurse I once met," he slurred.

Lucifer looked at the bartender and continued slurring, "I know why Satan put you behind the bar, wench; but remember I know why you're here so just pour the drinks and shut your tramp mouth."

"Now, see, Uncle, that's what I mean about the asshole

attitude. She was being nice, and that comment was uncalled for," I corrected.

Lucifer in a sarcastic tone added, "Sure, let's just forget why they're here. You want me to forget everything. You take my memories away like the woman at the lake."

"Uncle, I could never do that. All you've done made you the man you are, and in my eyes, I can only hope to be half the man you are, but there's always room for improvement or what's the point in existing," I asked respectfully.

Chapter 10 – Lucifer & Saliene

Shaking his head, Lucifer replied, "All I can say is I'll try, my boy. You have my word on that, just so you know I have a type and she's not it.

"Yeah, I kinda heard a little something like that," I admitted. "So, who's this siren of the sea, Uncle," I completed.

Louie's eyes widened, and he answered, "Come on, Ladies; let's dance. This is a family matter."

Lucifer glared at me and retorted, "Who told you about her?"

"I hear things, Uncle, and this mind reading thing is kind of helpful too," I responded.

Lucifer flipped me the bird and continued, "Well, then I guess I don't have to answer your question you must have all the answers."

"Not at all, Uncle, I don't. Do it to my family if you feel you need to hide something from me. It's cool. After all,

In Satan We Trust

I've hidden things from you, but I always tell you the truth when the time is right," I admitted.

Lucifer slammed down his fireball and ordered another round. "Keep them coming and I'm sorry for my earlier comment," he insisted. Lucifer looked at the bartender and announced, "I know why Satan put you behind the bar, Wench; but, remember I know why you're here, so just pour the drinks and shut your tramp mouth," he finished.

Lucifer in a sarcastic tone said, "Sure, let's just forget why they're here. You want me to forget everything. you take my memories away like the woman at the lake."

"Uncle, I could never do that, all you've done made you the man you are, and in my eyes, I can only hope to be half the man you are, but there's always room for improvement or what's the point in existing," I asked. Lucifer shook his head saying, "All I can say is I'll try, my boy. You have my word on that, just so you know I have a type and she's not it."

I grinned and told him, "Yeah, I kinda heard a little something like that. So, who's this siren of the sea, Uncle?"

Louie's eyes widened, and he said, "Come on, Ladies; let's dance. This is a family matter."

Lucifer glared at me and asked, "Who told you about her?"

"I hear things, Uncle, and this mind reading thing is kind of helpful too," I responded.

Lucifer flipped me the bird and replied, "Well then, I guess I don't have to answer your question since you have all the answers."

"Not at all, Uncle. I don't. Do it to my family if you feel you need to hide something from me. It's cool. After all, I've hidden things from you, but I always tell you the truth when the time is right. I'm a bit sad that I'll be stepping down as ruler of Hell soon," I replied.

The barmaid looked at Lucifer and announced, "This round's on me and thank you."

"Excuse me," I say. "This round's on you? There's no money in Hell. Everything here is free," I retorted.

Giggling, she replied, "Silly boy, around here we barter with time off our sentences."

"Aren't you a clever girl using my generosity," I questioned

Lucifer stated, "Nephew, I wasn't sure if you could fill my shoes because of your compassion towards mankind, but I see I have nothing to fear."

"I don't know just how much your mother told you about Saliene," Lucifer said, "but I haven't seen her since she decided that a red-faced horned demon calling himself

In Satan We Trust

Satan showed up at the ocean's edge many, many centuries ago. But she was almost as beautiful as your mother. We first met when I was still doing Father's bidding. Father has never cared for the ocean because of its vastness and depth. He had a hard time seeing into the world that lies beneath it, but he caught wind of the carefree lifestyle of the mermaids and was jealous of the fact that he could not rule over them. Your mother was to thank for that as she had a friend whose beauty had caught Father's eye and that dirty old man wanted to make the poor girl his sex slave. So, Nature created the oceans. She knew how powerful father was. Once upon a time, there were no oceans - just fresh water scattered all around the world, no continents no vast oceans; just large freshwater lakes for people to enjoy. While your parents were in Eden enjoying each other's company, Father appeared to Saliene and raped her. Nature felt this. After all, nothing happens on earth that she doesn't know. She came to her friend's rescue and used the full resources of her earth to stop him. That was the beginning of his hatred toward your mother. Father vowed to return and claim Saliene for himself one day as Nature banished him from earth. Your mother was the first one ever to dare defy Father. She knows the power of water and she decided then and there that the only way to save her friend was to join almost all the water on her planet to hide her friend. Come to think of it, that was the first cleansing of the planet. Saliene was so hurt by what Father did that she cried for a century and that, my dear Nephew, is why the oceans are salty. Little did Saliene realize that those tears cast a haze to the water making it impossible for Father to see into the oceans," he finished.

In Satan We Trust

"Now as I said, when I first met Saliene, your mother introduced her to me and I loved her from the moment I laid eyes on her and I believe she felt the same. We got quite close and it was around this time that I made my request to Father that I should have my share of his rule over all. I believe that request was why he started thinking about taking her away from me. I can't help but think I'm to blame for what happened," he finished as a tear ran down Lucifers face. "Thinking back, I realize that when Father kept me in Heaven to keep an eye on things while he was on what at the time he told me was a trial run to see how I could handle Heaven, was just so he could carry out his nefarious plan to capture my love. But I was naive and thought that he was telling me the truth, when in fact he was scheming again. Years went by before I once again returned to earth. Father told me other C.A.T's had attacked earth and that it was my incompetence that was to blame but he would give me a second chance to save face. He told me of this so-called siren of the sea who I needed to vanquish in order to regain his trust was to blame for what happened on earth. So I returned to earth and found the earth you see today. Nature, your mother, saw me searching the oceans looking for Saliene, but both her and your mother are, in their own rights, forces to be reckoned with and at this point in time neither of them were too happy with me. Thanks to, in great part, your grandfather. I often say Father's greatest power is one of manipulation. Anyway, Nature and Saliene teamed up on me and I would never harm either of them, so I returned to Heaven and Father knowing full well that I would fail the task he sent me on then cast me into Hell," Lucifer finished.

In Satan We Trust

"It was many years before I returned to earth's surface. My heart was broken by everyone I cared about, so I guess that's why I didn't question why souls were sent to Hell. I punished everyone without thinking about the individual," Lucifer said.

For the first time I saw Lucifer showing remorse and I comforted him, "Uncle, you were dealt a bad hand. A weaker man would have given up, but you never truly gave up caring. That's the most important thing," I convinced him.

Lucifer now with tears flowing down his cheek replied, "After all I've done, I figure I deserve to be in Hell. In fact, it's starting to feel like judgment day now; so, Nephew, what's my fate," he asked me.

Now crying hysterically, I answered, "Uncle, it's not my place to judge you, but if I was to pass judgement, I'd say you're free to leave this place, but I think it would be a mistake. I would ask you one thing first. I want you to think back at what you wanted to create and after I leave, make changes. Hell is going to get a makeover and you are the most qualified person for the job. You've given so much of yourself to assure that I was safe. I hope you can forgive me for ruining your life."

Lucifer grabbed me and hugged me while stating, "Forgive you? I want to thank you. You saved me, you little bastard."

"Wow, what a couple of pussies we turned out to be," I said.

In Satan We Trust

Now the tears running down both of our faces were from laughter and I prefer those kinds of tears. We were both so into our conversation that neither one of us saw Mother and Father come in and sit behind us. Mother meandered over and kissed me on the forehead and admitted, "I'm so proud of you, my baby, but what's up with the woman on the wall?"

"Well, Mother, this is Hell and even though I want to change things some people refuse to do the right thing," I confessed.

Mother interjected, "Is this really necessary?"

I scratched my head full of red hair and walked over to the woman and said, "I've got a proposition for you. Stay on the wall or I will turn you into a deer and then all you have to do is worry about hunters."

I took my fingernail and sliced open her sealed lips. The woman said, "I'll take my chances with the hunters."

I walked back to the line and let loose a blue orb. The woman's sins appeared in the mist. It was like watching the worst porn movie ever made. Mother looked at me saying, "I could have done without seeing that. Now, my son, I'd like a little time with you before you return."

Mother took my hand and demanded, "Walk with me, I'd like to show you the souls you've been gathering that make up your elite fighting unit."

As we walked, Mother asked, "So, how did you find out about Saliene?"

"I'll tell you; but, please Mother, don't tell Uncle. I would hate to lose my friend," I begged of Mom. So, I told her that Louie had told me the story.

Mother said, "Your uncle has changed thanks to you! He's starting to be more like the man I first encountered centuries ago. So, the little assassin knows more than we give him credit for. Don't fret, my baby, your secret is safe with me - Mommy's got your back. So I've come to realize you're always planning something, would you care to let me in on what's spinning around inside that head of yours this time," Mother asked her son.

"Ok, but this is just between us, if you don't mind. You can't even tell Pops. I know he would tell his brother and the element of surprise is the only way I'll be able to pull this off," I confided.

Mother whispered, "Baby, everything you do is a surprise; but, so far they have all been pleasant surprises. Tell me, do you know before the outcome before the events happen?"

Rolling my eyes, I replied, "Honestly, no. I don't I just follow my heart and trust that I'm making the right choice. I need you to tell me more about Saliene."

"Ahh," Mother says. "I can see what's going on in your mind now, I think. Baby, I don't know if even you can pull off this one, but I will help you as much as I can. My friend first came here back when I was very young - a mere girl in terms you'd understand. She didn't want to be left behind with all the self-righteous C.A.T.s. Back then, we were inseparable. Anyway, without her I could never have been able to make this beautiful jewel you know as earth. Saliene has the wonderful ability to create water and thus allowing me to grow all the beautiful plant life you see. I just wish mankind would care more about them than their greed. At one point, Saliene was so angry at man that she flooded the planet in an attempt to eliminate the C.A.T.s that your grandfather put here in an attempt to control our world, but I convinced her to save some of man. Looking back, that may have been my biggest mistake."

Mother continued, "After the flood, Lucifer was sent here to try and take control of our home; but, he arrived and at this time he was still a handsome young man with a will of his own - just like Saliene and me. He knew his father would, in time, destroy the beauty we had created so he misled his father. We could live in peace, but your grandfather's C.A.T.s here reported back to him about his deception. I saw a goodness in Lucifer and introduced him to Saliene and they enjoyed each other's company from the start and were inseparable. Before long, I could see they had fallen in love; but, Lucifer was still under his father's control and your uncle thought he could get his father to let him watch over the earth as ruler. Unfortunately, his father was a step ahead of him all the time. As you now know, your grandfather is a master manipulator and HE used Lucifer's inexperience to his advantage. When your uncle returned and tried to get his reward for being a good son, his father put his evil plan into motion."

I interrupted Mother by asking, "If you know all this, why did you two turn on Uncle?"

"Baby," she replied, "at the time we didn't know any of this and were led to believe by your grandfather that Lucifer was the one who planned the whole thing. But things are not always as they seem, remember? It took a very long time to unravel the truth; but, by that time, my friend was so calloused by her ordeal that I'm afraid that she was unwilling to trust anyone ever again. To this day, she still believes that Lucifer is still under his father's influence, so you see I'm afraid that even you and that beautiful heart of yours may not be able to sway her, so don't feel bad if you can't pull off what you're planning," she completed.

We arrived at my warrior's section of Hell. The accommodations were spectacular, strangely enough. A luxurious training camp, a soothing breeze blew continuously, giant shade trees were everywhere, and glorious thatch huts were all throughout. Paradise in Hell, what's with that? Hark, one of my childhood friends from this life of mine sprinted over to me and verbalized, "Sean, I knew you'd end up here someday! Just wait until you get used to it here; it's so much better than the life you have left behind, trust me," he said like a Jewish lawyer. "Who's the smoking woman," he inquired.

"Mike, I have a confession to make. I sent you here; it's me who is going to lead you into war," I stuttered.

Mike looked at me and spoke, "So, it's no different than when we grew up."

In Satan We Trust

"You're not mad," I asked him, feeling badly about cutting his life short.

"Mad," he asked. Shit, I was miserable on earth; you did me a great favor. I get to work out all the time and the people here are awesome. So that means you know Lucifer, Sean," he asked.

"Yeah, Mike, I guess I should tell you another little secret. My name isn't Sean, I'm Satan," I admitted. I guess you could say that I considered it official by now.

Suddenly everyone stopped what they were doing and hustle into formation. Mike's eyes opened like Irish tea saucers. "I'm sorry, Satan, I didn't know. how may we serve you," Mike inquired.

Stunned by the way they all snapped into formation, I replied, "Please everyone, relax. I just stopped in to ask you all to forgive me for cutting your mortal lives short."

Sounds of joy filled the air and Mike yelled out, "Three cheers for Satan!" And the crowd cheered like a scene from a New Year's Eve party.

"So, none of you are upset with me," I sheepishly asked. They all gathered around and started thanking me for freeing them.

"The afterlife is awesome; when do we get to kick some ass," someone asked.

"Easy, my friends; the time is not coming for two more years," I explained.

"Fuck," Mike interjected. "We better get back to training. It's sooner than we thought. May we get back to work now, Satan? We have plenty of time after the war to catch up," he finished.

"Do as you wish," I answered, and they continued training. Confused, I glanced at Mother. Mother smiled that Mona Lisa smile I assume won Father over way back then.

"Baby, I know you are still living mortal time; but, that doesn't apply here. Time is short to them and you're basically telling them war is this week. Don't worry, your troops are more than ready; but your time here is short before you have to return to the mortal realm," she explained.

"Mother, how can all these souls be so accepting of me knowing that I cut their lives short. I'm so confused," I told her.

Mother placed her hand on my cheek and whispered, "Baby, you need to thank your uncle for their loyalty. Those souls have been given everything they could ever wish for. Your uncle has spent countless hours in this section and in all that time, he has been kind and helpful with each and everyone here. He knows just how valuable they are to your plans. Watching him with them reminded me just what a great man he is - if only Saliene could forget her pain and see how much Lucifer still loves her. But every time I try to talk to her about Lucifer, she shuts me down and if I try to push the matter, she flees to the depths of the oceans."

I hung my head and stated, "If only I could talk with her, I think I could get her to understand that Grandfather is the one she should hate."

Mother grimaced and said, "Then talk to her. She has been watching over you. she's very fond of you and your uncle has been very cautious about her when he met with you. I think in some strange way he can feel close to her through you and I know he loves her so completely that he would give his life so she would never feel pain again." Teardrops ran down her face and she said, "Baby, you've done so much already; but, if you have half the power that I believe you do; please, please, reunite them. Your uncle has endured so much pain and all because he's capable of giving so much love to all he meets. Please help him and Saliene!"

"Mother, you don't have to worry. I have a plan and the best part of it is I pretty much don't have to do anything. Uncle will have his love. The one thing that is and always will be is that true love is always what it seems," I informed her.

Mother burst into tears. I cocked my head to the side with a puzzled look on my face as I asked her, "What's wrong, Mother? All the things I've done so far haven't been a given up to now and what happens after this will be another guess, but this is destiny. If I'm wrong then as far as I'm concerned, life is not worth living and the universe will discover just what Hell is. The bad rap it has been given will finally be true and no one will stop me."

Mother dried her eyes and looked shocked and a bit frightened while saying, "Well, let's just hope that you're right; but, Baby, you can't mean that last statement. You are supposed to save the human race, not enslave it."

I murmured and evil sound and replied, "Oh, but I do mean it if mankind has poisoned love. Then I condemn the universe and shall destroy it. So, if love fails Uncle for whatever reason and you wish to take on the task of saving mankind, you should kill me before my birth!" You see, it's not always as it seems.

We returned to the bar, called Kelly's Pub, and Jesus, Lucifer, and Louie were throwing axes at a bullseye, like a child tasting candy for the first time. I yelled, "I'm in and I've got to tell you I've done this before."

Louie puffed out his chest like a proud rooster and replied, "Well, Satan, you may be one of the most powerful C.A.T.s to come along, but I invented the ax and I have never been beaten."

Mother looked disapprovingly at Jesus and batted her eyes. Like a moth to a flame, he was in her arms. She stated, "You boys play. We have to talk."

It was clear that she was purposely using her womanly charm to bend Father to her will. I said, "See, Dad, that's how you put it. Mom's got class. She doesn't say things to make me uncomfortable."

Jesus shook his head from side to side and they headed for the great outdoors. Lucifer brought a round of frozen rum runners and I couldn't help but notice he seemed genuinely happy. His new look and the lilt in his voice fills me with joy. Louie handed me three axes and announced, "Alright, Satan, let's see what you've got."

Standing on the white line I asked, "What in Hell's creation is this shit?" I looked at the board, so why is it so close? I waved my arm and the wall pushed back is fifty feet. I suggested, "Too far for you? I can put it back if you're not up to it." Louie looked down at the board snickered and said, "Never let it be said that I've ever backed down from a challenge."

Lucifer decided, "Game on, boys!"

Pointing toward the target, Louie announced a second time, "Ok, Satan let's see what you've got."

I let loose and my first axe hit just outside the bullseye. "Hmmm," Louie said.

"I guess you have done this before," I finished. Axe number two was on its way and it found the bullseye. Lucifer, raising an eyebrow stated, "Looks like the boy got game."

I heaved my final ax and struck another bull. Handing Louie the axes, I boasted, "Now let's see what the master can do."

Louie threw his first ax and it hit low and struck the outer ring. Lucifer yawned, putting his hand up to his mouth clearly mocking Louie's throw as if he was totally bored.

Angered, Louie fired ax number two nailing the bullseye.

In Satan We Trust

"Just had to get used to the new distance I guess," smiled Louie. His third toss and another bull. Louie handed Lucifer the axes. Uncle stood at the line and threw one after another. His first axe struck the bullseye as does ax number two, but his third glanced off one of his first two throws and fell to the ground.

"Tough break, Uncle," I smirked. The game continued, and all came down to Lucifer's final three throws. Louie and I were tied. Lucifer stood on the line, when push comes to shove stick with what you do best. He waved his hand over the axes and turned them into his trademark pitchforks. One after another, he fired, turned his back to the board and first throw hit dead center. Number two Robin Hooded the first and his last one also did.

I conceded, "Uncle, well played."

Louie grunted, "My first loss."

Jesus and Mother returned to the bar. Lucifer teased his brother, "Damn, bro, talk about a minute man."

Everyone laughed but Dad. Funny guy, but we did just talk. He swiped his foot across the ground like a child who didn't get his way. Now we're laughing even harder.

"Son, it's almost time for you to return. Sorry, boys, but it's my turn to say goodbye to Satan. My love, why don't you teach these two how the game is played? Louie try not to step on your tongue gawking at my wife,' Father said.

It's Not Always As It Seems

In Satan We Trust

Lucifer retorted, "I'll make sure his pecker stays in his pants, little brother. Come on, Son, let's go for a walk."

As we walked, Jesus puts his hand on my shoulder and said, "My son, you have your mother a bit worried. She told me if you can't help your uncle, you plan on killing everything in the universe."

I replied, "That's not exactly right, Father. If I tell you something in confidence, will you promise me you won't tell anyone?"

He replied, "You're my son and I promise you I will never betray you. I know what that feels like first hand."

In Satan We Trust

Lucifer and Saliene

"I kind of knew that would be your answer. It's not me who's going to do anything. The fate of man depends on Uncle and Saliene. If they can't make love work, then, yes, I'm going to be more than upset and for all the goodness in me there is just as much evil lurking in my shadow. Now believe me when I say if Uncle or Saliene hears one word of this, it will no doubt end in disaster. I love Mother with all my heart, but I know she will want to help; but she's a woman and her nurturing instincts will do more harm than good. Love will always find a way. I'm just going to set the table. You, my father, are the only one I can tell what I need to ensure that when the time is right, the help I desperately require will be done with exact precision.

"Trust me, Father, you know that I wish to save man much more than to destroy everything," I replied.

"You can count on me, my Son. Just tell me what you need," he retorted.

Back in the bar, Mother was using all the tools in her arsenal to throw Louie off his game. That horny little guy couldn't drop a rock and hit the earth right about now.

In Satan We Trust

Father and I were standing outside the bar laughing. Mother is showing more flesh than I care to see but even I can see just how beautiful she is.

Father confided, "Your mother can make a rose look like a weed as she passes by or vice versa." I don't understand why he told me that as I had already seen these types of transformations Mom was so capable of.

Lucifer was on his last axe and nothing less than a bullseye can save him. Mother was standing slightly in front and off to the side of him, Lucifer started his throw, a sudden breeze blew, and mother's gown floated upward like that famous picture of Marilyn Monroe standing atop a New York City street grate. Uncle's eyes widened, and the axe slips out of his hand like melting butter and stuck firmly into the wall. Louie fell off his chair and Father sighed, "How I love that woman!"

Lucifer looked around at everyone enjoying themselves and stated, "I hate to be a wet blanket, but Satan must return. He has pushed his time beyond what he should. Louie, I'm counting on you to keep him safe."

Mother approached me and hugged me while saying, "Baby, I'll be near, too. I've got things to attend to on the surface and remember no matter how bad the climate gets, you are safe in anything I throw at mankind. I love you and I'll see you soon." Her embrace made me feel so safe and secure that it caused my heart to ache at the thought of having to leave.

Father winked at me and demanded, "Be safe, my Son. We'll see you before you know it."

Lucifer looked sad and admitted, "I'm really going to miss having you around."

I smiled and replied, "Remember, Uncle, you're going to brighten up this place while I'm away but keep your ears open as I'm sensing trouble and I'll need you right away when it happens. Louie's a great warrior but no one protects like family."

Lucifer embraced me and retorted, "Put your mind at ease, little one. I'll be there before you can say " Uncle Lucifer, Help."

With that, a tear rolled down my cheek. Turning back, I watched my family standing together happy and a whole a New Hel! had taken root.

Back in the realm of man, already my heart was heavy. I yearned for my family and I knew that I would see them again but being with them for such a brief time I already knew there was nowhere else I'd rather be. Louie seemed uneasy and asked me, "Satan can you feel it?"

Of course, I nodded and replied, "Yes, my friend I do. Treachery, deceit, and hate fills their hearts and I know now why the cleansing is necessary. Mankind cannot be saved so long as they are so numerous. The one thing that puzzles me is how will they decide who lives and who dies."

Louie got serious quickly and said, "The hardest part of being your bodyguard are the things that I cannot say, but now that I know if you wish to, you can see into my mind, so I feel that I can now speak the truth. You, Satan, decide who lives and dies."

"Louie, my friend, here among man you need to remember to call me Sean I'd hate to unleash Hell on these hypocrites because they feel they have God on their side and they think they can defeat Satan, silly humans!"

Louie grimaced and replied, "Anything you say, Sean."

"Now, Louie, I have something for you to do even though I know you will find it hard to accept."

Louie assured me that anything I asked for would be followed through to the letter. All 'i's would be dotted and all 't's would be crossed. I put my hand on his shoulder and told him, "I need to talk with Saliene. Mother informed me that she had been keeping an eye on me and is quite fond of me, so I have a plan to draw her out, but you must stay back out of sight and far away from any water."

Louie, displeased with my request, assured me it would be done even though Lucifer will punish him. I informed him I will guarantee that there will be no repercussions for obeying me.

We started getting close to the ocean where there's a park and a few beauties sunning themselves. Louie, the horny little dude, stared at the buffet spread out on the lawn and walked into a stop sign which caused me to just about pee myself laughing. I tried to speak, "Louie, I think this is a sign that you should stay here. It's far enough away from any water and I think you've earned some downtime."

Louie's perked up a bit and replied, "You're the boss, so if you think this is a good spot for me to wait, who am I to argue with you?"

"Well, I wasn't sure until you walked into the pole," I said.

Louie glanced up at the sign and uttered, "Oh, ruler of Hell and a comedian, funny guy."

I retorted, "Well, you made this one easy."

"It's good to laugh again. It has been a long time, but we're kind of far from the ocean and I shouldn't let you out of my sight. If anything should happen to you, your parents and uncle will draw and quarter me," Louie snickered.

I looked at him and informed him, "I told you in order to draw Saliene out, she can't see you or anyone from Hell. Besides, I've seen you in action and I can hold my own. I know you'll be there before I break a sweat and that's why they picked you."

Louie, feeling pretty good about himself, puffed out his chest like a strutting rooster and replied, "Ok, Sean, just call me if you need me and I'll be there." He headed off into the park and right over to the ladies.

Mother was doing her thing. The skies were dark and the winds were howling. I reached the ocean while the waves were crashing on the shore. The beach was as empty as

In Satan We Trust

Murphy's Pub at closing time which made the conditions just about perfect.

As I walked up to the edge of the ocean, I thought to myself only an idiot would jump in on a day like this, but I didn't get where I was by thinking about life. I just dove right into it and made life happen. Let's hope Mother's friend is who she thinks she is. As I walked into the waves and started swimming out, the riptide grabbed me, like a horny john grabs a hooker, and pulled me under. As I rolled along the ocean floor, the air was knocked out of me and my lungs started to fill with water. Just as I started to call Louie's name, the water parted, and a mysterious, pinkish bubble formed around me. Coughing up water, I'm on my hands and knees -not my best plan. Gazing upward, a beautiful woman stood before me and asked, "Just what kind of bonehead move was that young man?"

"Saliene, I'm Sean," I answered.

"Cut the bullshit, Satan. Why didn't you just call me, you, silly little fool," she asked.

As my face turned red, I murmured, "You mean you would have just walked onto the beach?"

Saliene looked deeply into my eyes, like a suspecting wife of a cheating husband, and told me, "Your mother is my dearest friend. How in her world could I ever explain her baby drowning in my ocean? I've wanted to see you in person for hundreds of years, but it would have been wrong for me to reveal the true world in which you belong. That was a job for your parents."

In Satan We Trust

By now I was shivering uncontrollably, like an interrogated suspect, so Saliene hugged me, rubbing my back to warm me up and continued talking to me, "Let's get you back on land."

As we strolled along the ocean floor, the mysterious bubble traveled along with us until our heads broke through the waves, like a pair of sharks escaping mankind's net. As we approached the beach, Saliene ran her fingers through my hair and exclaimed, "Hello, I'm happy to finally meet you."

Kissing my cheek, Saliene finally asked, "So, why are you here?"

Looking directly into her eyes; I lied, like a slimy bastard caught with his pants down, told her, "Mother told me about you. I finally found out who I am and that I'm part of a real family. I just wanted to get to know my kind. Do you have time to visit awhile?"

Saliene took my hands in hers and said, "Always for you."

Gripping her hands tight as a virgin, I admitted, "I have heard what happened to you." Panic appeared in her gorgeous, almond-shaped eyes. Now I held on even tighter as she tried to pull away. I said, "I'm sorry, I can't let you go until I show you something." Momentarily, we were standing in Heaven in front of Grandfather, still seared to the cross, like the beginning of a sacrificial offering of some sort.

Saliene started trembling. "You have nothing to fear." I

explained to her that Grandfather was powerless to free himself from the cross. I finally released her hands and a group of angels perceived this as a chance to take me down. They swooped down from two different directions, like the flying monkeys in *The Wizard of Oz*.

Sending a fireball at one group, I struck them down, like a perfect strike in bowling, and turned to the others, but Saliene withdrew the moisture from the surrounding clouds and, like a high-pressure washer, she used the water jets to slice their wings off, like an autopsy gone wrong. As they come crashing down, I looked to Saliene, grinned and said, "You're pretty handy with water."

Glaring at me with daggers in her eyes, she screamed, "How dare you deceive me? You shall pay for this."

"Easy," I said. "I brought you here, so you can attain your revenge on Grandfather."

As God looked down at her, in an attempt to pit her against me, He commended me, "Good job, Satan. You brought her to me.

Saliene turned her water jets towards me, but the water turns to steam, like a long-awaiting sex orgy.

"Easy, Saliene. Don't let him into your head. He's powerless to do anything. He's just trying to manipulate you," I begged of her.

Walking to Grandfather, I placed my hand on his chest as he screamed out in pain as the heat burned into his cold, dead heart like an icicle to fire.

In Satan We Trust

Devoutly looking at her, I asked, "Wouldn't you like to get even with him for raping you?"

Saliene, still angered at me; she corrected me, "Trying to rape me."

Confused, I asked, "What do you mean?"

"It's true he wanted to rape me, but your mother was there before he could do anything," she explained.

Happy as a pig in shit to hear this, I returned us to the beach.

Then, as Saliene headed back to the sea, I begged, "Please wait! I have no malice towards you; I just wanted you to see that God has been punished for what he has done."

She stopped dead in her tracks and walked back to me.

Saliene not quite as angered, explained, "Alright, Satan, only because your mother is such a good friend of mine and you returned me to the safety of the sea, I will give you a chance to explain yourself but no more tricks."

Feeling like a schmuck, again I begged, "Please forgive me, but I wanted you to see that there's no need to hide any longer and I couldn't chance your fleeing back into the depths. You see, Mother told me how you like to run from things that make you uncomfortable. I promise I will never stop you from doing what you want to do even if it means you want to run and hide. Just know one thing; you are safe now and there's no need to hide any longer."

Saliene looking so sad, asked, "You don't get it, Satan. I still am in danger. Your uncle is still out there, and he was working in conjunction with his father."

In between weeping, she explained, "Lucifer used my love for him to get me to lower my guard allowing me to be grabbed by his father. I do feel better seeing God imprisoned but be careful of your uncle. He's going to try to recruit you. He's the ruler of Hell and I believe he's after you as well as me. I don't think he could beat the both of us together and if he tries, I know your mother will also help us even though she wants to give him the benefit of the doubt."

"Time to come clean with you, Saliene. All I ask is that you stay around till I'm done explaining. Then you have my word that if you wish to leave and never see me again it will be so," I told her.

Agreeing with my request, Saliene admitted, "I've been watching you long enough to know you're a man who keeps his word and I've been yearning to talk to another like me. I can understand how you feel."
I replied, "I just recently left my family and already I want to go back. Now you saw God and I hope you know he can't harm you anymore. What you don't know is that Lucifer was by my side during the battle against God."
Saliene suddenly turned to the sea.

"Please don't run, you look like a sea lion that just saw a shark. I promise you can leave if you want to go now.

In Satan We Trust

Just walk away. I won't stop you, but you have nothing to fear from me. I only want to talk," I said.
Saliene looked sharply into my eyes and replied to me, "I don't know why, but I believe you. I will hear you out."

Music to my ears so I said, "Excellent, but do you mind if we sit somewhere as this may take some time and please feel free to ask me anything. I will tell you whatever you want to know."
Skipping off the beach with me, a tree rose up from the earth and two stumps popped up.
"I see your mother is still watching over you," stated Saliene.
Placing my hands on hers, I said, "Lucifer helped me battle his father, but what you don't know is he deceived God so that I could grow without God killing me for all these years, undergoing attacks for me putting his life on the line just to protect me. The man you believe to be God's servant is just the opposite and if you let me, I will show you that he has always loved you and still does. What I'd like to do is end all his suffering but I can't do that without your help."
Saliene bowed her head and gazed at the ground looking saddened. "I've been trying to put this broken heart and Lucifer out of my mind. I couldn't bare thinking about how he could let his father attempt to enslave and rape me; but still, I can't put it out of my mind I loved him so much. I think that's why I can't let it go," she told me.
"I think your fear and my grandfather's manipulation have caused you much pain, but I think I can end all this if you will trust me and put your fear aside for just a while longer," I asked of her.

Saliene wringing her hands, clearly agitated and

heartbroken, replied, "I don't know if I can. You want me to relive one of the most traumatic events of my life. As you may have noticed, I'm not what one would call brave."

Standing up, I started to pace. If I wasn't careful, Saliene would run back to the depths and I would have failed my uncle and the love of his life, the beautiful Saliene.

"Lucifer has never tried to find you in all this time. He has been tormented by the last time he saw you and the hurt and pain you were in so he has lived in a world of misery and loneliness, just so you would never feel pain again," I explained.

Saliene gave me a forced smile and stated, "Funny, that makes me think about the man I fell in love with."

"I know I have no right to ask you for a favor, but ask yourself this, why is it that you've been watching over me all this time? I feel like it may be that you know that my purpose is to put things right. I've been told I have a destiny and I believe now that I've found out just what it is. If you would indulge me, I think I can prove to you that Lucifer is still the man you fell in love with, but you need to trust," I debated.

Saliene apprehensively agreed to give me a chance to prove to her that I could make her see that I was telling her the truth. Now I just need to set the stage.

Walking along minding our own business, a hurricane rolled in fast and furious, while ripping houses apart and tossing cars full of people around like feathers in the wind. I start singing an Eddie Rabbitt song *I Love A Rainy Night*, which resulted in Louie starting to laugh. I glanced at him and admitted, "I know I can't sing, and I know it annoys people, but I don't recall my singing ever making people laugh."

In Satan We Trust

Louie ceased laughing and said, "Forgive, me Sean, but I just got a flashback to some of your past lives and the one thing that hasn't changed is your reaction to devastation. The singing is new, but still goes along with the way you act during past cleansings."

Confused, I asked him what he meant. He replied, "That's right, you couldn't possibly remember those lives. You were in a stage of your development where memories couldn't take hold, but you've been through a few cleansings. This one evidently prefers song, but when you were Nero, you fiddled; when you were king of the Mayans, you beat a drum; and when you were a pharaoh, you danced through the destruction. You say you want to save mankind, but there comes a point when they become greedy, hateful vile animals. You rejoice in their doom, probably because you know that one day they may finally realize just how to live in harmony."

Stunned by the realization of just how many of the lives I've gone through, I said to Louie, "From the sound of it, it sounds as if you have and will forever be my friend and for that I'm grateful and if you wish, I will allow you to be free to live your life any way you wish."
Louie stopped dead in his tracks and stated, "Satan, Lucifer offered you your freedom at one time. And you were insulted by it. So, I hope you can understand why I'm a bit upset with you."
Puzzled, I said to him, "Upset, I don't understand, my friend. I never said I don't want to be your friend, nor do I wish to do all this or that without you by my side. I just want you to do all this of your own free will. As I recall

after I said I didn't want to leave Lucifer, I got my powers. Would like the same deal?"

Louie no longer upset, started shaking his head and replied, "I appreciate the offer, but even if I wanted it and I don't, you couldn't grant me that."
Shocked at his answer, I asked, "Just what makes you so sure of that, my friend? I sense you are holding out on me."
Louie finally stopped nodding and retorted, "Satan, you are truly my friend. I know if you wanted, you could just read my thoughts; but you don't. You were created to be a C.A.T. My species is completely different. Lucifer never gave you anything except for the choice to be yourself. Your family had always intended to let you become whomever you wanted to be, but biology is destiny. As for us, we will be keeping company for a very long time and I don't want to miss a moment of the wondrous new world you're going to create."
He outstretched his hand for me to shake and as my hand grasped his, thousands of images flashed through my mind. Louie smiled and assured me, "Don't worry, my friend. In time, you will come to understand what just transpired."
I didn't understand much, but I was sure that he meant no harm to me, but I need to know one more thing, so I asked, "Louie. Does anyone else know what you are?"
Once again Louie laughed merely nodded and said, "Not at all. They just know I'm your faithful bodyguard."
The storm continued raging on, power was knocked out everywhere and the devastation was widespread. The cleansing had started.

In Satan We Trust

Louie, looking like a drowned rat asked, "Sean, could you ask your mother to ease up a bit? I hate being wet. It's most uncomfortable."
Suddenly we were in the eye of the storm. Through the rustling of the leaves, I heard mother's voice, "Stay in the eye, Baby, it's going to get crazy outside the eye."
The sun began beaming on us now. Louie, happily announced, "I love your mother. She is always watching out for you."

Continuing on our way, we climbed over the wreckage. Some dirtbag looters noticed us coming and one of them pulled a knife and rushed us. I started singing again - *Shot to the heart and you're to blame. You give love a bad name*. A jagged two-by-four flew into the eye where we were standing and stuck into his heart, killing the looter. I started laughing like a hyena and blew mother a kiss. I recognized her handiwork. His fellow looters witnessed the whole thing and came towards us. Again, I heard Mother's voice in the wind saying, "Baby, tell them to stop."
I did as she instructed as they were standing about 12 feet from us. Louie was ready to fight, like the little 'fighting Irishman' mascot. I told Louie to relax because Mom 'had' this. One of the looters asked me if I thought it was funny that his friend died, to which I replied, "I laughed didn't I? But, it's not nearly as funny as this," as I pointed to the sky. Looking up, a huge bus crashed down on them. Louie gazed at me and joked, "I guess I should feel good that when she was mad at me, she only cracked me across the ass with a sapling." We both start laughing. Like they say my friend, you don't mess with Mother Nature. Mother walked like a soldier to battle, into the

eye. "Baby, you don't need to see this. Besides, don't you have better things to do, she asked me.

I pouted, "But, I just wanted to see you. I miss you and Dad so much already."

Louie was still laughing, and Mother looked scowling at him and asked, "You find this humorous?"

Louie tried his best to stop laughing and answered, "It's not that.......a bus; that was awesome, Mother Nature."

The softer side of her showing, she giggled like a young Catholic school girl and retorted, "What can I say? I already had it in the air and I think you should just call me 'Nature' from now on. You've done an extraordinary job watching over my baby and he's quite fond of you."

Louie, as happy as ever said, "Thank you, Mother; I mean Nature. And I promise that before anything happens to your baby; I, myself, would have to be killed first."

Mother turned her attention once again to me and scolded, "Now, I love hearing how much you miss me; but I think it's time you got busy. Your father said you have a task for me, but he wouldn't tell me more. I hope whatever it is, it's worth my taking time out of my work, but if your father won't tell me what it is, and you haven't told me by now, you're probably not going to tell me either. Just remember it's not nice to fool Mother Nature and I can predict a NorEaster in a flash."

She embraced me and kissed my forehead just like an affectionate mother would do. "Now, Baby, it's time for you to get to work and I know how much you like a thrill, so Mommy has a special treat for you. Tell me where you want to go and get ready for the ride of your life," she warned me.

Louie sprang up, like a porn star's erection and announced, "I'll meet you there. I'm not big on rides."

In Satan We Trust

Mother whispered, "Sorry, Louie, children aren't allowed to ride alone." And with that two small twisters scooped Louie and me up and we were off on another adventure. Mothers, gotta love them!

The twisters brought us to an isolated section of a forest. As we neared the ground, they disappeared and left us safely on the ground. Louie dropped instinctively to his knees and kissed the earth. Still shaking, Louie stammered, "Please, let's never do that again."

As for me, I was pumped! Mother does know how to amuse me. She should have owned an amusement park.

"So, Louie, I need you to go see my Dad tell him it's time," I implored.

Louie answered, "As long as I can travel my way. I'm still shaking from the trip."

I chuckled, "You've ridden in my sleigh and have been thrown out of it and that ride we just went on scared you? You, my friend, crack me up."

Louie replied, "Believe me, that scared the crap out of me. I thought my life was over. Luckily for me, angels aren't all that bright."

Placing my hand gingerly on his shoulder, I told him, "Those were the worse days of all my lives. I've lost friends before, but watching you plummet towards the earth and the feeling of being completely helpless to save you broke my heart."

Louie tried to console me by answering, "My life means nothing next to yours. You have so much to accomplish. I don't want you to feel badly no matter what happens to me."

I snapped, "Never let me hear you talk like that. Your life is as important as anyone, including mine."

Louie thanked me and said, "I believe you mean that, and

In Satan We Trust

I will always remember you are my dearest friend. I have a problem though; your uncle told me to stay by your side at all times."

My answer gave Louie no peace of mind, "I've gone against Uncle's orders before. What's one more time?"

"Ok," responded Louie. "Let me try it this way - if I should leave you and something happens, I could never live with myself, not that your uncle would let me live that long anyway," he continued.

Now I had to pull rank on my friend by saying to him, "Louie, my father is waiting for word from me and I can't stress this point enough. Don't let Lucifer see you. Don't worry, my friend, I can handle myself. Now go."

Louie was always by my side. You've gotta love him for that at least.

As I walked deeper into the forest, I realized that I wasn't where I thought I was going to be, but I knew I had been there many times before. It had just been there in the winter. After all, Mother did say 'just think of where you want to go'. I remembered the twister which reminded me of the sleigh ride and was wondering if my reindeer were doing well. Huh, I guess I'll have to be more careful flying Air Twister next time Mom offers me a 'lift'. I supposed the location didn't really matter; it's the guest of honor who's important. I frantically searched the area until I found the perfect spot to put my plan into action. So, I entered a clearing and what I found was better than my wildest dreams. This was *the* spot! I paused for a moment and soaked in the beauty and all the sounds of the forest. Then I discovered myself saddened and wondering how I wish I spent more time there as a mortal. I also considered just what I was about to become when I was reborn. Oh, well; enough of that. Back to work.

All those years as Santa Clause were paying off as I carved out two chairs from large fallen trees. I mean, these chairs were royal.
Using only Cain's blade, I created two seats worthy of kings..... And why not? Two kings would be seated at the table I will be carving shortly; right after the chairs are completed. Stepping back from the clearing and admiring my stage, I told myself that King Arthur could kiss my ass. This was a work of art. I then reminded myself how I hated, with a passion, the word 'King'. Tapping into my Santa magic one more time, I allowed Cain's blade to whirl around and created the finishing touches. Just once more, I told myself.
Easing backwards while carefully examining my latest project, the finished product of my labor, my masterpiece was complete. A royal table and chairs in a clearing truly was truly a place for family to chat. As I was critiquing, images flashed through my mind almost as if I was shaking Louie's hand once again. With my mind fully clear, the hairs on the back of my neck stood up and instantaneously four angels in white came screaming in through the canopy from directly in front of me. To the left, I caught a dozen or so doing the same. The four were almost upon me when from the right, the ground rumbled. Then, crashing through the trees, faithful Koda, the mighty Hell Hound, burst forth. He mercilessly snagged the four angels like a show dog catching frisbees with his mouth, gnawing them into three gory sections. Turning back and heading directly at me, the next wave of angels was not far behind him. Koda dropped his massive head arranging his nose against me flipping me

delicately on his back and ran into the forest with the angels in hot pursuit. Now I spied two more squadrons of angels coming in from the sides. As they closed in, I readied myself with Cain's blade. Koda swished his tail, slicing an angel's wing off. Another nasty angel cleared the tail and was on me. I sliced him down the middle, like an undertaker beginning an autopsy. I laughed as he exploded. Feathers were flying everywhere. The angel who lost a wing slammed against a tree with a defining TWHACK. I laughed again and told Koda, "That's gotta hurt, fella. Good boy," as Koda's tail batted another one off into the woods. Koda moved his head toward me and growled. At this point, I kind of felt he was pissed that I was enjoying myself, but Koda's in the zone.

Fucking angels were always screwing with me!

Koda turned on a dime and headed towards the squad. On the right, the angels behind us adjusted their angle and began closing fast. Koda turned a second time, now bearing down on the angels who thought this was just a stupid earthling dog. Koda, however, earned the name 'the Mighty Hellhound' for a reason and now they were about to see this was an intelligent beast, like no other. He leapt into the air, like Superman, his paws straight out and the size of a compact-sized car, each with razor-sharp claws. As they collided, the unsuspecting angels were shredded like pieces of pitiful confetti. Too bad a ticker-tape parade was not on the schedule.

The poor bastards who came in between the claws would be seen again.......when Koda was to take his morning constitutional, hemorrhoids or no hemorrhoids. That's how thought this was! As Koda began running faster, I Suddenly realized the flashes that I saw were parts of the battle. Again, Koda maneuvered around and looked at me and growled, "Aarrrrrrrr". I nodded at him proudly, like the father of son whose military career awarded him every ribbon or medal possible. "Don't worry, boy, we're about to get some help," I promised him. Koda raised a brow and obediently returned to the business at hand. The others, who were closing in quickly, heard a familiar whooshing sound in the air and angel feathers were once again everywhere. These fucking feathers were like the craziest pillow fight at Karate camp. Koda glanced around confused, but continued hurling himself through the woods, to the point that he didn't realize what was actually happening now. I patted him on the side and convinced him, "My reindeer are here. Be a good boy and don't eat any of them, ok? They're here to help".

With another group of angels closing in from the side, Koda swiped his tail, like a knight thrusts his sword, shattering a giant redwood. These shattered wooden splinters were the size of javelins and impaled most of them by sticking them against the surrounding trees, like needles in a pin cushion. I couldn't help but think how handy that redwood would have been for the royal table and chairs I had just finished creating. The reindeer jolted through the trees so quickly that the other angels barely saw them. I, however, had become so accustomed to being with them and seeing the blood-soaked antlers as they whiz by making it really no great shock to me.

"Koda," I shouted, "Back to the clearing!" Koda, still running like the wind, tilted his head back to begging, "Nnnnnnoo."

"Don't you tell me 'no'. Wait, did you just talk? Never mind - just get back to the clearing. We have more help back there," I demanded. The last thing I needed in this chaos was a talking dog. But, then again, nothing would surprise me at this point. Koda, obeying my order finally, bolted for the clearing. Upon reaching the clearing, the angels surrounded us. Koda howled and Jesus arrived and started ripping angels apart with his bare hands. With that, tree branches started swatting other angels. He rose up next to Koda and I demanded, "SATAN, WHY WOULD YOU COME HERE AFTER WHAT YOU DID AT CHRISTMAS? DIDN'T YOU THINK THEY WOULD BE WATCHING YOUR REINDEER?"

Now Louie leapt from the trees and assisted Father in dispatching the rest of the reindeer. Realizing that they had no chance of reaching me any longer, the few remaining angels fled like a defeated baseball team, kind of like moving their wings to the ground saying, "Ah, shucks, we lost!"

Mother, clearly angry, looked around at the bodies and asked, "Do you have any idea how lucky you are? Just what were you thinking by coming here?"

"I'm sorry, Mother," I said, "but it was totally by accident. You didn't tell me that I had to think about my destination the entire time. My mind wandered, and I ended up here, but this place is perfect. I just need your special skills to finish the stage."

Mother glanced around and asked, "You still plan on doing this with all these bodies around?"

"Well, I hadn't planned on it. I just need to talk to someone first, but I think I can use this to my advantage," I conceded.

Mother gazed questionably at Father and then back at me before saying, "I should probably be worried that you can still go through with whatever you have planned with a massacre all around. Don't you think it's time to let me in on your plan now?"

I hugged her while answering, "Yes, I do; but let's get everyone on the same page now. Follow me."

Strolling over to a tall oak tree with a long flowing moss curtain hanging down to the ground, we walked behind that curtain. There was a small crystal pool of water behind it babbling calmly down a hill. I walked over to the pool and said, "Saliene, I need you." And moments later, Saliene ascended up out of the water, which made Mother smile. They lovingly held each other, and Mom said, "It's been too long. How in Hell did my baby get you to agree to this?"

Saliene, obviously so happy to see Mother again, wiped a streaming tear from her eye and reminded her, "He's a smooth talker and for some reason, he makes me feel safe. I guess I've been a bit stubborn, but he said he could prove everything he told me earlier. After all, he is your son!"

Saliene asked, "Are you ready to do what we discussed earlier, Satan?"

"Yeah," I said, "about that, a small hiccup arose. The angels attacked me while I was working on my plan, but if you want to know the truth, I can actually use it to my advantage. I have to warn you that it's not going to be pretty out there."

"Out where," she asked as I took her hand and paraded her around the other side of the mossy curtain. Saliene's eyes widened like Irish tea saucers as she viewed the carnage. "Did you do all this," she demanded to know.

"Not exactly. I had help from everyone here," I informed her.

Saliene gazed back at us while stating, "You promised me I'd be safe and from what I see, I don't think I have to worry about God's angels with all of you here. So, prove our earlier conversation to be true. I'm only going to go through this once, so make it good. I'll be in the pool listening".

"Ok, Mother, I need you to get the animals to drown out the sound of the water and thicken the mossy curtain. Make it look like the battle took its toll on this area and then I need you to all hide from Uncle," I instructed.

Mother waved her hands like a magician with his wand and I was in awe at the result. The tree looked even better than I thought it would.

Chapter 11 - It's Showtime

"Ok, everyone, hide - it's show time," I announced.
Standing in the clearing, I shouted loudly and clearly, "UNCLE LUCIFER, HELP...."
Before I could finish my request by saying 'me', Lucifer was there ready to fight. He searched for someone to kill and saw me and said, "Nephew, I don't understand. Why did you call me? It looks like you can handle everything on your own."
Running over to him, I began sobbing. Then he lovingly hugged me and asked, "What's wrong? Are you hurt?"
"Uncle, I can't do this. I'm just not strong enough. Before this all happened, I was going to bring you here. This isn't who I am. I can't take it. You must help me, please. Don't tell Mother and Father. There must be a way you can help me; after all, *you* have been *me* for so long. You must know how I can end this all," I begged for answers.
Lucifer, looking heartbroken, compromised, "I was kinda hoping you would end my suffering, my dear Satan. I comprehend your fear, but I also know that you've already changed things in Hell so much for the better that it won't be like it was all this time that I reigned. You have love inside you - the kind that can win out over your hate. you've created *A Whole New Hell*. You need to remember where there is greed, there's generosity and

where there is love there is hate, where there's truth there are lies; but, you, my Boy, have deep feelings and your love is so strong that it's contagious. Just look at me. I'm almost kind and caring again, that's all you! And look around, my Boy. You can handle anything. Unfortunately, now I also feel pain and if you love me like I think you do, you can take that blade you carry and cease my suffering. It's been so long already, and I can't go on any longer even in *your* world.

"Well that's my bid; but I also know that if you feel that way, I love you, too; and I can't make you go through the pain I've endured, so if you truly want out, I will try to free you," I declared.

I glanced to the table and chairs all toppled over by the mossy curtain and I walked over to them, beginning to stand them back up. "I carved these, so we could sit and talk," I bragged. I held one for Uncle to sit on and as he sat, I said, "Uncle, I didn't know you were hurt so badly, but if I take on this role, how could I do this without you? But how could I be so selfish? If you're in so much pain, is there anything I can do to stop the pain?"

Grabbing a chair for myself, I also sat down. As hard as he tried to smile, Lucifer just couldn't do so. My heart was torn apart, like a person's first break up, seeing the look on his face. I must be Satan; this is torture unlike anything Lucifer could ever think up, but I must get him to talk. I hate myself so much right now. "Uncle, I will end your pain, but you must tell me why you feel you can't go on," I compromised.

Rubbing his head while pausing at the spot where Lucifer's horns *used to be*, he admitted, "Nephew, when you fall in love, true love; cherish every moment of it like your mother and father. Never let it slip through your

hands, like sand through an hourglass. Everything you do, ask if this will hurt her, will she be safe, will she be proud of me, and most of all - will she still love me?"
Tears streamed slowly down his leathery and worn cheek. "For when she looks at you with hate in her eyes, you will spend every second of the rest of your life wishing the pain would go away, but it never does. It only hurts more and more. You'll drive yourself insane wondering what you should have done and when you see two people in love with each other like your parents, it's like someone is squeezing your naïve heart in their unsympathetic hand. I had that once and lost it and now she hides in the ocean, but if you remove me from this world perhaps in time as she sees what a wonderful world you're going to create, she will come out of hiding and actually live. So, Nephew, how much do you love me," he inquired.
Lucifer started sobbing hysterically now and the forest was completely silent as Koda howled in sorrow for his friend. The world heard the pain in the air from the Mighty Beast, Mother cried in the background and Lucifer, with his face hidden, was dying a slow, painful death inside. Upon seeing that, tears filled my sympathetic eyes. Saliene came from around the curtain and softly touched Lucifer's shoulder, and told him, "I never stopped loving you. I was ashamed to look at you."
Lucifer turned and saw her smiling down at him and waterworks then filled Saliene's eyes, too. What a bunch of crybabies we all became.
Wrapping his arms around her waist and resting his head in her midsection, she started weeping and rubbed his worn head with her delicate, petite hands. As I got up and walked away quietly, Mother was standing at the edge of the clearing wiping tears from her own cheek. I had to pass Koda while walking toward Mother. He snuck

a wink at me and lapped me with his tongue, which was like a wet, king-sized waterbed mattress, and it knocked me squarely on my ass. Mother smiled her Mona Lisa smile, came over to me, helped me to my feet and embraced me like only a mother can do.
"I could never have done that. I'm so proud of you, my Baby," Mother told me.
Dad approached us from out of the forest, his eyes red and bloodshot. "That's my boy," he told me.
We headed into the forest where we come across Louie, sobbing behind a rather large tree. This was beginning to take on the feel of a funeral, all the crying and all. Hey, as long as it didn't involve a machete to me, all was fine.
"Satan, you continuously amaze me. Hell's the best thing that ever happened to me. I never want to leave," Louie confided.
As we strolled practically hand-in-hand through the woods, Mother and Father could clearly see that I was still upset about my deception. Mother approached me and held me maternally in her arms saying, "Baby, calm down. You did a beautiful thing. Why are you so sad?"
"Mother," I replied, "I can't help but feel that I may turn into Grandfather one day because I manipulated Uncle Lucifer and those are the tactics that he uses".
Jesus stopped me while assuring me, "Son, never let me hear you say that. What you did was nothing like your grandfather. His manipulations are all designed to achieve personal gain. Wat you did was out of pure love and compassion. You, my Son, will never be like your grandfather. I am worried about one thing though. Do you really feel like being free of your place in the world, because if you do I will take on the task with your mother and you can be anything you want to be."

I hugged father as I just needed to get Uncle to open up. "I know that you'll both be around to guide me and as long as we stick together as a family, we will be fine," I told them.

Watching Koda lumber off into the forest I excused myself by asking, "Could you all excuse me? I need to thank Koda for his help. I'll catch up with you."
Mother insisted, "Go, my Son, and let me just say your grandfather would never worry about a dog's feelings; but you do. That's how I know you will never be like your grandfather."
It was finally time to give Koda the recognition he deserved.
Finally catching up to Koda after running into the woods I asked him, "Just what do you think you're doing leaving without giving me a chance to say goodbye and thank you for saving my life? Even for a Hellhound, that's just bad manners."
The Mighty Koda cocked his head and murmured to me, "Heh?"
Koda turned back and we saw Lucifer and Saliene holding on to each other as if they feared they may once again be separated, for life this time. Koda smiled, looked back towards the forest and hung his head. Then he started prancing away like a reindeer, of all things. I sprinted up to him and jumped up on his back again, and said, "So I was thinking Lucifer is going to be busy for a while, what do you think about hanging out with me and Louie for a while? We're going to have some fun and you will fit right in."
Koda's tail whooshed back and forth, like a set of windshield wipers during a massive rain storm. His ears

shoot up, like a shooting star, and in a deep rumbling voice I heard, "Coool". What the fuck!?

"I know you're talking, and I've got to know - do you have a large vocabulary," I asked.

Koda sat at my demand, I slid down his back, he curled his tail and dropped in front of me. Looking straight into my eyes, he replied, "Nuff, sup?"

I stared at him for a while and said, "So, being of few words myself, I can respect that".

My articulate dog tipped his head into me and I scratched behind his ear with my two hands and said, "We're going to hang out here a bit just in case the angels try another assault. Lucifer's guard is down and we gotta keep an eye on those two star-crossed lovers." Koda nodded his head and replied, "Yup".

We kept a reasonable distance from Lucifer and Saliene, keeping an eye out for signs of an attack. Koda jolted his head and he growled quietly, "Something is coming." Upon hearing the growl, my trust and loyal reindeer bound out of the forest and Koda was on his feet immediately. "Easy, big guy; they're our friends," I assured my dog.

The reindeer began checking out the Mighty Koda by sniffing. They appeared to be sizing him up while I told them, "Ok, you guys leave our new friend alone."

My words didn't stop them as they still seemed anxious and kept playing silly reindeer games with the Mighty Beast. Koda growled, "Sssnnaack"!

"No, Koda; I need them. I have two more Christmases to get through before they can retire," I explained to him.

Once again, we heard earthly footsteps in the woods and Mother, Father and Louie come strolling in. Mother waved her hand and the apple tree near us started dropping apples, blueberries burst out on the bushes, the reindeer forgot about Koda and started filling their bellies with the new-found fruit. Koda whimpered watching the reindeer feeding. Mother waved her hand again and a heard of buffalo started rampaging across a distant valley. Mother strolled over to the giant beast, rubbed his cheek and said, "Go eat, Koda. we will wait here."

He glanced back to the clearing, but I pushed him and demanded, "Go on, we can handle any trouble that arises, at least until you get back."

Koda grinned a toothy canine mouth and bolted towards the buffalo, the reindeer leapt into the sky, Koda thrashed his head back and snickered, "Heh,heh, heh"!

Mother and father sat on a bench she recently whipped up and Jesus waved for me to come over. I looked at Louie and suggested, "Come on, Bud. Evidently Pops has something to say."

Louie retreated ever so slightly and replied, "Hey, this is probably a family matter. You go and I'll wait somewhere safe."

I laughed, "Congratulations, you've just been promoted to FAMILY. Besides, I want you to hear firsthand when I shift the blame on you," while nudging him towards Mother and Father.

Standing before both of them, Mother said, "Have a seat, boys." Roots twisted and turned making two chairs, so we sat just waiting for the upcoming.

Father started, "Now, let me begin by telling you that what you did for your uncle was one of the nicest things to happen to him in a very, very long time. I just want you to know that we are so proud of you, both of you."

I elbowed Louie and said, "See, you thought we were in trouble and you're not."

Mother chimed in, "Oh, but you are in trouble. Do you have any idea what could have happened if Lucifer didn't have Koda following you two around?"

"Yeah, the bodies of angels would be lying around a lot closer together," I answered.

One of the roots on my chair flicked my ear, like a Catholic school nun. "Son of a bitch, that stung," I said.

My words made Mothers eyes open like clams in a steam pot and informed me, "If you don't want another one across your backside, young man, you'll watch your language."

Realizing how serious she was, I apologized, "Sorry, Mom. I was just trying to lighten the mood."

Jesus shook his head saying, "Son, the angels still have a slim chance to stop you, so you need to start being more careful."

I told a smug-looking Louie that I wasn't supposed to leave him alone.

Louie yelled, "Ouch," while rubbing his red left ear.

In Satan We Trust

I laughed, "Stings, doesn't it? OUCH," I got another. "What was that one for," I asked.

Mother simply curled her cute, little button nose at me answering, "Louie didn't laugh when you got flicked, so why would you?"

A bit mad, I said, "It's not my fault. He doesn't have a sense of humor. OUCH, ok, enough. I get it, I get it."

"I'll answer before you even ask. The answer is 'cuz I'm the Mommy," Mother said. That answer made me think of the dinosaur TV show of the 90's where the baby said, "Not the Momma, not the Momma".

I sat there rubbing my ruby red ear with Louie grimacing immediately covering his ears with his hands and asked, "May I be excused? This doesn't really need to include me," getting up from his seat.

Mother started moving her hand and Jesus put his hand on her hands stopping whatever she was thinking about doing.

"Let's all relax, Louie. Sit down. You need to hear this too," he told Louie.

Jesus looked at mother and implored, "Honey, enough ear flicking."

I was was holding back from laughing also, but I don't want to get flicked. "Boys will be boys," Jesus defended us.

Mother rolled those gorgeous eyes of hers and stated, "Men, no matter how big you get, you're still children."

Louie sat down as instructed, still covering his ears. Mother peered over at him and requested, "Put your hands down. You look silly and you know as well as I that if I wanted, nothing you can do would stop me."

See looked serious, so Louie lowered his hands out of fear alone.

She continued, "You were lucky this time, Baby; but things are only going to escalate in the remainder of time on earth. If your father hadn't told me that you were going to need some help, things could have turned out a whole lot different in a very, very bad way. I have to get back to work now so I'll let your father finish up. I need to make another volcano erupt, quell man's technology and return them to having to interact with each other. That should get them killing each other off."

Lucifer and Saliene appeared and Saliene asked Nature if she was going to leave without saying 'goodbye'. Mother told her that she was actually thinking of asking her to give a hand if the two lovebirds could tear themselves apart.

Lucifer knew exactly what Mother has planned and told her, "Nature, I want you to promise me you will not let anything happen to my sweet Saliene."
Mother agreed and vowed to Uncle that his love would return after the coastal communities were devastated. Lucifer begged of Saliene, "Promise me you'll come back, my love."

In Satan We Trust

Saliene advanced to Lucifer kissed him softly and promised, "We will never be apart again, but we all have our parts to do in this event."

She looked at me saying, "And you, my sly one. I hope you live up to all the hype."

"I look forward to witnessing A Whole New Hell from the beginning," was my answer.

Father looked pleased and added, "We're all looking forward to that."

Mother split a crack in the earth over to the pool. In the clearing the water rushed over to us. Saliene liquified into it and yelled, "See you on the west coast."

Mother sunk back into the earth, like a swallowed earthquake victim and then they were both gone. The crack closed, and the water trickled back to the pool, just like that.

Lucifer reminisced, "How I've missed the sound of water flowing." A tear slowly and sadly rolled down his cheek. Jesus looked to Louie and me saying, "Now back to the business at hand. You need to do your best to keep away from man. Things are going to get violent, Son. I know you feel they should be saved, but the time is coming when you will have to defend yourself. Louie, you just kill any threat to my boy, but let him fight too; it's important he sees the evil in man if he's ever going stand a chance to change man in the rebirth."

In Satan We Trust

Koda jolted back over to us, plopped downs and licked the fresh bison blood off his paws, like a warrior licking his wounds.

Lucifer looked to his brother and asked, "Jesus, you want to go to the inner cities and incite violence into the mind of man?"

Jesus answered jokingly, "Hell, yeah; we'll be home long before the women and twice as many people will die when we're done. Man's so stupid. It's not even a challenge."

They meandered off and Lucifer called out, "Koda!"

Koda looked at me so I inquired, "Uncle, would you mind if Koda tags along with us?"

Lucifer shrugged saying, "He's hard to control and I don't think he understands too much."

I looked at Koda and asked my dog, "Doesn't he know you can talk?"
Louie glared at me and said, "No offense Satan, but I've known this beast for centuries and he's not all that bright. Koda don't just sit there, say something. Koda yawned and lied down.

"Well he's big and scary so there's that," I say, "Louie, why don't you go get us some meat and we'll have dinner. Everyone else ate so we may as well. Just don't kill any of the reindeer."

In Satan We Trust

Louie headed into the forest while I looked at Koda angrily because he made me look like a fool and asked, "What's up? Everyone thinks you're dense. Doesn't anyone else know you talk?"

"Just you," rumbled Koda.

"Ok, my friend. Have it your way, but I think you should let a few more into your life," I suggested.

The sound of a gunshot was heard which caused Koda to flip me on his back and head toward the noise of the shot. We arrived to find Louie standing over a hunter's body. Louie ran into the woods, so we followed him. Approaching, we saw him crouched over one of my reindeer working feverishly on the new hole in its leg.

"Aww, not Dasher. Is he going to be ok, Louie," I queried.

Koda pushed Louie aside and garbled, "Mmmee". Holding Louie back, Koda licked the wound, like a deer to a salt lick, and the lead from the bullet was easily lifted. His next step in the process was to drool on the wound. Koda continued speaking, "Nnneeedss rrresst". Although a very tragic situation, at least now Louie knew Koda could really talk, because I was concerned that I may end up in one of those earthly asylums if word got out, I was hearing voices…..from a dog! Desperate times call for desperate measures, as Mother used to say.

The mighty Koda laid beside Dasher so I spoke to Louie, "Louie, let's leave them alone. Koda will watch over him."

In Satan We Trust

Louie glanced quizzically at me like I was crazy and screamed, "The beast will eat your reindeer in the night. Let me dress the wound and hide him from the beast."

I snapped back, "Do not doubt me! Didn't you hear him talk? Koda is an intelligent animal, a lot more intelligent than some humans I know." Of course, I was including Louie in that group of unintelligent people.

Koda growled, "Just you".

"Don't you hear his words, Louie," I asked again.

Louie, still thinking I was going nuts replied, "Maybe this is one of your abilities, so I'll go along with it; but I'm going to keep an eye on you in case the strain is getting to you. I'll try finding us food. You just stay right here and watch over Dasher. Do not move from this spot."

With Louie gone, I tried in vain to convince Koda to let Louie hear what I heard, but Koda wanted no part of it. Returning hours later with a wild boar all cleaned, Louie spoke, "I remember how Lucifer cooked my venison." With that being said, I simply waved my hand and roasted that boar straight up.

"It's a bit charred, but; hey, not bad for my first attempt," I boasted.

Throughout dinner, I tried to explain everything to Louie as best I could. After all, I *was* Satan. As he rubbed his head while trying to comprehend the information that I was *trying* to give him, he queried, "So, you want me to believe that the beast is so intelligent and for centuries he has convinced everyone that he's just a giant killing machine?"

"Louie, my friend, all I ask is that you keep his secret. After all, you've got a secret also and you trusted me with it, so I don't think it's asking too much to keep this from our new friends," I returned.

Louie assured me that Koda's secret was safe with him especially since he thought I was going crazy, if not totally insane because all *he* can hear was a dog! But he trusted me, and our friendship had endured so much already. We called it a night and all the other reindeer kept guard over us, like the tomb of the unknown soldier, so we could attain the rest we needed so desperately.

With daybreak upon us, we woke to see Dasher standing up feeding on apples. Koda was instinctively close by, like a new mother guarding her baby. My other reindeer were all giving the Mighty Koda the respect that such a magnificent being deserved. Louie, now realizing that I was not going insane spoke, "Satan, forgive me for having doubt as to your state of mind, but there's always a slight chance that one small event has the power to change a person forever and it's my job to watch over your development. But I will not be so quick to doubt you in the future."

I approached Dasher in an effort to check out his leg. It still seemed tender upon my touch and it looked raw, like a fresh piece of beef hanging out back in a butcher's shop, but I could tell his muscles were still strong by squeezing them. Calling the reindeer to me, I informed them, "My faithful steeds, I need you to spread the word throughout the forest that all the carnivore hunters will not be tolerated in *this* forest. For if anyone sees one, make them fear for their lives. If they refuse to be frightened off, maul them like a shredding machine, but leave them well enough to crawl painfully out of the forest."

"Satan, don't you think that letting the hunters get out of here alive will only bring in more of them and put the animals in danger," asked Louie.

"Well, that's exactly the plan. If they come to us, I'm not going against Mother's and Father's orders to stay away from man; but if they come seeking revenge, we will teach them that revenge is detrimental to their health. Soon no one will dare hunt in these woods and armed men will at least have a slight chance. It's still not going to help them, but I know hunters and they are clever and will work together. That will give you a chance to hone your skills. We will need practice before the war with man comes," I explained to my dear friend.

Louie, looking puzzled and a bit concerned asked, "What if by some chance a hunter kills you? My life won't be worth a fucking dime."

Trying in vain to ease Louie's mind, I told him, "Louie, half a mile east of us there's a hunter in a tree stand. Go see for yourself and don't worry about me; the animals are here and they will keep me safe".

Louie hesitantly headed out as a loyal friend would do. I sensed he needed to know that I would not fall victim to a hunter's bullet. Koda glared at me and demanded, "Mmmee gooo wittth," and he trailed behind Louie.

I began to wonder that maybe the Mighty Koda wasn't as intelligent as I gave him credit for. Watching him disappear, I didn't hear a sound from the massive beast - not a twig breaking, no limbs cracking, and the color of his coat morphed to match the surrounding terrain. My concern ceased, and I was secure in my belief that the Mighty Koda was everything I thought and more – much, much more. After all, how could a very heavy weighted animal not make any noise rummaging about?

Having been so long since I had been alone with just the reindeer, I noticed the spark in their eyes desiring my undivided attention. Dasher nudged me and performed a little dance, like a Rockette. I scratched behind his antlers while I told him, "I know what you're looking to do, but I think you need to rest that leg." He was clearly trying to prove me that he was ready for anything. He didn't want to be sent to the glue factory just yet. He was not yet quite ready for retirement!

Dancer raced across the field and back to me, paraded around me and nudged me in the direction of the practice sleigh. Looking around with a devilish smile on my face, I said, "This is a bad idea, but what the Hell. I have always done what I wanted to do. OK, team, the sky's the limit, even though there are footprints on the moon. I know what you're capable of so let's have some fun. After all, you did me proud every time we encountered stupid angels and I know we can handle them if they should try anything today."

Chapter 12 - Reindeer Games

Hooking my arm and moving me to his side, Dasher forced me to climb on his back and then we were off to the sleigh. He leapt one hurdle after another, like a high school track star. The show off was proving he was good to go. Hooking up the team and grabbing the reins, I hollered like only Santa Claus does, "Let's hit it!" The reindeer just gazed at me but did not move. "Are you guys serious? You want the poem? Fine, but its Satan's ride today:

"On Dasher, you, rash little dude.
Off Prancer, I find you quite crude.
Now Comet and Vixen, don't be such prudes
Off Dancer, no moonwalk that's rude
Hit it Cupid and Blitzen, let's get in the mood
And as for you Donner, make let's this ride smooth, for Satan's driving and has an attitude."

The team burst forth with such force that I almost flipped into the back. Had there been Christmas gifts back there, I may have crash landed.

Soon I realized how I missed the feeling of riding in the sleigh, the wind whistling through my freaky red hair, but suddenly something wasn't right. The sleigh seemed to be dragging and it wasn't cutting through the air like it should have. The team was still fast, but even the reindeer seemed to feel the resistance. They were always happiest when they were soaring through the air with me. And then I saw it. Devilish-looking angels darted out of the cotton-candy looking clouds and reared towards us. The team had no choice but to bank hard, widening the gap. As we shot to the forest canopy, a gunshot rang out, an angel got hit in its already slightly damaged wing and spiraled out of control, like an exploding rocket ship. Louie, perched atop a tree with the hunter's gun, peered down at the hunter lying dead on the ground. The angels were closing in and I realized now that the cold air of winter was thinner allowing the team to fly effortlessly while pulling the sleigh. I cared too much about my team to see them butchered by the angels, so I leapt out of the sleigh onto Donner's back. Pulling Cain's blade from my jacket and cutting the sleigh free, I watched it crash into the ground. Now the team widened its lead on the angels and felt the time was right to cut Comet free and get Louie, my boy, to join us in the forest.

Comet sped towards Louie knocking an injured angel out of the way and Louie jumped, like a javelin thrower, from the tree and followed him down. Comet scooped him up within just feet before the forest floor. Cutting the rest of the team loose, we all entered the forest, causing the remaining angels to concentrate all of their fruitless efforts on getting me. This allowed my team to circle to the side. They all knew me so well and understood just what I was going to do, so they intercepted seven angels tearing them all apart. Leaving only two angels on our asses, we screeched across a field when I suddenly heard

In Satan We Trust

Koda dive as we slightly scraped the ground. Just as the Mighty Koda revealed himself, we cruised under him and the angels were a most welcomed and deserved dinner for my favorite Hellhound!

While Louie paced back and forth, he fretted, "Oh, we're in big trouble! I should never have left your side. Your mother is gonna be angry with me."

I assured him, "Louie, my friend, we didn't do anything wrong. Angels attacked and simply and quite magnificently, if I do say so myself, we dispatched them. That's all, plain and simple.

Louie, still a bit freaked out, cried, "I left you alone again and they attacked. This all comes down to me screwing up again. How can your parents be happy with my incompetence?"

As I became irritated, I yelled, "Louie, I'm Satan; thus, that makes me your boss and you need to do as I tell you."

Louie retorted defensively, "You're not Satan yet. You need to be born first and if the angels succeed at their plot, all is lost. Try to realize at this time and on the earth in that shell, you are Sean, not Satan. That's why you couldn't use your fireballs. The mortal controls this body as long as it's on the earth's surface!"

Louie, sitting on the ground, appeared extremely worried so I tried to convince him, "Louie, forgive me; I cherish your friendship because in all my lives, friendship and love have eluded me and each time when I thought I found a friend, they were taken from me, like an alienated grandparent, so perhaps I've become jaded. I'm trying my best not to have such feelings about you. At Christmas, when you were tossed out of the sleigh, rage filled my heart. But after the fight was over, I was so saddened that I was consumed with sorrow and all I could think was that the world will suffer tenfold. Hate, anger, and rage were my driving force. I want to confide in you, my friend. I fear that just as Uncle Lucifer became a ruthless ruler; I, too, will fall into the role that has given Hell such a bad reputation. But now that Lucifer has been reunited with Saliene, he and Father can rule together and make a kingdom of goodness and purity. The only thing standing in their way is their belief that I am the answer to the problem. I remember the conversation about how I could also become the worst tyrant that will ever be. I've been thinking that if I am never born, Father and Uncle could create *A Whole New Hell* in memory of me. Just think of it, my friend. Everything could work out just as they hoped and all that I have to do is sacrifice my life."

Louie, looking shocked like a trauma patient, I continued, "Louie, I trust you will not divulge my plan. You said you're my friend, so I'm trusting you with my secret. My father sacrificed his life for man. My uncle sacrificed his life to save me. Saliene sacrificed her love for Lucifer. Mother sacrificed her beauty for me. It just stands to reason that in order to accomplish the goals set before one's self, that the answer lies in sacrifice. Things aren't always as they seem!"

Jumping to his feet, Louie bellowed, "Why you selfish spoiled little brat. I should slap the shit out of you. How dare you think like that. Centuries of planning for your arrival and the sacrifices your family made for you and now you want to just end your life so you don't have to work a little? You're acting just like an insignificant little baby. You have no idea just what the consequences of your actions could do - a chain reaction that could destroy all of those lives you think you would be helping would be set into motion. You think Lucifer was cruel before? Just imagine what breaking his heart again, so soon after he has had his heart healed, would do. As for your father and mother - your mother would be so filled with sorrow that the earth would wither and die and your father would blame himself because he'd feel you must have thought he was as untrustworthy as his father and that would hurt him so badly. I have no idea what would happen to him. Saliene would see Lucifer taking his rage out on man and would be so frightened that she'd once again return to the depths. Then there's me - you say I'm your friend, but you would leave me here to face all of their wraths? I'd be tortured every second of my life. Some friend you are. Let me just end by throwing your favorite line back in your face - Things aren't always as they seem!"

Instantaneously, Mother leapt out from a tree, Saliene arose from a nearby creek and they approached us. They did not look very happy. Saliene whispered to Louie, "I'd like you to walk with me, Louie. This is a mother and child reunion which excludes you and me and it doesn't need an audience. Consider it an intermission of sorts."

Louie, nodding in agreement, skipped like a child over to the creek.

Mother put her arms around me stating, "Baby, I know you are scared and will have doubts about the future but know this - you are loved completely by everyone around you and we are here to help you through all your doubts and fears. But if you can't come to us and talk openly and honestly, we plainly can't help you. All I can tell you is that you will never be alone from here on out. I apologize for eavesdropping, but your friend is wise, and you may not know this, but he's more than a friend. He looks at you like a big brother watches over a little brother. Could you hurt someone who loves you that much? I realize that you may feel overwhelmed, but you're just a baby and I expect you to make a few mistakes. However, what you are thinking of doing now will result in all that Louie told you. Did I do something to hurt you? I don't understand why you would not want to be part of our family. Or is it that you just wish us happiness and you are searching for a way to make that happen? Baby, trust in your family and you will see that there's nothing we cannot do or overcome."

Saliene motioned Louie to sit down on a rock and began, "I have watched you caring for Satan and I must commend you for becoming the man you are this day. Of all the people who have had the right to become cold and uncaring, you could have very well become one of the most ruthless killers known to man; not even after tragedy struck you and your wife was killed, you still maintained a sense of justice and I just want you to know that you will be glad to know that your wife has been preserved in the icy cold depths. But only Satan can revive her when the time comes."

Wow, Louie thought to himself as tears well up in his genuinely looking eyes. "But I saw them toss her into the sea. Are you saying she's alive," Louie begged for an answer.

Lowering her eyes to his level, Saliene regretfully informed him, "No, I'm not saying she's alive, but she's not dead either. By the time I reached her, all I could do was preserve her. I know Satan has the power to restore her life; unfortunately, there are still a few more trials you must pass to make this happen and it saddens me that I cannot tell you more. Just know that you have been an intricate part of the grand scheme. I know you think that you were a cruel assassin, but you were actually a law enforcer and all those you killed were slated to die - if not by you, by another of the chosen ones. I shouldn't have told you this, but we heard you talking to Satan. Nature and I both agreed that it is the least we could do. You see, we feel your pain and we just want you to know how much we care about you and just how proud we are of you."

Sliding down the huge boulder he just placed himself on after Saliene requested he sit, Louie embraced Saliene, like a soldier is welcomed back from deployment, and broke down in a stream of tears.

Just then, Jesus and Lucifer returned. Lucifer eyed his little assassin and asked, "What's wrong with Louie? I've never seen him so vulnerable."

Saliene motioned for them to back off. She knew Louie needed to shed these tears. It was holding him back for a long time. As for now, he had a much harder test to face shortly and if he failed, his love will be lost forever. Not a happy thought, it was strictly a lose/lose situation should he not pass.

In Satan We Trust

Wiping his tears away out of embarrassment, he confided, "Saliene could you cover for me? I'd like to be alone for a few and I know Satan is safe with all of you."

In an effort to reassure him, she said, "Take as much time as you need, you, wonderful man, and please consider yourself family."

Trying to digest the wondrous news he just learned, Louie journeyed off into the forest. He needed to meditate and understand the situation.

Saliene joined us and Lucifer asked, "What did you say to Louie? I've never been able to break his spirit and there he is crying like a baby in your arms; but now for some reason, seeing him like that I feel bad for him".

Saliene's face glowed as she explained, "I just told him we consider him family. He's fine. I don't know about the rest of you, but I'd love to have a family meal. It's been something I've been dreaming of."

Mother, realizing that her friend was trying to switch the subject, started shifting the foliage, creating a dining environment fit for kings and queens. It was like watching a dance marathon, minus the judges. It was just so much fun watching Mother work her magic.

As we sat at the table, she bended the river closer to us and then Saliene waved her hands. Fresh fish rose from the water, jets of water cleaned and filleted them, and Mother produced a platter from twigs for the food to be placed on, plates of a sort. Lucifer called to Koda, "Go get Louie. It's dinner time."

Saliene ordered Koda to stop and he did – he ceased immediately in his tracks. She whispered to Koda, "Give Louie some time. He won't be long. Trust me," said like a dishonest attorney," "He will be back in time to join us," she finished.

Turning her gaze to me, Saliene questioned, "So, I know you didn't know I was there; but why have you stayed away from water most of your lives especially since water is so important to your survival?"

Puzzled by the question, I respond, "I've never given much thought to that but……" Once again images flashed through my mind, I snapped to my feet, like a soldier to a commander's order for attention and demanded, "KODA TAKE ME TO LOUIE!" I thwarted my body onto his back and we bolted into the forest like wicked warriors.

Everyone started following us and Lucifer sensed something was wrong. He ordered Mother, Father and Saliene to stay there while he handled the situation. Then he followed them into the forest.

As Koda neared Louie, I saw what was becoming an all too unwelcome site. Ravaging angels were swarming my friend, like flies to shit. Pulling out Cain's infamous blade, I took stance on Koda's snout and dove, like an Olympic swimmer, headlong into the battle. My trusty blade sliced through those evil angels like a hot knife through butter and once again, feathers exploded here, there and everywhere.

In Satan We Trust

Koda began ripping them apart like rag dolls. Scooping Louie up and placing him on Koda, I shouted, "Save him." The Mighty Hellhound burst off with my friend and the revengeful angels had what they came for – me! Carefully using each explosion of feathers to move from one to another of the winged vermin, they realized the hard way that they had a habit of underestimating their enemies. Casualties were high for the injured and dying angels, but the sheer numbers they sent this time were taking their toll. Just when I thought all was lost, a familiar site appeared before my eyes - fiery red balls everywhere! Lucifer had arrived, and I became blinded by the fiery explosions so close to me. Just as quickly as they attacked, the cowardly angels retreated once again only to have denied their goal.

Lucifer kept his distance as I continued whipping Cain's blade all around like a crazy man from *One Flew Over the Cukoo's Nest*. I still couldn't see, but I sensed the angels had left. Lucifer called my name over and over until I finally realized the battle had ended as I considered what could happen if I should accidentally hit Uncle. With that in mind, I dropped to the ground, and yelled out, "Fuck this mortal shell. I'm exhausted."

Uncle screamed, "Nephew, I'm coming to you; stay calm!"

My answer was, "I understand, Uncle".

While Lucifer held me carefully checking me to see if I was hurt, my sight returned slowly.

"Louie. Uncle, we must find Louie, I blurted out obviously tired.

Lucifer called Koda and we heard Koda yelp and then Lucifer grabbed my hand and we hurried hand in hand to the sound where we thought the yelp came from. "Uncle, you can let go now. I can see. Let's move it," I suggested.

Reaching Koda, we discovered that Louie was beaten pretty severely. I called Dasher and he came crashing through the thick woods like Lassie, the hero dog! He sensed something in my voice that let him know I was on a mission and it wasn't mission impossible. Jumping on back but just before Dasher leapt into the blue sky, Lucifer tackled me off his back and reminded me, "Nephew, killing yourself isn't going to help Louie. You want to help your friend, calm yourself and stay here."

I gazed at Louie, he glanced slowly at me and coughed up quite a bit of blood. "You should see the other guy," he mused. I tried to muster up a laugh, but I was heartbroken thinking all this was my fault. If I leave any angels free to roam, everyone I love will be in danger. Deep thoughts were going through my head and all I could do was sigh in confusion, like being torn between two lovers.

Grabbing me by the arms, Lucifer demanded, "Nephew, snap out of it! Sorrow has no place in healing. Think of the love you have in your heart and think about the zeal that Louie puts into everything he does. Now, put your hand on his heart and think about how you wish him to be."

In Satan We Trust

I thought Uncle just wanted me to face death head-on. After all, on earth I'm mostly just another man; but Uncle had never led me astray before. So, I placed my hand lightly over Louie's heart, but nothing happened. Lucifer slapped me and reminded me, "You're the son of Jesus and Nature. You are more than you can imagine. Now believe that and save Louie. I don't know about you, but I can't imagine life without my little assassin."

Reminding myself that Lucifer cared deeply for him, I came to the realization how nice it was to hear that he cared again about anything. Then I began reminiscing about all the fun we had and miraculously I felt Louie's heart beating, stronger and stronger. Just to be sure, I checked for a pulse near his carotid artery. My head starting spinning, like Regan in *The Exorcist* and all went black.

Opening my eyes slowly and carefully, I made out the faint images of my family looking down at me. The concerned looks on their faces thankfully turned to smiles, ear to ear smiles. When all seemed fine to everyone, Lucifer announced, "See, I told you he'd be fine".

Our Lord and savior, Jesus, punched him in the arm like a hardened boxer. "Don't ever risk his health like that again," he exclaimed.

"Don't ever sucker punch me again," Lucifer said to Jesus.

My head, pounding like I just drank for three days straight, was all over the place. Louie popped up in front of my face scaring the Hell out of me.

"Satan," he said, "Why would you risk your life to save me; not that I'm not grateful, but this last week watching you lying there was the hardest thing for everyone; but *my* guilt was tearing me to pieces", Louie finished.

"Uncle, how can I ever thank you for showing me how to save him?....... Wait did you say I was out for - a week," Satan asked.

Mother held her precious soft hand against my forehead checking for a fever and told me, "Yes, Baby, we tried everything but none of us could help you. Your uncle should have never tried to get you to do that you aren't ready for, a stunt like that; but as usual, he does as he wants. We think you've taken after him in that respect - two of the most pigheaded individuals I've ever seen, but I wouldn't have it any other way".

Lucifer once again put his hand in mine, like a father/son walk across a busy street and I thought to myself 'not the hand-holding thing'. "Thank you, Nephew. You saved Louie and none of us wants to lose him. He's one of my most reliable demons and a good friend, not to mention part of the family now.

Hearing those words expelling from Lucifer's mouth nearly caused Louie's jaw to hit the floor. Trying to sit up with my head still pounding, I apologized, "I'm sorry that you've had to put your lives on hold watching over me."

Saliene, looking happy announced, "After all you've done, we would have stood here for years waiting to see you open those baby blues." Talk about being on cloud nine!

In Satan We Trust

A few days after my resurrection, so to speak, I was back on my feet and on steady ground again. But Mother hadn't left my side since I helped Louie. Now we were all seated at the majestic table. Mother told me I need to eat, and I replied, "I can't!"

"No offense, Saliene, but how do you survive eating fish all the time? It tastes nasty," I blurted out.

As Louie excused himself from the table, he answered, "I'm glad you said that. It just so happens I've got some meat right here. Lucifer would you do the honor," he inquired. In a flash, like an unexpected bolt of lightning, we had perfectly cooked venison – medium rare to be exact.

Saliene, appearing disgusted retorted, "Satan, how can you eat that - being so fond of your reindeer and all?" I had to admit, to myself only, she had a point.

Now, my actual answer was not at all what she was ready for. I simply stated, "The reindeer realized I needed meat to survive and I remember back many, many Christmases ago that Cupid's father got too old to work and I got snowed in these very woods and my first venison meal was *him*. The old boy ran into a low branch and broke his neck but wait until I tell you just exactly *how* it was broken. I still remember the wink he gave me before he snapped his own neck with his own paws. Not only was he one of the best flyers I ever had, he was also one of the best meals I had ever eaten." How was that for a comeback?

In Satan We Trust

Looking as if she witnessed a ghost, Saliene demanded, "You're making that up, right?"

Looking clearly at the reindeer grazing, I answered, "I wish I was, but it's a true story."

Lucifer giggled, "I remember that Christmas. It was around that time that I realized this boy had what it takes, and I guess I wasn't too far from wrong".

Jesus, frustrated by our relaxed attitude inquired, "Can we get serious here for just a bit? Need I remind you the angels know we are here, and they've been pretty brazen and we're making it way too easy for them."

Mother served me a multicolored fruit-looking masterpiece on my plate and spoke, "Eat this, Baby. It has everything you crave in it."

It was unlike anything I've ever seen, but I'll try anything once, so I bit into it. The flavor exploded in my mouth, my salivary glands in utter happiness. I couldn't help but chow down the odd fruit, licking the plate clean as if I was starving.

Mother seeming extremely pleased with me and said, "I thought you'd enjoy that. It has never been tasted by anyone before and no one but you will ever have the pleasure."

Saliene, looking hurt by my comment about fish tasting nasty, I decided to apologize, "I may have misspoken when I said fish is nasty. I remember having swordfish and it tasted very good and I have eaten fish and chips many times, so I hope you can excuse my earlier remark. I guess I do like *some* types of fish, and because of your looks, I hope more women start a fish diet."

Snapping his fingers in my direction, Lucifer scolded, "Uh, Nephew, you're kinda young to be trying to put the moves on my lady."

Scowling, I answered, "Uncle, we're on earth now. I guess my host here speaks up every now and again and he's a dirty old man."

Placing her head in her hands and shaking her head, Mother looked shamed by my remark. Dad let out a huge, Santa Claus-type laugh, and Uncle joined in unison. Saliene winked at me and continued, "Well, I'm actually heading to the coast. Would you like to join me? If so, I can treat you to a nice swordfish dinner on the beach."

My jaw dropped like raindrops from a cloud, Lucifer threw his hands out to the side with a big grin on his face and answered, "I'M RIGHT HERE"!

Saliene, looking that playful look of hers, said, "Oh, Lou, you know if I did anything with him, that would be how he would die." That was the first time I ever heard her call Lucifer "Lou". At first, I looked around for Louie, but after a moment I figured it out. Her being playful, that's all it was.

With a shit eating grin, I stated, "Well, if I get a final say in the cause and manner of my last death, that would be my favorite choice so far."

In Satan We Trust

Mother, having had enough of this conversation, told us, "I'd Rather discuss the weather and then I would simply make the weather". It's not always as it seems!

Looking quite serious, Saliene asked, "Well, what do you think? Want to see the power of water? I know it makes you uncomfortable, but I promise I won't let anything happen to you."

Nodding approvingly, Mother insisted, "I'll be around too, Baby, and I need to tell you something about that fruit I gave you. It should build up your abilities here on earth. With the angels being so brazen lately, your father and I feel you should be able to access your fireballs and that fruit will let you do just that, but every tenth fireball you unleash, you'll need to replenish your strength. Just walk up to any fruit-bearing tree and place your hand on it and another fruit will sprout. But only do it if you need one. Never let an angel get their hands on one of them. Should your grandfather eat one of these, he will become strong enough to free himself." Wow, that was intense.

Louie frowned and added, "I know you will be safe by the ocean, Saliene, but there's no cover for Satan and we'll be sitting ducks".

I started laughing and told Louie, "That's right; you don't know how I went about finding her. Allow me to set your mind at ease, my friend. She can protect us and we will be able to walk on the ocean floor without getting wet.

Koda growled, "Nnnno wet".

"Saliene, I'd love to go, but Koda won't be able to stay hidden," I explained.
Saliene, looking sheepishly and innocently declared, "I can keep him dry and under the surface."

Koda squealed like a pig and said, "Fuuuu k nnno."

Looking straight at Uncle, I asked, "Do you think Koda can hang out with you while we go on a field trip?"

Lucifer meandered up to Koda, pat him and said, "Well, my old friend, it looks like we're on our own again".
Saliene whisked us over to a river, we said goodbye to everyone and grinning she said, "So I hear you enjoy a thrill ride. You're gonna love my mode of transportation".
Louie rolled his eyes and begged, "Can't I just meet you there? I'm still recovering from Nature's ride. See, I called her Nature, not Mother Nature."
I laughed and informed him, "You're my bodyguard. You go where I *say* you go. You can't tell me a little ride scares you. After all, we battle angles constantly and they want to kill us and I know Saliene isn't going to hurt either of us."
Saliene called Nature, "Nature, the boys are going to need a boat, a sound one though and maybe a hand grip or two."
Mother maneuvered her hand again like a juggling clown and vines twisted and turned until a pretty slick race boat took shape.
"I know you well, Saliene. I figured speed was going to be involved," Mother snickered to Saliene.
"Ok, boys, hop in and let's ride the tide," Saliene suggested.

In Satan We Trust

Louie catapulted in front, I hopped in the back and Saliene dove in. Swirling around the boat, like windsocks on a stormy night, the water actually launched us down river. With the current picking up speed and the waves growing larger and larger, almost like mogles on a dirt bike track, we propelled over them in the same fashion. Approaching a lake, we thrusted into the air one more time. Just before arriving at the lake, a whirling, gaping hole opened up in the water and our boat shot into it. We ultimately corkscrewed straight through the tunnel, shooting out the other side of the lake and a waterfall was revealed directly in front of us.

Appearing quite pale, I wondered to myself if Louie was going to puke soon. And the adventure continued. Just prior to reaching the waterfall, we grabbed our earthly little asses and then the falls spun the boat completed around and we descended over the edge backward and the sudden drop brought up Louie's dinner.

Saliene curled the water out like a kid's sliding board and we skipped across the river below, like two silly school girls. Finally, we reached a crystal lake and our boat stopped suddenly. Saliene arose out of the water, like Jesus on Ascension Thursday, and stood beside the boat. Louie, still reeling from the ride, saw Saliene standing beside us and climbed out of the boat dropping like a stone into the water. Saliene sunk like an anchor below and reappeared with Louie in her long, gangly arms. dropping him back in the boat brought on tears of laughter from yours truly.

The dip in the lake brought Louie back around. I told myself, 'Damn, I thought that it was too good to be true'.

"Saliene," I said, "You teach my father that trick. I read something like this maneuver in the bible one time".

In Satan We Trust

She told me she was there that day and it wasn't anything like the war manual said. She continued, "So, hold on, boys. The final ride's going to start, but I'll make it smooth all the way, but fast as Hell".

Chapter 13 - The Lighthouse

Jetting down rivers and streams, twisting and turning all the way, but as promised, it was as smooth as silk. The wind, however, was almost too much to take.

Arriving at the ocean, Saliene raised our boat, like a profession marina worker, to the top of a cliff. Pointing to a lighthouse she inquired of us, "Why don't you two get up top and enjoy the show?"

Mother was seen summoning the winds calling in the cyclones. Saliene pulled the tides out, like the conscientious observer she was. It appeared that together they were going to flood the coastal communities. Louie assumed what was about to happen and raced like a greyhound around the inside of the lighthouse, returning with a long, twined piece of rope. Opening the window, he tossed it out tying it off on the stair railing. He then jolted down, grabbing the boat and tied it off like an experienced sailor. As I was laughing at him, I heard mysterious-sounding footsteps coming up the stairway. Peering slightly behind, an older man emerged to the top with me.

In Satan We Trust

"I'm the lighthouse keeper. You shouldn't be here. There's a nasty storm coming and it's going to be big," he said in a gruffy voice. Pictures again flashed in my head. Then Louie was heard coming up the stairs.

The keeper snapped again, "This is private property; not a shelter! just what right do you have here trespassing," he asked us.

Louie started towards the keeper and suddenly the keeper lunged at him, like a high school wrestler, pinning him against the wall. I grabbed the lighthouse keeper and pushed him down the staircase. Louie started down after him, but I took hold of him and pulled him back.

"He's going to be right back. Just stand back, my friend. This is my battle," I told him. I removed Cain's blade from my jacket once again. This was beginning to become an everyday thing, like many scenes from *Groundhog Day* starring Bill Murray.

Rushing up the stairs like a college linebacker, the keeper advanced on me as I thrusted Cain's shiny, metal blade into him with the precision of a surgeon - exploding, like the angels before him, into a bright flash of light. Louie looked slightly confused and asked, "What just happened?"

I had to admit that I, myself, was confused also. I declared, "Louie, you put these images into my head. You should have seen this coming before me".

Louie, shaking his head vigorously replied, "You don't get it. All those images you saw when we shook hands were images of your life I hold inside me. Images of everyone I am acquainted with trying to keep track of everything would drive me insane. I gave you those images because I believe you will usher in a new world of peace and harmony. I've only done this once before and it didn't work out the way I hoped."

My curiosity got the best of me now and I asked, "So, my friend, who was it that disappointed you?"

Hanging his head lowly, he replied, "I'm ashamed to tell you because you have been so kind to me from the moment we first met, and I mean even when you didn't know who I was and when I tell you, I fear that will all change".

Louie continued, "A very long time ago, I met another of your kind. His powers were great! He could have created a paradise, but when I passed along my knowledge to him. He used it to his advantage and not to help others. That being was none other than your grandfather."

I assured Louie that I knew all along of his association with grandfather through the images he passed along to me and that no being was without flaws and the best intentions quite often don't go the way we wish them to. This event brought me to the realization of how the C.A.T.s have managed to escape the cleansings and now, thanks to Louis' gift, I will be able to find the others much easier.

"Louie, I have one more question for you. Is there any way I can tap into the images and look ahead so I can better prepare for upcoming events," I inquired.

Biting his lip Louie answered, "It's possible, but I did that with your grandfather and you see how that went down, so I hope you can respect my wishes not to revisit errors that I promised myself I wouldn't make again."

I spoke, "No, my friend, I would never ask you to do anything that would go against your better judgment. I thank you for what you've given me already and I won't let you down."

There was a lull in the storm, but a huge wave approached the lighthouse. Vines buckles and rotated around the structure climbing to the top. No surprise that Mother and Saliene appeared outside the dome. Mother seemed worried until she viewed both Louie and me standing inside. "Well done, my son. You found a spy, I see, and dispatched him. Did you have any trouble doing so," she asked.

I fluttered my eyes at mother and answered, "If they're all this easy, I'm going to be rather bored hunting them down."

Mother and Saliene made their way back to work and as the winds picked up, the storm surge rolled in. Thirty-foot waves were crashing inland and increased in size with each new set of waves. Louie pointed out that the ocean's wall of water was building on the horizon. He informed me, "It must be three hundred feet tall and rolling in fast. The humans have already started evacuating the coast, the highways are packed, and mankind is doing what he does best trying to save his own hide."

In Satan We Trust

Mother summoned gale-force winds, knocking down derbies across the highway and stopping cars dead in their tracks. People frantically tried driving around the downed signs and cars got stuck in the grass bottling up the escape route. Now they were getting out of their cars, fighting one another rather than helping each other. Stupid humans. Little did they know that their last act would be one of rage and selfishness. If they only worked together, they may have been able to survive the flood waters bearing down on them. It is not always as it seems.

Some of the locals scurried their way to higher ground and attempted to open the door to the lighthouse. Louie, battle ready, I informed him it was time for us to leave the safety of the lighthouse. We made our way down the stairs and opened the door. Exiting the building and watching people trampling each other trying to save their own skin, I shook my head and told him, "As you can see, Louie, man cares very little of his fellow man and self-preservation is his driving force. I can't stand to be here any longer. It saddens me to be this close to such petty beings."

Louie located our boat and we exited away from the quarreling mass of people, fighting to get themselves to safety. We eventually reached the water flowing inland and took to the safety of our boat. Saliene must have been watching over us, as the debris cleared a path for us and a most convenient and welcomed current sent us off to our next stop. In the water, injured and half-drowning bodies were seen floating among the debris.

In Satan We Trust

The tide whisked us safely to another location where Mother was standing. As we attempted to get out and walk up to her, the tide was like an anaconda moving steadily up to its prey engulfing everything in its ravenous path. Those who foolishly chose to weather the storm in their homes didn't even have time to regret their decision before being crushed by the water and debris. I remembered thinking how glad I was the wind and waves were so loud. This way I didn't have to listen to their screams and pleading to a God who, even if he could help them, wouldn't.

Mother asked curiously and seriously, "Why did you leave the safety of the lighthouse?"

I glared at her and explained, "The townsfolk came to the house and I decided my work was done there and watching those poor wretches fighting to survive was bumming me out." That was a real buzz kill plus!

From where we were standing at this point, we noticed the ocean rise up and over the edge of the cliff surrounding the lighthouse and on the incoming tide, a giant orange buoy had broken free of its anchor and was headed straight for the tower. Moments later, it thrashed with such force that the lighthouse and its frightened occupants were no more! It's not always as it seems! Why don't earthly humans get that?

Gazing off in the distance, I viewed a house, solid and well-built, sitting on a mountain of solid granite. Again, images flashed in my head and I announced, "Mother, it's time for Louie and me to go. If you would hide us from the view of that building's inhabitants, that would help us greatly and ask Saliene to send us our boat in a couple of hours."

As we scurried along, the winds howled, like a horny Koda, all around us. But Louie and I didn't even hardly realize that there was a category five hurricane all around us. I was chuckling by this point. Louie looked at me quizzically and I told him, "Look at all the crap flying by us - boats, parts of cars, bodies, and remains of houses, but no trees. I just find that humorous." We must have an "in" or something.

Louie grinned, "You do tend to enjoy the little things in life, but why are we walking all this way just to seek shelter when your mother could have provided us some."

Chapter 14 - Visions

While slapping him on the back, I assured him, "I'm sure you know that I'm going hunting, now my friend. The visions you gave me have shown me how the C.A.T.s have survived the cleansings and each time I eliminate one there's a slight glow, and now I can see it on them before I kill them, and I can swear that I see that glow around that building."

Louie nudged me with his elbow, the look in his eyes revealing a bit of a nervous appearance. He motioned with his head for me to look in back of us. In the calm behind us, the animals were enjoying the relief from the wind and rain. I shrugged my shoulders and said, "Not to worry, Louie, they won't bother us. They know why we're here and they're all for it."

With doubt in his eyes about the big cats, wolves, and bears, Louie asked, "How do I know that?"

"Hmm I'm not sure. Must be something I picked up from Mother but believe me they're good and you never know when they may come in handy," I replied.
As we reached the building, we realized that it was not going to be easy to gain access because the battered, old

door was reinforced, and the walls were made of stone. Louie suggested we just start pounding on the door and demand they open it. I looked at him in disbelief, and reminded him, "These C.A.T.s have survived all these cleansings, I don't think they're going to open the door knowing that another cleansing is beginning. We don't want to scare whomever is inside. I think I have a plan that will get them to open the door on their own. Wait here and keep an eye on the place. I'll be right back."

Louie, all freaked out yelled, "You can't go off on your own. Every time you do, something horrible happens, so I'm coming with you and the only way you're gonna stop me is with one of your fireballs!" I threw my hands in the air and I reinforced," I can't hurt you-you're my friend even though you're pissing me off, but you make a valid point".

Walking over to the animals still hanging in the calm, I asked, "Can you guys watch this place for a few? I've got to make plans and then we'll be back".

The trusting animals dispersed, so I surrounded the building and quietly sat still. Louie and I walked down to the water's edge and whispered into the air, "Saliene, I need to speak to you."

Obediently, up from the water Saline emerged and replied, "You called me? I hope you realize we are kind of busy wreaking havoc."

I answered, "Yes, I know, but we need you to fold that building up there. I know you can get water anywhere and I need to get whomever is inside to open the doors".

In Satan We Trust

Saliene attempted to penetrate the building but unfortunately, she had no luck. Mother appeared and began an earthquake. The building cracked slowly and noisily. Saliene started flooding the building and we heard the door start to open, like a safe cracker's delight! The door swung open and a lovely woman stumbled slowly out of the doorway. "Louie, I need you to approach the woman but go slow. I have to get into position," I demanded.

As I tip-toed to the back of the building, I informed myself that it was time for a little Christmas magic of mine, so up on the roof and down the chimney I proceeded. Louie hesitantly approached the trembling woman in the doorway where two figures lay in wait inside the building. Depressurizing the room by opening the door, the seal inside the chimney's flue cracked allowing me the ability to bring a special present for the unsuspecting figures in the shadows of the room. However; before they realized what was happening, I subsequently released two fireballs, removing the threat to my companions outside.

Rushing the woman in the doorway with a silvery blade in hand, he made his attempt at lunging at her; but just as he began his descent, I halted his assault by sternly grabbing his arm. The blade, at that point was merely inches from the terrified woman's heart.

Perplexed as to why I didn't allow him to complete his mission, he stammered, "I didn't know we were going to take prisoners".

In Satan We Trust

The trembling woman raised her shaking hands, like a surrendering prisoner, placed her hands to her face and her mouth opened slowly and only slightly. But no words came out. Just what seemed to be fear in her eyes and defeat upon her face were all that remained.

Peering deeply into her eyes, I placed my shaking hand on her heart feeling for a pulse. "You have nothing to fear. I know you can't speak and that you were held here against your will. Please try to relax. The animals sense fear and they don't quite know what to think of you," I comforted.

Louie interrupted, "The animals aren't the only ones confused".

The unidentified woman closed her eyes and placed her hand on top of mine, which was still on her chest. Hanging her head and exhaling a nervous curl as if a smile hasn't been on her face in ages, she gave way, like a motor boat to a sailboat, to a look of relief.

"Mother, could you come here I," asked aloud. Not surprised at all that she didn't appear again, I sent a second request, "Mother, you can trust this woman and she and I both need you. Please help us."

Mother soared up to us and Louie backed up to what I guess he figured was a safe distance away from what was about to happen.

"Baby, I know you think you know everything, but I don't make appearances to people. This woman has to die now," she firmly stated.

In Satan We Trust

Stepping in front of the woman, not that mother would stop in any way from ending her life because of my gesture, I begged, "Mother she's not human. Well, she is; but she's kind of in the same situation as me. To be honest, I don't know exactly why I want her to live, but I know she has to".

Making eye contact with the frightened woman, I admitted, "I'm Satan and I give you the choice to walk away freely or to go with my mother and be put somewhere safe. I promise you will be safe. It's just that we have much to do right now and you're going to need to wait till we finish before I can talk with you. I realize your first instinct will be 'why would I trust that Satan's promise would be followed through' and I understand and don't blame you for felling that way." I probably wouldn't believe me either, telling he that I was Satan.

Chapter 15 – It's Not Always As It Seems

The trusting soul clutched onto my arm with both hands and held herself tightly against my side. Her lips quivered, and her eyes begged to not be sent away from me. It's not always as it seems!

Hanging my head lowly, I shared, "You're breaking my heart; don't be afraid. I promise you will be treated kindly in my absence. Believe me, no one wants to feel my wrath, but I will also grant you safe passage wherever you wish to go, and my friends here will go with you," motioning to a pack of wolves. The wolves appeared and sat around us. I continued, "So, it appears you're a dog lover or the big cats would have come to you."

She reached out cautiously and scratched behind the alpha's ear.

Mother saw the wolves' reaction to the woman and said, "My dear, I apologize for being so curt, but these are dangerous times for all of us; but I've never known wolves to be a bad judge of character. So, I will do as my son asked if you so desire."

In Satan We Trust

The woman, who we decided to call Uno Noon, an alias for 'unknown', looked cautiously at me, then stepped toward Mother and curtsied. I gazed over to Mother and stated, Classy, isn't she? I think she must have assumed we are royalty of some sort. Now I'd like it if you would escort her like a prisoner of war, to Hell and place her in my chambers. Tell Uncle to have any of my elite warriors guard her as if she was on suicide watch until I can return."

The wolves bayed to the sky, the woman dropped to the ground in front of the wolves and she began petting them.

I reached down to pat the alpha and inquired of our newest guest, "Would you like the wolves to join you? They are great companions." The woman eased up from a somewhat kneeling position to her feet, embraced me somewhat as a teardrop slowly cascaded down her soft complexion. She held a look of acceptance, so I stepped into the pack. "You guys go with her and do what you must to keep her safe." Tails wagging, the pack pranced, almost like my reindeer, around the woman. It was as if she was one of them. And I thought to myself 'it's not always as it seems'.

Mother assessed the storm clouds above and decided, "This is strong enough to be on its own. Saliene, stay by my child and watch over him while I take her to Hell. "My son, I hope you know what you're doing. This isn't normal protocol; outsiders don't last long down there."

Taking Uno Noon's hand and placing it affectionately in Mother's I debated, "Humans don't last long; she's not human, but have Uncle look in on her and if she starts to look like she's not doing well, return her to me. Louie, you ready to do battle? I've seen something big and I believe we are going to be in for our biggest challenge yet."

The ground began to shake, a hole opened up and a tunnel slowly morphed. Mother summoned to the woman, Uno Noon, to enter. Beginning her descent down the tunnel, the woman turned backward and gave me a little wave, the kind of waves the beauty queens do in a parade or on stage. she looked worried, but advanced down anyway, the wolf pack by her side. Once inside, the tunnel closed, and the ground seemed as if the passage was never there. Oh, Shit; it's not always as it seems. As I stood there perusing the spot where she disappeared, I asked myself 'what the fuck happened to her'. Though she spoke not a word, luckily my abilities allowed me to grasp without a doubt that she didn't mean any of us harm. I simply had to believe that. I only hope Uncle treated her better than the angel I brought down with me on my last excursion. This could very well be the perfect ending to a horror book.

Suddenly I became aware of Saliene and Louie watching me. Sure enough, I heard Saliene's voice, "Satan, you have to keep your head; a distraction like that could cause you to make a mistake that could tip the scales in Heaven's favor." They were all referring to me as 'Satan'. Perhaps the torch had already been handed to me maybe during a black-out period? I wasn't sure, but I had to find out somehow.

Glancing up in an effort to locate her, even her face would do, I screamed, "What do you mean? I feel certain inside that she's not one of those who need to die. I refuse to harm any C.A.T. who is innocent!"

Louie barged in, "Cut the boy some slack. He probably doesn't even realize that he's crushing."

In a very defensive state, I let them both know, "Hey, you two are way off; I know my task and indiscriminately killing everyone is no way to win a war. Those kinds of tactics are God's way, not mine! Imagine if we just killed everyone around us in a battle and after we won, those remaining who lost loved ones by my hand would harbor resentment towards us. Then another enemy would rise up; one who I might add has a righteous cause. I don't know about you, but I personally feel that that is a war I don't want to fight because that's a war you cannot win. If that happened, in our situation, it would be a total lose-lose to us and a win-win for the others. Do you really want to chance that?"

Saliene and Louie let the conversation die there, but they both sensed that there was more to it than my reasoning and they gazed at each other and both smirked.

"Whatever. Let's just go - we have a bit of a journey ahead of us," Satan acquiesced.

"Saliene, would you take us west? Forces are joining there, and we may want to get them while they're all gathered together strategizing. We could pull a quarterback sneak like the Japs pulled on us at Pearl Harbor." Our boat cruised uneventfully up to the flood water's edge and Louie placed himself in back this time.

In Satan We Trust

He figured if he couldn't see what's coming it won't be so bad.

"You don't mind taking the front this time, do you, Satan?"

Rubbing my hands together, I replied, "Not at all, my friend. I actually wanted it the first time around, but you beat me to it."

Saliene whooshed our boat westward, we were clear of the storm and we finally reached a point where Saliene couldn't get us any closer. So, we abandoned the boat and began walking quietly using military maneuvers along the way so that if we were heard, we would appear to be the militia instead of a small group of guerillas.

I informed Saliene that she can stay behind in the safety of the water. Rejecting my suggestion as if she never heard it or just outright ignoring me, she reminded me, "Your mother told me to keep an eye on you and from what I've seen so far every time you're left alone, you seem to find trouble, with a capital "T" and rhymes with "P" and stands for 'pool'. I can handle myself and you could always use an extra hand if trouble finds you."

I thanked her for her support and explained, "I hope you don't think me ungrateful, but I'd appreciate it if you would stay back and safe unless I absolutely need your help. You and Uncle just got reunited and I would like both of you to be able to enjoy centuries of love and happiness together. You two are like "New Jersey and You – Perfect Together!"

In Satan We Trust

As we paraded through the woods as if we were in search of a missing person, a wall of thick brush appeared around us like a prison. Mother was back! As she rose up from the ground, she placed a thin, frail finger up to her lips whispering, "Sshhhhh, they're coming."

A group of defiantly looking angels soared overhead and down into a ravine. "Son, you've bitten off more than you can chew this time," Mother scolded. "The angels are meeting with C.A.T.s and they are getting ready for you. You're heavily outnumbered this time. I don't know what you're thinking but it was paramount to suicide," she completed her lecture.

I stroked my straggly, red beard and yelled, "Louie, time to do what you do best to get me some intel and we'll make a game plan."

Like a thief in the dark of the night, he slipped silently into the darkness.

"Uncle, I need you," I begged.

Appearing with a fiery red glow in his eyes, it was apparent that Lucifer was ready to defend his true love with his life. He boisterously asked, "What's going on? This doesn't seem to be an emergency to me."

Explaining the circumstances to Uncle, I was forced to tell him that it was time for my elite warriors to join me for battle, but they must be quiet and use stealth. Mother told Saliene to return with Lucifer. After all, she did stay with us and they deserved time together before the craziness began.

In Satan We Trust

Saliene joined Lucifers side and promised, "We will both be back to join you when the battle begins. After all, family sticks together, like crazy glue, in times of great peril. Jesus appeared to announce, "That won't be necessary. I have decided to fight. I've been taking shit for far too long from Grandfather and his minions."

Checking Father carefully, like a pet owner looks for ticks, I realized he looked differently - like a prizefighter in his prime with a deep coldness in his voice. It appeared Jesus was prepared to no longer turn the other cheek.

"Son, I've hidden for far too long as you've said time and time again and I control your destiny," Jesus blurted to me as he approached. "So, too, should I, as your father, be teaching *you* not *you* teaching *me*.

"Father, in all the lives I've endured to reach this stage of development, I have been learning from all of you. I don't pretend to have all the answers, but what I do have is family and a strong desire to see them happy," I told him.

Lucifer held Saliene securely while speaking, "I can die a happy man now knowing you still love me and well, if I don't fight to make Hell a better place and something happens because I wasn't there, then it's all for naught and we would be hunted down without allies so when we return to Hell to get Satan's elite I will be returning with them to fight and you will watch over those remaining in Hell."

Saliene forced her hands on her hips while saying, "You don't believe that I'm going to miss out on the greatest change of all time. I intend to be right by your side - we all win or we all die to fight the good fight."

I chimed into the conversation, "Easy, people, this is just a skirmish. The real fight is yet to come, so don't think I don't appreciate your support. But I don't want any of you here for this battle. I promise you we will return, but Father, I would love it if you joined me in this one. I'd cherish the time together. It will be a definite father/son memory forever."

Lucifer intended to open a fiery gateway to Hell, but I stopped him in his tracks by saying, "Uncle, you can't let them know we're here. Just let Mother open the door and remember, my warriors must not be seen."

After returning shortly thereafter, Lucifer and Saline disappeared like ghosts into the tunnel, when Louie exclaimed, "We're in serious trouble just as you predicted, Satan. the C.A.T.s are gathering humans down there along with the angels."

Nodding my head ever disgustedly, I told him, "Well, this is a good sign. We've got Heaven scrambling. If they're already willing to sacrifice their mortal followers this early, we must have done more damage than I thought."

Mother does what she does best and created a dense undergrowth to shelter us from the angels and told me, "Baby, your warriors are ready to come up."

"Father, I need you to go over what we discussed earlier. Tell them any human they spy must die – none are to escape, no prisoners! I'm not quite ready to let the world know what's coming," I instructed.

Jesus began his journey before saying, "Son? For someone who wants to save mankind, that's a strange order to give. Are you now ready to kill man?"

The image of my parents looking deep inside me as if they're worried that killing is becoming too easy for me now caused me to reply, "No, no I'm not; but in my heart, I know that any human out there right now is exactly the type of human that they want to eliminate with the cleansing. Besides, Uncle trained my elite warriors. I'm not going to have to kill any of them, of this I am sure".

Mother and Father, more than satisfied with my answer, travelled off to speak with my troops. Louie, in full-on battle mode armor and all cried out, "Satan, it doesn't appear you're very worried. I've seen the data, so to speak, and we are greatly outnumbered, like the IRA verses the Brits. I really suggest you take a look for yourself. You may want to call for more troops."

I retorted, "Louie, have no fear, my friend. Unless they fill that ravine with soldiers, they're the ones who are outnumbered. Remember, you, yourself can kill 100 or more and my warriors can do almost as well. To tell you the truth, I feel badly for them as they may feel an overconfidence now, but all Hell's about to bust loose and then they're all going to find out that this is little more than a training exercise for us."

As my warriors came forth, Louie's jaw dropped, like a 60- year-old woman's tits after being released from her bra. Louie re-asked, "There are a lot of women in that group. Are you sure they can handle themselves in battle? Staring Louie down I uttered, "Women are vicious. Try taking away their credit cards and you'll witness this if you haven't already. And I've picked some beauties. Aside from their fighting skills, they inspire the males to show off their talents. Let's not forget Father and Mother. They are not to be messed with even on a bad day and today these idiots want to hurt me. So, they both have their A games going today."

Hanging my arm around Louie I reinforced, "Now all we need is the bait and since that is me and you, the one who's always by my side......Hey, what do you know - you're right; we should be worried." I cackled as I motioned to Louie to follow me.

Louie sauntered alongside me pushing and shoving me and voiced, "I see you get your sense of humor from Lucifer."

Louie, fumbling nervously with his jacket, replied, "Well, even though you're trying to get us both killed, this is for you," pulling out of his jacket a one-pound chocolate bar and presented it proudly it to me.

"See, things like this are how I know that we're friends. I was just craving something sweet and look at this," I exclaimed.

Breaking it in half, I offered Louie a piece and he admitted, "Yeah, thanks; but no thanks. Candy makes me feel sick and makes me fat. I don't know anyone who eats candy like you. I get it. It's a Satan thing?"

Approaching the opening to the ravine I announced "'SHOWTIME'."

In Satan We Trust

While Louie readied himself for an ambush, I suggested he relax but by that time, our guys were already in position and that we were just bait, like chum to fish. Louie, who has eyes like a hawk, whispered, "There are men with guns in that group of trees. Just how do you plan on handling them?"

No sooner did he finish his question when out of the trees some of the elite dropped silently, like parachuters during the VietNam war, and removed the threat. The same thing took place all throughout the dense woods. All around us, the angels commenced their attack from high atop the ridge. More of my warriors leapt off the edge and hit the angels from above, bringing them ramming to the ground. As more angels dove down into the ravine, Mother now joined in weaving a net across the top, closing off the angels' retreat. Without room to fly freely, the angels were forced to the ground to fight. While my warriors advanced, the angels flapped their wings together and razor-sharp feathers spurted out, carving into my warriors, like a Thanksgiving turkey. Jesus advanced to the front of the line as the angels let loose another barrage of feathers. He proceeded to hold his hands out and a brilliant white light radiated from the holes where he was nailed up to on the crucifix. When the feathers hit the light, they were turned into what looked like confetti. Jesus yelled out to the warriors, "It's party time," and the warriors were all over the angels julienning them apart like carrots in a food processor.
Stampeding through the battle and Louie was hot on my heels each time a threat appeared in front of me. One of my warriors appeared, like an apparition, from out of nowhere and opened the way for me to advance to my

objective. Reaching the clearing where the C.A.T.s were waiting, I figured their one mistake was thinking I wouldn't live long enough to reach them. As we closed in on them, they used their feeble powers to attempt to stop me, but their energy blasts were likened to a mosquito bite – annoying, but not life-threatening by any means and much like a mosquito, they were about to be squashed like a pancake. Unleashing my fireballs killed almost every C.A.T.

While trying desperately to remove the last remaining enemy, I discovered I had nothing left in my tank. My opponent fired at me by surprise and based on my weakened state, I was merely a sitting duck. Quack, quack! Louie arranged himself in front of me, taking the blast meant for me. I shuffled, like a scene from *The Walking Dead*, to a tree, placed my hand on it and waited for a fruit to appear. Not only was it not nice to fool Mother Nature, also ….Mother knows best! The last C.A.T had me in his sites while everyone else was busy with their assigned task.

My cocky overconfidence looked to be my downfall. As my enemy prepared to take his shot, two figures hit him, knocking him to the earth's ground and I spotted two wolves earing him like he was the appetizer before the last supper. Another figure leapt onto the C.A.T. and the fruit finally showed itself on the tree I just touched. Plucking and eating it swiftly while the C.A.T. tossed the figure against a tree of some sort, I realized it was Uno Noon, the woman who was supposed to be in Hell waiting for me to return. The enemy rotated around to kill her and just then I felt my strength return and I fired, killing him softly and slowly. This was the 'fruits of my labor'.

The wolves assembled around the woman, and she used them to get to her feet. Rushing to Louie, I strongly sensed he was unconscious, but breathing, nonetheless. Mother and Father approached and started working with me to save Louie's life.

Weakened by the battle, I didn't have enough strength to help Louie and the woman. Realizing our catastrophe, they made their way to us while placing their hands on mine.

Mother then placed both of our hands on Louie's chest and the familiar glow radiated from our hands and Louie began breathing normally again. While opening his eyes, he barely whispered, "They say C A.T.'s have nine lives, but it seems like they should say Louie has nine lives and then he choked slightly.

My heart, beating wildly replied, "You, my friend, need to be more careful. One day, I may not be able to help you recover and I thought that was this day. Luckily, this woman, Uno, has a gift and she was gracious enough to share it with us."

Turning my attention to Uno, I faintly heard her thoughts. Evidently there was a plan in place to kill me which was much more elaborate than this latest attempt. The woman was worried that I was going to send her away once again.
Visions

Then it hit me like a hammer to a nail. "Your name's Harmony isn't it?" He wasn't quite sure how he knew that. It could have been a real vision, or a fake vision placed by someone else and the only one he knew that could do the vision placement thing was Louie. But Louie was his dearest friend wouldn't think of doing such a harmful act. Or would he?

Her eyes beamed with excitement a smile stretched across her face and she stammered, "Sssau Ssaa." She tried her hardest to speak my name, but her smile gave way to the frustration. I took her hand and told her, "My mortal name is Sean, it's easier to pronounce." So, from then on, the name Uno Noon was never mentioned again.

By now Mother, Father and Louie wondered just how I could be carrying on a conversation with what they perceived as a mute woman.

Mother queried, "What's going on here, Baby?"

Rubbing my forehead, I explained, "Mother, the reason she doesn't speak is she's never heard spoken words before. She's been held captive all her life."

The woman, Harmony, as they all came to know and call her, clutched my hand securely, Mother opened another tunnel to Hell and announced, "We should take her back to your chambers to keep her safe until we can sort out just who she is and how to help her.

"Owwwww," I screamed, as she squeezed my hand. "Relax, Harmony; you don't have to go if you don't want to. I told you before you are free to do as you want, but please don't break my fingers just yet. I need them to fight."

In Satan We Trust

Setting my hand free, she covered her mouth. In her mind only, I heard "I'm sorry; I don't want to leave. You're the first person who ever seemed to care about my well-being."

Reaching out and touching her elbow I comforted, "Not to worry, you are more than welcome to join us on our journey. It will give us time to get to know each other."

Mother had her doubts about the strange new woman. Father pulled Mother aside and suggested, "My love, I think you should let them spend time together. He looks at her like I look at you, besides Louie's there to keep an eye on them."

Mother's protective instincts kicked in and asked, "Am I the only one who finds it odd that a pretty girl shows up at such a crucial time in his life? I may have been born at night, but it wasn't *last* night!"

Harmony reminisced about how Mother knew her parents and wished she could tell her she had nothing to worry about. I realized that Mother was worried. After all, don't all mothers worry about their children? I questioned, "Mother, do you remember Kitty and Rock?"

Curious about my question, Mother queried back, "How do you know those names? They were way before your time."

Chewing my bottom lip, I admitted, "This is going to be hard for you to believe, but they are Harmony's parents."

Mother instantly advanced towards Harmony, peered sadly into her eyes and a tear cascaded down her face as she noticed the family resemblance.
Mother pivoted to me and asked, "How do you know all this? iI seems improbable that you've ever heard of any of them."

I shrugged my shoulders and confessed, "It's just one of the abilities I possess. I've got to tell you, mother; every day my senses become more defined like right now Harmony is wondering if you know where her parents are."

Bewildered by the question, Mother's face appeared deeply saddened. She continued, "I was under the impression they left earth to escape your grandfather's evil invasion, but I also thought they took her with them. I felt so foolish. Had I thought for a moment that they were still on earth, I promise you we would have done everything in our power to find them. I hope you can forgive us, Child. I feel sick now. Your parents were my friends and I was upset when I thought they left without saying goodbye. Now I hope that we may yet find them and reunite you with them."

Poor Harmony was devastated, and I could see how badly she was treated for so long and she thought to herself that her parents may very well have been killed by people like the ones who held her captive. I felt her sorrow so, being Satan or Satan-to-be and all, I decided to do something I hated more than anything. I lied, "Don't be sad, Harmony. I can sense that your chances are good that they are among them."

In Satan We Trust

And now with that one little lie, hope was revealed in her eyes.
Jesus threw the man at my feet and as he glared up while attempting simultaneously to catapulted toward me, promised, "I'll kill you".

Seizing him by the throat, cutting off his air, a massive amount blood oozed quickly from his neck. As my nails sunk into his flesh, I thought to myself, 'Damn humans; such violent beings and so little compassion, the more I see of them the more I think the cleansing is necessary.' "Now you little piss ant, what are you people planning," I asked.

Attempting to speak, he forced out, "Go to Hell!"

Gurgling as I tightened my grip on his throat, I told him, "Silly human, you'd be lucky to go to Hell, but before you find out what Heaven is like, where are this girl's parents?"

The man cockily answered, "Even if I knew what you were talking about, I wouldn't tell you."

Beaming like the cat who swallowed the canary, or the kid caught with his hand in the cookie jar, I informed him, "Today's your lucky day. I'm going to let her hunt you down and kill you. So, you'd better run now because she's not really happy with your answer."

I tossed him backwards like what you do with salt for good luck and then he began jogging away.

In Satan We Trust

Louie retreated after him, I held him back and declared, "Harmony, show them what you've got."

Harmony produced a yipping noise, the pack of wolves that have been with her ran off into the trees after the man and moments later screams enveloped the air accompanied by the sound of the wolves tearing him apart, piece by piece. Big high- five to all!

I asked Father why he was willing to die for such despicable beings. Jesus replied, "From the very beginning, my father had driven the story of salvation into him and after he met Mother and Grandfather realized that we were going to live our lives outside God's will that's when he decided to take what Mother created and enslave her and kill me.

Then he sealed me in a stone cave. However, stone is the one thing your mother can't control on the earth, like kryptonite is to Superman. That element was a creation of Harmony's father. He was one of your mother's best builders and a master of materials that were excellent for making structures that could withstand any weather. Just look at the pyramids - they've been here for ages. And the one thing your mother can't see into, an unfortunate side effect that allows the C.A.T.s to hide from us." Wow, that was a history lesson and a half!

I finally realized what one of the images that I had seen meant, so I explained, "I think it is time we travel the world and commence the destruction all around the planet, starting with Egypt then China and everywhere else where stone is an intrical part of each culture. That's where we can find your friends. That's how the C.A.T.s have kept them hidden, but if we get close, I'll be able to see them."

Mother and Father, becoming all fired up, replied, "Ok, son; but we're going to need help. Your mother and I need to go get your uncle."
With that, mother unsecured yet another tunnel to Hell and they marched off.

"Harmony, I need you to stay behind. There's someone I want you to meet and work with," I declared.

Harmony thought, "I want to come with you if you're going to find my parents. I'd like to be there," she suggested.

Peering into her earthly looking brown eyes I answered, "I understand how you feel, but I have someone who I need you to work with. I know that you're not mute and I may regret what I'm about to do, but I have a speech therapist I'd like you to work with. I'm sure your parents can't read minds like me. Wouldn't you like to be able to communicate with people, especially your parents?" After all, I said to myself, 'if Koda could speak, why can't Harmony'? Stranger things have happened. It's not always as it seems!

Harmony frowned but agreed that it would be nice to have her thoughts heard. Mother, father, Lucifer and Saliene returned and I stopped Mother from closing the tunnel. "Louie, please escort Harmony to Hell and find my teacher friend and tell her she gets to teach again," I ordered.

In Satan We Trust

Louie journeyed down with Harmony and rotated back, then asked, "You are going to wait for me to return, aren't you? I'd hate to miss out on all the fun."

I told Louie a battle just wouldn't be the same without his presence, but before he returned, I needed him to be sure that some of my elite guard her while we were all away. They disappeared into the tunnel with the wolves right on her heels. She thought I needed protection. Hence the reason for the pack's presence.

Lucifer shuffled over to me and spoke, "Well, Nephew, it seems like you're expecting a major battle if you want all of us by your side."
Mother interjected, "It was Jesus and I that thought it was a good idea to have you along with us. The C.A.T.s and angels have banded together and are using humans now, too.

Lucifer scowled, "Good thing I have Satan's elite waiting in the wings. I've instructed them to wait for us to open a tunnel and to be ready to kill his enemies."

Pacing back and forth, I began thinking about the angel problem and asked, "Wouldn't it be better if we just took the fight to them? I could simply transport us all up there and wipe them all out leaving the C.A.T.s alone with just humans to help them fight us."

"Nephew, if you did that earlier it would have been the best tactic, but you burned up almost all the time your mortal shell could handle in our realm. You couldn't handle a battle there without collapsing, leaving us all stranded. Your mother and Saliene would fall next and your father and I might be fine until they finally overwhelm us."

Feeling rather foolish now, I apologized, "Well, I would never knowingly endanger any of you. I'm sorry I suggested it."

Lucifer smacked my back and replied, "You just keep thinking, Nephew. That was an excellent idea and who knows? If I didn't play so many games with you and told you the truth about who you were and exactly what was going to happen, you may have come up with that plan in time to execute it. My Bad!"

Louie returned from his trip to Hell laughing, "Your elite squad saw me open the tunnel and started after me. I had a bitch of a time convincing them that I was meeting you and that they weren't needed just yet. Luckily, Mike was there to take control of them. I guess he's a powerful warrior that not a lot of them want to tangle with."

Nodding my head, I added, "Even as a mortal he was a tough mother. I'm not surprised by the fact that he has taken up a role as leader."

Lucifer explained that Mike, aside from being one of my closest friends, also scored highest among all my elite warriors.

Mother conceded, "Now, if we're going to Egypt, I think Saliene should stay behind. The desert isn't a place where her abilities are very strong.

In Satan We Trust

Saliene chimed, "I can take water from anywhere. Don't worry about me. Besides, I can fight as well as the next guy."

Father attempted to quell the concerns of mother by stating, "Remember when you two joined forces before? Your opponents didn't stand a chance and we really should be moving. The longer we wait, the better organization they can achieve.

Glancing at Father, I inquired, "What do you say to a cyclone ride, Pop? I figure a nice sandstorm on our way in will mess them up and it will also hide the tunnel when my warriors arrive. And I'd love to watch an angel try flying into a cyclone. I'd probably piss myself laughing."

Jesus's answer just about killed me, "You and me both, but you're still a baby so pissing your draws wouldn't be nearly as bad as me doing that. So, I hope we don't see that. Your uncle would never let me live it down."

Mother interrupted us, "You boys, the stuff you say - I swear I'll never get used to it."

Lucifer grimaced, "I'm coming along. I've yet to ride in one of those bad boys and I want to be right there when the shit hits the fan."

Beaming, I added, "The angels being the shit, and you the fan, aye, Uncle."

Louie lowered his head like a scolded child and continued, "Well, this is going to be an interesting ride I'm sure."

In Satan We Trust

Nearing Egypt, I recognized the glow of the enemy while Mother called out to Father, "There are hundreds of men hiding in the sand; but don't worry, I have a surprise for them."

Rounding the corner to the pyramids, I was shocked to learn that no angels had moved in on us. Father informed me, "The air around here makes it hard for angels to fly very well. They won't show. They would be sitting ducks around here. Perhaps they want us dead, but not at what would result in basically suicide. They don't perform suicide bombings here like in Iraq."

Clearly or shall I say not so clearly, sand was floating everywhere. And from underneath the sand, men with long, harmful-looking rifles darted up. This is where the robot, from the old TV show, *Lost In Space*, would say, 'Danger, Danger, Will Robinson'.

Mother instinctively collapsed the ground under a bunch of them. The remaining raised their rifles and Mother directed sand into the rifle barrels as the men fired. The guns exploded up in their faces, the tunnel to Hell reopened and my warriors raced out slicing the throats of the men struggling to get out of the sand. We touched down at the base of one of the pyramids and yet, another image of another battle flashed through my mind.

Father glanced at me, asking, "Son, what's going on in that head of yours?"

Sauntering over to a stone and pushing on it, an invisible door opend and Lucifer wandered in first and then he lit the corridor. "Watch out for hidden passages. I don't want or need anyone getting killed needlessly," he cautioned. Continuing through the passageway, we annihilated everyone we found, like the Nazis to the Jews. We extinguished all the pyramids of C.A.T.s like a finely tuned killing unit and as we exited the last one, Mother had an appearance of disappointment. When she noticed the look of puzzlement on my face, she told me, "I was hoping that we'd find Harmony's parents; I fear she's going to be heartbroken."

Brushing the sand off my clothes I promised Mother, "Don't worry; we're not finished here just yet, Mother. I saved the best for last. I figured they would have expected us to go for the hostages first then they would come in behind us and surprise us, but they don't know that I have an edge. We need to forge to the Sphinx; there's someone being held there, and we need to free him."

Mother asked, "Only one? Who?"

"I wish I could tell you who it is, Mother, but I don't know any of them," I secreted.

"Well, Baby," Mother said, "I just happen to know all about the Sphinx. I watched the construction and there's a vast expanse of tunnels. We can enter it through the tomb of kings."

Not totally sure that Mother knew what she was talking about," I justified, "That seems like a long way for a tunnel in this kind of soil, but Mother Nature knows her planet."

So, she hurried us off to the valley of kings, under the cover of the sandstorm. We jogged right up to the entrance, killing every human along the way. It appeared that they had been expecting us. Lucifer held Saliene's hand, gazed into her eyes and begged, "I wish you would return home. I don't want anything to happen to you."

She assured him, "Lou, you should know that I do what I want, and I want to be with you through thick and thin. What we're doing is probably the greatest thing that's ever happened since your father poisoned paradise and I'm going to do all that I can to return Earth to paradise even if it means dying. The child needs our help and it's important for him to understand just how much his family is behind him."

Lucifer's face said it all, "Family, how I like the sound of that"!

As we entered the tomb of kings, we were greeted by a C.A.T. "Please don't kill us. We've been awaiting your arrival and we don't want any trouble,' one begged. Lucifer restrained him and demanded, "Why don't you give me one good reason why I shouldn't end your pitiful existence right now and it better be good."

The 'being', for lack of a better word, appeared calm and confident by saying, "First let me warn you by opening the door you've no doubt caught the attention of the warriors in the pyramids and they plan on coming in behind you and trapping you between our men and them. So, you should get ready to face them before you continue on. Second, we have a prisoner that we were supposed to be guarding, but once you see him, you'll realize we're sincere. And finally, we'd like you to have this as a gesture of good faith." The being stretched his arm toward a long wooden box, opened it and pulled out a beautiful sword, which he presented to Lucifer.

Lucifer scowled, "You're offering it to the wrong person, Asshole. And no one's coming to your aid; you're simply stalling for time. You can't fool this old guy." Clearly, Uncle was testing the man.

"I assure you that they are coming. If you allow me, we've got a plan to let them in and trap them the way they planned to trap you," he insisted.

Lucifer motioned to me suggesting, "You should be giving that sword to Satan."

The guard, glancing at me and then back to Uncle, declared, "We've heard you like to use deception and trickery, but believe me we don't have an ulterior motive, Master. You can talk straight with us".

Uncle faced me asking, "Satan, why don't you show this fool who the real master is!" I thought to myself how weird this was – Lucifer calling me 'Satan' because as far as I knew, he was still holding the torch.

Retrieving the sword and just holding it in my hand, I noticed sword was glowing red. The guard fell to one knee, like a proposing groom to be does. "Forgive me, Master, but we've known this man as Satan for so long and have been waiting for him to arrive for quite some time. God and his angels have spent a thousand years trying to kill him. We assumed he was the true prince of darkness," the guard stuttered.

Angered, I placed the sword up to the guard's neck and threatened, "Never call him that. God is the only prince of darkness and I've already punished his sorry ass."

I asked the guard, "So, you believe me to be the prince of darkness? You are quite bold thinking that someone like that would have allowed you to live this long and you wish to join the darkness?"

The guard glanced down saying, "I beg your pardon. I misspoke. It's not my place to explain our situation. May I suggest we eliminate the reinforcements coming first? Then we can continue on our way and our leader will explain our position."

I motioned using the sword pointing it towards the tunnel and suggested, "Let's get moving. We have already killed everyone at the pyramids. You have no backup on the way and if one more of you losers use the expression 'prince of darkness', you're all dead! Evidently, I have a reputation to live up to."

Strolling through the tunnel using military precision, Lucifer commented on the number of treasures along the way. There were golden statues of angels encrusted with jewels, vases, crowns, vast kegs of water and wines, and the mummified pharaohs of time gone by. The guard was glaring at me and making odd movements while nodding his head forward. I decided it was time to see what he was thinking, so I commented, "Yeah, so what are you thinking, Gatekeeper?"

The guard thought to himself, 'damn for someone who's supposed to be all that, you'd think he'd realize I'm trying to warn him about the angels lying in wait to ambush us. Now we're all going to die because this guy is too dense to see I'm trying to warn them, and I don't even have a weapon to kill one of the angels to prove that we really don't want to go to war with them.'

I moaned a little and asked, "Hey buddy, what's your name?"
The guard answer was "Josaiha."

"Well, Josaiha, I'm weary after our last battle. Why don't you carry this fine sword for me a while; give my arms a rest," I asked. Handing the sword to him, Lucifer being the greatest warrior of all, realized immediately that danger was ahead and moved Saliene to the rear telling her, "My love, why don't you open a couple of kegs of water, so we can freshen up a bit? I could really use a drink." Now *everyone* knew something wasn't right.

Josaiha was telling himself that at least now he could kill an angel or two before he died then maybe I wouldn't kill off my friends and family. I batted my eyes at him and told him, "Don't worry, Josaiha, you're not going to die, at least the way you think. Josaiha, baffled, thought, 'It's almost like he's reading my mind. Wouldn't that be nice! Then I could explain that I couldn't tell him about them because of their excellent hearing.'

I needed to protect my family as best as I could. I said aloud, "Family is very important. I'd do anything I could to protect them."

In Satan We Trust

Josaiha sighed and looked as if the weight of the world had been lifted from his shoulders, or at least relieved that he may have saved his people. Up front in the tunnel, I viewed a large dome-shaped room and I called Louie up to me while reaching into my jacket and pulling out Cain's blade once more and held it in my hand in back of me motioning for him to take it. While retrieving it, Lucifer appeared shocked that I would entrust him with such a powerful weapon. A few steps before reaching the room, I started singing *Bat Out Of Hell*. Louie remembered that I like singing during times of destruction and he prepared for a fight of all fights, hiding the blade inside his sleeve. While entering the room, I noticed about 50 angels on the walls and they really blended in nicely with the statues we passed earlier. The odds weren't in our favor, so I decided to tip the scales *in* our favor. Maneuvering myself quickly into the center of the room, I asked anyone listening, "Man, have you guys ever noticed just how ugly these statues are? Evidently only goofy, ugly people go to Heaven and the whole wings thing must be so people can recognize them as the fat ass turkeys ready for a Thanksgiving Day slaughter and talk about ugly birds. The other song by Meatloaf, which starts out *Good girls go to Heaven, But Bad Girls Go Everywhere*…….entered my mind at that very moment.

The angels became sick of listening to my insults and they escaped their perches and swooped down towards me figuring they could take me out before anyone could stop them, but alas, to say Father and Lucifer were ready for them was an extreme understatement.

In Satan We Trust

Louie, rushing to my side with Cain's blade in hand while a group of angels remained in the air clapping their wings in front of themselves sending their razor-sharp feathers in my direction, Father once again fired light, reducing them to snow. Louie began slashing through the flurry of angels while Saliene sent water along the floor beneath us then she blasted it upward knocking the angles backwards. Lucifer fired the largest fireball I had ever seen, killing most of them. Josaiha wielded the sword like a professional as I managed to sink my claws into a few angels. And to my delight, my fingernails released a toxin that disabled those they cut into. As the last angel fell, Josaiha continued slashing and stabbing them

"ENOUGH," I screamed. They're finished. I'll take my sword back now if you don't mind," I continued.

Josaiha ceased and then he wiped off the sword on the robes of the dead and returned the sword to me. "Let's get out of here. We still have much to do," I demanded.

Proceeding through the tunnel, I suddenly felt a sharp pain in the center of my chest. Leaning against the wall, holding my chest as the pain subsided. I felt something. Unbuttoning my shirt, I discovered a small hole about the size of a BB and a glowing light inside me. With my family gathered around me, I realized that they weren't concerned, and Mother had the happiest little smile on her face surprisingly enough.

"Times growing short, my baby. You're so close to being born that it is just one of the signs," she explained.

Now everyone has a strange look of contentment on their faces, everyone that is, except for Louie. Instead Louie appeared sadder than anytime I could remember. As much as I didn't want to, I couldn't help but look into his mind. He was hard to get into especially since I've told him of my ability, but he's no match for me. I finally penetrated his defenses and viewed just why he was so sad. What do you know? Louie had a secret and I'm sorry that I peeked into his mind, but now I need to figure out how to ease his pain without letting him know that I know. Perhaps it was time I stop looking into his mind because it's not always as it seems! Plus, it could be detrimental to see some of the ideas in his head.

Josaiha informed us that were about to enter the Sphinx. While entering a room, all decked out in gold, we noticed in the center of the room was a banquet table with about a dozen C.A.T.s standing on the other side of the room. Lucifer growled, then whispered to me, "For centuries, these douches have lived like royalty. Why were we giving them a chance? We should kill them all."

Finding it tough to keep a straight face, I asked uncle, "If one thing they say is untrue, then you will get your way; but if we don't have to kill them, then where's the harm in showing mercy?"

Lucifer grunted, "Mercy has been in short supply on this planet for centuries, but pain and suffering have been plentiful."

One of the men stepped forward and announced, "Please sit down. we want to discuss our surrender."

Placing the sword on the table I inquired, "Where's your hostage? We would like to see him."

The leader stated," I beg your pardon? Guest, not hostage! The only reason he's locked up is to keep him

In Satan We Trust

safe. The angels would surely have killed him if we didn't keep up the façade."

He motioned to one of his 'people' and that person exited the room returning with another soul. Mother rushed over to the new arrival and uttered, "Rocky I'm so very happy to see that you're alive and well."

"Nature," he said excitedly. "I knew one day you would free us. Tell me, have you freed my family yet," Rocky queried.

Not wanting to really answer, Mother simply bowed her head. I shuffled over to the soul replying, "Your daughter has been found and she is safe. Your wife, however, is still among the missing."

Turning to the leader of the Sphinx I informed him, "I think it's time you told us everything you know. I grow weary of the games you vile creatures are playing. So, if you don't start singing, I'm going to let my uncle do what he does best."

Rocky, moving me aside spoke, "Boy, I don't know why Satan has you along, but you need to step back before you get hurt."

Like a flash of lightning, Louie had Rocky on the ground. Rocky retaliated and threw him off the wall, I got a hold of Rocky by the neck, raised him up and said, "Your daughter was much more grateful when I saved her. Don't make me kill you. I'd hate for her to have to mourn your death by my hand!"

It's Not Always As It Seems

Mother shouted, "Satan, he's a dear friend. Don't hurt him!"

Dropping him, he bowed to me apologizing, "Forgive me, Satan. I had no idea you were Satan. My deepest apology, but you're a human. I had no way of knowing." There he went calling me 'Satan' again. Curiosity may have killed the cat, but it also got me wondering if I had been unofficially re-born without physically experiencing the feeling.

I scowled, "Go stand by my mother and be quiet before I lose my temper."

Lucifer told me, "Nephew, you have learned a lot hanging out with me."

Pinching Lucifer's arm, Sailiene interrupted, "You need to correct him when he is scolded, not instigate him."

"Now, Josaiha, just who's in charge here," I asked.

Josaiha glared in my direction and retorted, "Why you, of course, but before you arrived, we answered to Jacob."

Jacob, stepping forth, interjected, "I hope you believe me when I tell you ever since this war started, all of us in the Sphinx were against war. So, we remained here in an effort to not offend you, but God had his angels keeping us from trying to warn you of their plans. It's just that we'd like to leave the planet when you've finally defeat God, so he doesn't hunt us down. We will, however, fight by your side to earn our freedom. I'm ashamed to say we were too scared to go against God in the beginning, but while here we knew that in order to be free, we would have to fight when the time was right."

In Satan We Trust

Eyeing Jacob up and down I suggested, "Let's cut to the chase, huh? Where and how many more hostages are being held by you people?"

Jacob, singing like a caged canary answered, "There are four total - Rocky's family and two others. His wife is in the Vatican, his daughter, you already found, it seems. Another is in the ruins of a Mayan temple, and the last is in a castle in Ireland. If you tell us what you'd like us to do to earn our freedom, then we will do anything you command."

Shaking my head furiously, I requested, "Uncle, a doorway, if you please. I need some of my elite."

Lucifer displayed a passageway and my warriors began pouring out. the C.A.T.s eyes filled with fear as he stated, "My man, Michael, stands before me, my friend. These sheep are not to be harmed; at least not as long as what they told me is true."

Michael nodded in agreement to do as I've instructed and said, "I wish I could spend more time with you, my friend, but there's still much to be done."

Michael replied, "It's cool; I've made lots of friends here. You sure know how to pick good people."

I called Lucifer asking, "Uncle, can we talk privately?"

Sauntering back into the tunnel I admitted, "Uncle, I'm worried that something is wrong with me. I don't want Mother to know, but I can't seem to transport anymore. That's why I have been letting Mother supply our transportation lately and now this hole in my chest. Can you help me?"

Lucifer, placing his hand on my shoulder replied, "Nephew, there's nothing wrong. Your body is morphing right now, so you are using more of your power in other ways causing other abilities to go dormant for a while. Soon you will be almost like a newborn. it's going to be hard for you after having gotten used to using them so much and just let me add that you've used more than anyone I've ever seen before. Just remember, it's all part of your development and don't stress over it." That was it – I was finally on my way to becoming Satan...or was I? It's not always as it seems, is it?

It was time to visit the Vatican again. Had I had some of the abilities that I have now, my first trip to the pedophile complex would have gone quite differently and I may have very well taken the lives of a few of those wretched 'holier than thou' assholes; but now it's time for a bloodbath.

I inquired, "Uncle would you get some of my warriors ready to prepare to lay surge on the Vatican?"

Lucifer, fluttering his eye, replied, "I'd be more than happy to. You may want to stay back from this one, Nephew. Your father has been wanting to visit the Vatican and I don't mean to admire the place; in fact, I don't think he will need any help laying waste to that place."

Grinning foolishly, I replied, "Maybe so, but I just want my warriors to have some fun too."

In Satan We Trust

Lucifer unsecured a door and he and Saliene traveled back to Hell to gather my troops.
Mother fired up a twister, like a boy scouts lights a campfire, and scooped us up and we were on our way to Vatican City.

Eyeing Father, I told him, "Jesus has fire in his eyes. I've never seen him like this. His body is shaking." The holes in his body glowed red and Rocky unsurprisingly looked as cold as stone. Hence, his name fits him perfectly.

Louie, relaxed, I asked him, "My friend, why so calm?"

Shrugging his shoulders, Louie answered, "I'm just going to sit back and enjoy the show. I want to thank you for bringing me along, Satan. I know you don't need me anymore, but I am grateful."

Resting my hand on his shoulder I spoke, "You're my friend and you will always be welcome to join me unless one day I find love. Then I'd better not see you by me."

Louie assured me, "You will find love one day, this I'm sure of because if you can't, what hope is there for me? What about Harmony? She's hot and one of you."

With hearing that, Rocky's head whipped around and screamed, "Don't talk about my little girl, you little insignificant piss ant, or I'll kill you."

Instantly my hand was on his throat and I yelled, "*You*, my pushy friend, are the piss ant and if you wish to see your girl, you will treat my friend with respect or its you who will die!"

Mother touched the twister down on a small island and bellowed, "SATAN! Let him go. We all need to calm down."

Pummeling Rocky into a tree I continued, "Ungrateful fuck, just because your captors were easy on you, you think you're special but hear me now - you will learn your place or else, believe me when I say I won't take your shit much longer."

Mother ushered Rocky away quickly and suggested, "We all need a rest, Rocky, let's take a walk and cool off."

Disappearing into the woods, like Hansel and Gretel, Louie thanked me and said, "I'm not sure about that guy, Satan. Maybe he should wait in Hell with Harmony."

Jesus stared at me saying, "Son, I know you have every right to be upset, but do me a favor and wait until we free his wife. I promise you he will be a different man when his family is back together; besides I really, really want to get to this next battle – this one's personal."

Lowering my head, I apologized, "Forgive me, Father, he just rubs me the wrong way."

Louie asked if Rocky would likely be joining us after we freed his wife. I responded, "If the prick doesn't smarten up, he may not even last to the pedophile palace."

In Satan We Trust

Mother and Rocky appeared back in sight. Jesus frowned sternly at me saying, "Remember, Satan, it's just a little bit farther, and Louie why don't you hold your tongue until we all finish up this battle?"

I nudged Louie and stated, "Don't worry, my friend, we'll have our fun with this prick later."

Nearing Vatican City, images careened through my mind. "They're ready for us. This is going to be one of our toughest battles yet," I predicted.

Mother called forth another storm and bolts of lightning bombarded the grounds. Touching down, Louie and Rocky attacked, and angels rained down on us, but Jesus shielded us from the razor-sharp feathers. The ground unleashed itself and Lucifer and Saliene emerged, my warriors hot on their heels. The faithful to the church rushed in from the town and a gory bloodbath ensued. I viewed an angel just hovering in the air. He raised a horn to his lips and played a high-pitched note and I watched my family and warriors drop to their knees grasping their ears, screaming in pain. Lucifer cried out, "It's Gabriel!"

With the opposition beginning to slaughter my warriors, I started to feel myself giving in. Then rage encompassed my body and I thought about Gabriel and I then appeared directly in front of him. Before he could do anything, my hand was on his throat, crushing his windpipe and his pain must have been excruciating as his horn fell from his hands down to earth. A horny little fellow, he will never be again. With my free hand, I removed Cain's blade from my coat and vanquished the mighty Gabriel.

In Satan We Trust

Rising to their feet, my warriors once again gained the upper hand.

"Mother," I cried out, as I felt my body go limp and plummet towards earth. Then all went black.

I struggled to open my eyes, but they closed time and time again. As I finally regained consciousness, I noticed Koda's massive head over me, two huge limbs cradled me, and I was in the forest surrounded by animals and my warriors. A woman scuffled up to Koda's feet. "We will take it from here," she informed us. Koda gently placed me on a bed of moss. The woman knelt beside me, like a true Catholic does in church, and softly kissed my forehead saying, "Satan, thank you for saving my family and me. We are forever in your debt."

Still groggy, it didn't register in my mind who she wass. Louie, standing at my feet blurted out, "Satan, you have given us quite a scare. I'm glad you finally woke."

Propping myself up on one elbow, I inquired, "How long have I been sleeping Louie?"

"Two earthling weeks," was his reply. "Kitty has been watching over you for most of that time." Terror rushed through me instantly, so I asked, "And Mother and Father, are they alright? And Uncle? What happened? Did they make it," I continued with my questions.

Thinking the worst, I tried to get to my feet, but it was no use. Louie dropped down beside me, placing his hands on my shoulders confiding, "Everyone's fine. You must relax. Save your strength. I'll go spread the word. Your family has been fighting with a vengeance. They're not happy with the angels or their followers. They need a break and hearing that you're finally awake will surely get them all back here for a while. In my absence, Kitty will tend to your needs."

A deep voice added, "Koda too!"

Kitty giggled and stroked the mighty Hellhound's paw. Louie bounded off to deliver the ecstatic news. Kitty raised one of Mother's special fruits to my lips so I could eat. "This is a special animal right here. He told me he likes you and you can understand him too," Kitty spoke.

Swallowing the last of my fruit, I replied, "Yeah, but no one else seems to believe he's more than just a dog. Kitty informed me, "It is a rare gift you have being able to understand animals."

I corrected Kitty, "Koda is the only one I hear. Well, that's not exactly right. When I arrived in Hell in my nursery, I swore I heard the animals singing one of my favorite songs."

Kitty took my hand while saying, "Just listen a little harder." The wind howled, and Mother came sliding in and she embraced me with a look of relief on her face crying, "Baby, I know you had to help us, but you must not try to access your abilities from here on out." She unbuttoned my shirt and the small, glowing hole in my chest was now the size of a quarter. Time was growing short for me!

Father and Uncle arrived, Jesus looked discussed and announced, "If it's this stressful awaiting your birth, I can only imagine what your life is going to do to our nerves."

Lucifer patted my head with his hand stating, "That was impressive, Nephew. You shouldn't have been able to pull that stunt off, but I'm glad you live by your own rules."

Sighing, I answered, "Uncle, I fear I've lost Cain's blade in my haste. Please forgive me."

Lucifer retorted, "It was yours, Nephew, and I know one day you will get it back but until then, you've gained another weapon." He presented me with the horn of Gabriel. "I'm astonished that none of their arsenal seemed to have any effect on you," he finished.

Glancing over at him, I queried, "Uncle, are you kidding me? When he blew that thing, I almost died - such a no talent, **bitch killing music** that way and harming my family. Prick deserved what he got."

When Louie returned with Saliene, Jesus became concerned for everyone's safety over the loss of Cain's blade. "We need to stay vigilant now that Cain's blade is in the angel's possession. They will be coming for the ones you love, my Son, with the hopes of getting to you," he suggested.

"The angels don't have Cain's blade," Louie said as he reached into his jacket and proudly presented me with the blade.

In Satan We Trust

Lucifer pat him on the back and exclaimed, "You certainly have proven yourself time and time again, Louie."

Mother conjured up another fruit and handed it to me. As I ate, I declared, "Louie, how's about you getting us some meat? My host is starving! Getting up to go hunting, Kitty stopped him demanding, "Rocky, lend me a hand. Let's show him how we do things."

Rocky maneuvered his hand through the air and a sharp boulder appeared. Saliene called out and an old buck stampeded out from the trees and jumped across the sharp boulder, hanging himself up in the branches, effectively gutting himself. Louie wasted no time and got to work butchering it. And then Uncle cooked it to perfection like a five-star chef.

Sitting at the table, enjoying our feast when a doorway to Hell burst open and out came Harmony hugging and kissing her parents. She made her way over to me saying, "Thank you, Satan."

I blushed slightly and replied, "So nice to hear your voice. But you can still hear me, even if I don't speak."

I agreed, "Yes, but others can now, too. I enjoy talking with you too."

Peering around the table, I continued, "So, I wish you could fill me in on what's been going on since I have been somewhat incapacitated."

In Satan We Trust

Lucifer began, "After we shook off the effect of Gabriel's horn, slaughtering their forces was like a smooth summer breeze."

Louie added, "You would have laughed your ass off watching your father grabbing priests, shoving one's man-up, another ass making a chain out of them. It was like watching the grossest game of barrel of monkeys ever played."

Mother looked at me admitting, "I'm glad I took you back here during the battle. I don't like it when your father goes all ballistic."

Winking at Dad I inquired, "You feel better now, Pops?"

Jesus grinned answering, "I've dreamed about taking that place down and I'm happy to say it was better than I thought it would be."

"So, what about the two weeks after," I inquired.

"Well, we took down the Mayan temple and then the underground temples at Stonehenge and Easter Island. Now Mother and Saliene have been causing devastation all around the world. As a matter of fact, as we speak, the three C.A.T.s we rescued are leading demons in protest, causing dissension among humans. They're about ready to turn on each other. Just a little more time and we will be ready to put the final plan into action," he commented.

"That's all well and good, but it's nearing Christmas. It's going to be here soon and I think maybe we could cut back a bit till after the holy holiday. After all, it's about showing respect for my father," I said.

Jesus answered, "My boy, don't you think we should just let it go? They don't have much longer."

"That's alright," I said. "I refuse to end this tradition. Granted, humans suck but at Christmas, they act differently, - they smile and actually get along a bit. And as long as I'm around, I'm going to keep on giving them hope," I finished.

Lucifer chuckled, "I told you all before this boy dances to the beat of a different drum. Despite the danger and ungrateful masses, he still has hope and I'm all for letting him do what his heart tells him to do."

Mother snipped, "Well, it's not that easy to restart all the storms around the world if we ease up now. We do have a schedule we're trying to follow."

Defiantly I responded, "Well, it's only one month I'm asking for and it's up to you, but I'm flying everywhere again this year and next year, too; so, if you want to make it more of a challenge for me, so be it."

Mother, not totally thrilled by my independence, glared at Jesus querying, "You want to chime in here, Dear?"

Jesus outstretched his arms as if he was surrendering, stepped back retorting, "Hey, the boy has been doing this for almost two thousand years, honoring me. I refuse to tell him to stop now. We all know that the month of

December renews his belief that mankind can change for the better."

Mother, clearly aggravated by now marched off into the woods, Jesus sighed and started after her. Saliene stopped him asking, "Why don't you boys stay here? Kitty, care to join me?"

As they headed out to catch up to Mother. I overheard, ok eavesdropped may be a more succinct term, "Saliene, just wait until he gets a look at our other C.A.T.s out fighting with the demons. Now that will be interesting."

Jesus extended his arm into his shirt and retrieved a bag demanding, "Here, make sure you keep eating. The vessel you're in needs to fuel itself."

Unzipping the bag, I discovered it was full of jerky. This was awesome, as I just adored this stuff.

Jesus, quickly blinking his eyes at me revealed, "Believe me, Son, I've been watching you all along and not to be mean, but you're crazy……but in a good way. Your mother worries about you but just between us, I've never laughed as much as when watching your unique way of coping with people and situations. The jerky, by the way, is moose. I used the spices you generally use, so it should taste close to the way you make it. Let me know what you think."

While biting into it, Jesus very kindly filled a glass with water and Offered it to me. "Oh, yeah," I said, "That's got some heat," I finished saying.

In Satan We Trust

I began drinking the water, but good old Dad turned it into my favorite beer. "You're the best, Pops. Is it possible that I'm gonna be able to do this little trick, too, one day," I asked sheepishly.

"I'm pretty sure you can. Just concentrate, my Boy. It's pretty simple. You've already done things fifty times harder than this."

Lucifer interrupted us announcing, "Now let's not forget, Uncle Lucifer, I know this boy better than anyone. I knew you were going to start thinking about Christmas and I also knew that you still planned on doing the whole Santa thing." So, Uncle, like a game show host, pivoted his body and pointed to the sky and gliding by, like a precision squadron of jet fighters, were my reindeer and sleigh with my man, Louie, at the reigns.

Landing the team safely in the field beside us, Louie exclaimed, "Hell, yeah, Satan; the reindeer are in amazing shape this year especially for it being so early. I've never seen them so strong."

Still chowing down the jerky, I offered Louie a piece informing him, "You gotta try this stuff. Dad made it and it's great!"

Lucifer stopped him before he received any requesting, "I need to talk to you, my little assassin."

As they stepped aside, I could tell something was up and asked, "So, Pops; did that strike you as odd?"

Jesus retorted, "Your uncle must have a task best suited to Louie's expertise".

Rocky was huddled with his daughter and Harmony was actually heard speaking. Her voice was so soothing and sweet that I was feeling much better since eating the meat Father made me, so I approached Harmony and her father requesting, "Rocky, would it be alright if I stole Harmony for a few?"

Rocky stared at me like I had two heads and inquired, "Don't you think we have time to make up for? After all, we have all been prisoners for a long time and I would like to spend some time with her."

"I can understand that, but I'll be leaving soon, and I'd just like to say goodbye," I begged.

Reluctantly, Rocky gave her permission to go with me, so I lead her over to the reindeer. I told her, "I'm so I'm glad we could find your parents safe and sound. Some of the enemies claimed they just wanted to leave when this is all over. I'm not sure what your father has planned, but just in case you leave, I wanted to say goodbye. I'm getting the feeling he doesn't really like me."

To my pleasant surprise, Harmony started talking, "I guess he's different with me. You know, being his child and all. Truthfully, I don't remember much about my parents." As she spoke, my mind drifted off and I thought to myself that Harmony was the perfect name for her. "Excuse me, excuse me," a little reindeer is heard saying. Comet bumped me, and I snapped back to reality as I realized she had caught me daydreaming.

"What's up with that smile on your face? Are you even listening to me," she asked me as she glanced at Comet. "Thanks, big guy. Someone needed to get his attention because it seems like I can't hold it," she finished.

Embarrassed, I confessed, "Forgive me, but you have the most beautiful voice. It just seems to calm me down and I just got lost in it. It's been kinda stressful for me the last year or so, everyone wanting to kill me and all that. That beautiful voice just gave me a tiny well-needed vacation. I truly hope you and your family stay after its all over because I could really use your help molding the lucky few humans who are chosen to survive."

Harmony blushed or at least I thought it was blushing. For our kind, I guess I could understand that, but as far as I knew she was not 'our kind'. She replied, "Your mind is always going a hundred miles an hour. I'm glad I don't carry the weight of the world on my shoulders like you have to".

While embracing me tenderly, she hugged me saying, "You saved me and showed me nothing but kindness."

Shying away I reminded her, "Your Dad's getting annoyed."

Peering over my shoulder at her father she inquired, "How could you possibly have known that?"

"It's just part of me. It's a double-edged sword - good *and* bad. A lot of times I wish I could turn it off. Feeling something doesn't mean you act on it, but knowing what people think always makes me guarded," I admitted to her.

Swaggering over to Comet I chastised, "You're no help, Buddy. I might have caught myself."

Comet grunted and pranced which made Harmony giggle. And I must have taken to heart what Kitty told me because I heard Comet and understood him as he said, "Please. You are so busted. I was just trying to stop the bleeding."

Returning my attention back to Harmony I whispered, "So, you're like your mother in respect to hearing animals?"

She replied, "Kind of - our winged animals are easier to understand, but I get the gist of most animals."

Still pounding down jerky, I offered some to Harmony. Again, Lucifer interfered, but now he had to show his hand demanding, "Don't eat that. It's just for Satan." How rude, I thought to myself.

Raising an eyebrow, I caught sight of Louie and could see he was deeply troubled.

"Uncle, I know you would never harm me, but I also know that you're up to something. I think it's time for you to come clean," I exclaimed.

Lucifer, bowing his head answered, "Just know, Nephew, I did what I did only to make sure you survived."

In Satan We Trust

Curiosity got the better of Jesus and Rocky about what was going on.

"Uncle, this has something to do with this bag of jerky doesn't it," I inquired.

Jesus stared at Lucifer demanding, "Brother, what have you done?"

Lucifer, guarded by now responded, "Hey, I've been protecting this little guy for his entire development and now the angels are trying harder than ever to kill him, so I put some life everlasting in with your spices."

Father went crazy on Uncle screaming, "We were supposed to destroy that shit. Why would you do that?"

Lucifer snapped back at his brother, "Satan is too close to being born and the only one I trust to save Satan *is* Satan himself. He has done spectacular things already and this will allow him to continue at full strength."

When Mother returned, Jesus told her what had transpired. But rather than anger, she was showing signs of shock and a bit guilty. Then she confessed, "I'm sorry, Dear; but I, too, have been worried for his life and I also put some life everlasting in your spice."

Louie smacked his hand against his forehead and shook his head in disapproval, like a scene from *The Three Stooges* and then he journeyed off into the forest.

"Koda", I said, "Go with Louie and keep him safe."

In Satan We Trust

The mighty Hellhound rushed off like an obedient pet would do.

Jesus was speechless, so I asked, "Father it's ok. I know they only wish to help, but why does this bother you so much? Louie doesn't seem too thrilled either," I finished.

Taking a deep breath and for the first time in an earthling's month, I didn't feel a shooting pain from the glowing hole in my chest. So, I opened my shirt and it appeared to have healed. Patting Uncle's shoulder, I reminisced about my favorite lake in New Hampshire near the Old Man in the Mountain, which was a tourist site with the natural formation of a man's profile. Before I knew it, we were standing right there, and it was exactly how I remembered it over time.

"Now that we're alone, I have some questions I want you to answer without any reindeer games," I requested of Father.

"I need to know how this shit is going to affect me, Uncle," I requested.

Lucifer, with a glowing face, kind of like the first trimester of pregnancy, explained that the drug had been administered. "Well, Satan," he began, and I already didn't like the sound of this. "You know how you just got us here? Now, as before, you can travel anywhere your heart desires and not have to worry about your body giving out."

Confused, I asked, "Ok, then why is Louie so upset? This shouldn't affect him, but he's different ever since that hole opened up in my chest. He should be happy that it healed. Why isn't he?"

Lucifer lowered his head saying, "I did my best to turn his heart to stone and I thought I did a pretty good job of it. Then you ended up making him feel like a friend, then family. He still has to do his job and truly caring about you has turned his job into a monumental task. Don't get me wrong, I like the little assassin, but you're my nephew and you, above all, are my number one concern."

I grimaced saying, "Nice job dancing around the answer, Uncle."

Lucifer curled his lip and replied, "He has never been a fan of being called out. Sorry, Nephew; but that's the best answer you're going to get from me."

I returned us to the forest where we left the family and informed everyone, "I have an announcement to make. I'm returning to Heaven. It's time to put those rats with wings in line and show them who's in charge now and the only ones who are going with me are Louie and Koda. Mother, why not go with snow to cause devastation? I've seen how well you have used it in the past and my team doesn't mind the snow. I'll see you all before Christmas. Promise."

Jesus extended his hand suggesting, "Son, why don't you give me that jerky back until you return?"

I compromised, "You can have it when I get back." And quick as a wink I was gone and in front of Louie and Koda. Still walking away from the others, I called out,

"Hey, Louie, you quitting on me? I mean it's okay, but we're friends. I'd at least think I deserve a goodbye."

Louie, looking nonchalant, but I could tell his mind had him somewhere else, convinced me, "I will never leave you. I just needed to get away for a few." I looked into Louie's mind again, even though I promised myself I wouldn't. Hey, I'm not fucking perfect!

And what I saw convinced me even more that I shouldn't have done it. The conversation I saw involved Mother, Father and Louie. My 'parents' were discussing with Louie the possibility of him becoming Satan instead of me. They may have just stabbed me in the heart with my own blade to put me out of my misery.

I couldn't reason as to why they would do that to me, their only son! What had I done to upset them? They did show a small degree of disappointment when I killed that girl named Erin. She deserved to die – she was blonde, after all. Had I not done that, she would have gone ahead with her plan. And that plan of hers was to kill her twin brothers, Frankie and Kenny.

While doing her bid in prison after this crime-to-be, she was heard on an infamous phone call with dear old Mom, who now had no sons and a daughter behind bars. Mom screamed into the phone to her, "And you told me you put those large, heavy crystals in Frankie's and Kenny's pockets to keep them from having to carrying the heavy load in their hands. What the fuck would have been the difference? Heavy is heavy, whether or not they were in their pockets or their hands!"

Erin replied to dear Mom, "Mom, I also wanted to keep their hands warm, so they could keep them in their mittens. They wouldn't have been able to keep their hands *and* the crystals in their pockets at the same time." Mary, Erin's Mom, replied, "You're such a fucking dumb blonde. They didn't have to keep their hands in their pockets if they were wearing mittens."

"Oh, yeah, didn't think of that," Erin said. So, that was what would have led to the 'accidental' sliding on ice on Lake Hopatcong and crashing through into the water causing hypothermia and drowning. And I wasn't about that to happen to twins or non-twins. So, Erin died a slow and painful death.

You see, it wasn't that Erin wanted an immediate inheritance. She wasn't willing to kill her parents also and get rich. She was willing to wait; however, when they died natural deaths in years to come, she wanted to make sure she was the sole survivor and the inheritance need not be shared with two little brothers, twins or not. I would do it all over again, too, if I had the chance.

This was the same stupid blonde when told that Jimmy Hoffa was found in a freezer and that the owners of the house where he was found tried to push the discovery as a pig, and the police ignored their claim because a Teamster badge and a name plate were found on the body, her reply was, "Really, I have to google that." Blondes!

I hopped on top of Koda like I was jumping into my sleigh and looked down at Louie. "Well, my friend. I have good news for you. The three of us are taking a trip.Let's have some fun and leave the adults behind," I informed him.

Louie, looking up at me, cracking an ever so slight smile, catapulted up on Koda's back. Then he giggled, "You know they're gonna find us pretty quickly and normally I'd try and talk you out of a stunt like this, but they kinda pissed me off; so, screw whatever punishment I get/ Let's just do this! By the way, where are we going?"

Stroking my long, red Santa beard, I winked devilishly at him. "I was thinking we should pop up and visit Gramps and his winged vermin," was my suggestion.

Louie's face went blank. "That's your idea of fun? I gotta say I could come up with like a million other things that are way more fun than dying," he told me.

Swatting my hand in the air, I retorted, "Have I ever led us into harm's way?"

Louie rolled his eyes and said, "Oh, so many times; but I also know there's no use trying to talk you out of anything."

With a mischievous grin, I said, "We'll be fine. I had more visions, so you know it'll be ok." I simply opened the door about the visions, but he didn't bite. His expression didn't even change a single bit. Perhaps he didn't remember I had visions.

Louie wrinkled up his face like an old prune and answered, "I'm sure. Fuck it, let the fun begin!"

In Satan We Trust

After those words were no sooner said, we appeared in front of God, the angels advanced towards us and I maneuvered my hands towards the ground. At this, they all dropped to their knees. I yelled, "You bitches like worshiping at someone's feet? Fine, stay like that until I finish what I came here to say. I grow weary of swatting you flies, so I tell you what I'm gonna do. You think that Grampa up there is a merciful God and that's what you want, so I'll show you mercy. I offer you this option. Stay the fuck here and never leave or I will vanquish each and every one of you bastards."

I raised my arms in the air and released the mangey angels. As they rose, I continued, "I could conjure up a barrier and force you to stay here, but it's easier to kill all of you."

Waving my hand again, a thousand angels burst into flames. "Now, as you can see that took no effort at all. A thousand angels for the thousand years of darkness you told the people I would bring. So, if you wish to continue to exist, you will stay here. If just one of you pieces of shit leave, I will kill all of you. So, do you want to die now, or would you like to take my offer," I finished.

The angels glanced pitifully at God hanging on the cross and looked to him for guidance. But God sneered at me saying, "Cocky little fuck; you'd better kill us all because you're not leaving here alive. Kill him my children!" The angels didn't move, not even the slightest, and this time it wasn't because I stopped them. Nodding to the angels in approval, I rewarded them with, "Very good. I will leave you to contemplate your existence and as long as you abide by my rule, I will leave you in peace."

God screamed at them like a young kindergartener, "You will do my bidding or suffer my wrath."

I floated up to Grandfather, like a child does in a pool, seared to the cross and placed a finger over his lips and told him, "Shhhh." My finger glowed red and God's lips fused together. "I've grown tired of listening to your psycho babbling and now none of you need to worry about him talking to you. Live in peace," I finished. Placing my lips next to Grandfather's ear, I slowly whispered, "When I said I would kill everyone, I didn't mean you. Old man, you're staying right here. I want you to suffer like you've made my family suffer. You could have been great; but instead you had to be cruel. Welcome to *real* Hell. You've been here all the time."

Louie bellowed to me, "Satan, why don't you just kill him and be done with it?"

"Louie, you really don't know about the images you put in my head. That's exactly what he wants. It would only free his essence. Then he'd be able to hide anywhere," I explained. And then it hit me – he did remember my ability to see in minds. He put the conversation image in my head. But, why? Was he hoping I would give up the throne willingly if I had 'known' my parents were debating that issue? Not hardly! But then again, it's not always as it seems!

Louie's gaze kept focusing on a table full of weapons. It seemed like he was unable to stop himself. "My friend, "If you see something you like, just take it. They have no use for them any longer," I finished.

Louie sauntered over and picked up a battle axe saying, "This was my father's. He died saving me." Tears welled up in his eyes.

An angel sang out, "Yeah, but it's mine now. Your father was unworthy of such a fine weapon so after I killed him, I claimed it as mine."

I sensed the rage flowing through my friend instinctively and spoke, "Louie, you can just take it if you choose or reclaim it in the manner in which your father lost it."

The angered angel retorted, "Better just take it, Dwarf. You're not half the warrior your father was and I ended his life in record time."

Shaking my head vigorously I replied, "Yeah, you're gonna regret not keeping your mouth shut."

Louie stared, like a guy's first look at a naked female, straight through the angel's soul crying, "Miserable pigeon. I saw the fight. You didn't even take him down alone and you *will* die alone."

"Louie," I begged him, "I can't interfere in any way, so do me a favor and don't die." Was Louie prepared to die for me or for the purpose of being reborn and taking Satan's role?

The angel unveiled his sword and plunged towards Louie. Louie grabbed the axe and as the angel thrust the blade at him, Louie swung the axe twice, like an experienced baseball batter. The first swing shattered the sword into pieces and the second removed the angels head.

"Case closed," I replied.

Louie glanced over at me exclaiming, "Well that was anticlimactic, but, oh so satisfying. What do you say we leave this place Satan?"

Koda limped over to the body and chomped it down.

"Well, everyone it has been a hoot, but let's not do it again," I finished like a glorious Olympic winner. I blinked us all back to the forest where Mother was standing with her arms simply crossed saying, "Young man, we need to talk."

"I'll be right with you, Mother, but first I need to keep my promise. Walking slowly over to Father, I handed him the bag of jerky as a peace offering. I really should have handed it to Mother.

Jesus removed the bag from me while scolding me, "I'm a bit surprised that you handed it over so easily. All those before you who used that stuff cared about only the drug and it always ended badly."

Pivoting toward Mother to accept my punishment, but then spinning back to Father, I reached into the bag and took one last piece, like a kid in a candy store.

Jesus grinned consoling me, "Don't worry, Son. I know your mother and you're not in that much trouble. She just worries, like all mothers do, but take heed in her words. She's just concerned for her baby."

I hugged Father and told him, "I'm sorry that I'm so much trouble, but I'm doing my best to figure out just how best to become what fate has thrust upon me."

Jesus's heart grew sad for he knew all too well that turmoil was going on inside me as his life had taken a similar path. He comforted me, "My boy, you are doing just fine. Be true to your heart and know that will be all you need to be the man you can be proud to be. Now go put your mother at ease."

Approaching Mother, I noticed tears welling up in her eyes. I asked for forgiveness, "Mother, please forgive me for causing you such sadness."

Mother held me tight stating, "All your father and I wanted was a family. We had no idea just how hard things were going to be on you. As your mother, I just want you to be safe and happy. It tears me up inside having to watch you doing things that your elders cannot do. I just hope that after all of this you can become a just man with love and compassion for others."

Lowering my head, I convinced her by saying, "Mother, all I can say is that right now sadness is in all of our hearts, even Uncle Lucifer. So, if his heart changed in such a short time, I can only hope that when it is time to rebuild, we can all look back at what transpired. And we, too, can grow as a species. After all, no race is above growing to become better for if not, they seal their fate and will perish."

In Satan We Trust

With my family and friends in my vision I announced, "We all have much to do, so I ask you all to sit down for one last meal before we part ways to do what we must to ensure that peace and joy is the order of the next generation."

With that being said, everyone began whipping up a feast worthy of kings. As we dined, laughter filled the air and memories of time long past were the topic. By the time dessert was being enjoyed by all, the discussion became more current and much less joyful.

"Father", I inquired, "Could you please fill everyone's glass as I wish to make a toast."

Jesus shook his head and replied proudly, "No, my son. You may have the pleasure and I'll bet when you do, it will be better than anything I could produce."

Lifting my cup high into the air, I miraculously felt the weight change and all the others smiled as their glasses filled so I toasted, "Here's to family and friends. Though we are entering one of the darkest times, most of us have been witness that we are ushering in a time of peace and even though the things we must do seem cruel, do understand that man has brought this upon himself and with the next rebirth, man is on his final chance to exist. For if they are truly unable to correct the apparent flaw they suffer from, I myself will extinguish the flame forever more. May you all go forth and complete your task, so we may all meet back here to celebrate friends and family once again. CHEERS!"

In Satan We Trust

One by one they said their goodbyes to each other and headed off to bring Armageddon to man. Stumbling into the field after perhaps one too many toasts, I sat down on a quite large boulder and began working on sewing a Santa jacket. I wanted to create my finest coat yet, as this was sure to be the last joyous Christmas for many years to come. As I contemplated the coming days, water works from my sensitive being fell on the material and formed a snowflake pattern. The reindeer were thinking about their fate, wondering if this was to be their last run and what was to become of them. Finishing my jacket after a few hours, I slipped into it and informed the reindeer, "It's ok. I promise you each year we will make the trip. the magic of Christmas must live on. I believe that it's the only hope for mankind!" I must admit, the Santa suit fit just about perfectly, enough slag for comfort and tight enough to look like the sexy Santa I was.

Louie patting my back with his hand and reminded me, "Santa is in your soul again. May I be the first to wish you a Merry Christmas season?" He outreached his arm presenting me a candy cane. "This one's for you," he finished. And I loaded up the sleigh with enough candy to last the entire season. I start eating my candy and suddenly all my worries faded away, like a worn-out paint job.

During the next couple of days, Louie and I walked among the humans passing out candy canes when through the crowd appeared Lucifer. "Nice jacket, Nephew. You've really outdone yourself this time." Could he be here possibly to officially hand the torch to me? Only time would tell.

In Satan We Trust

Helping himself to a handful of candy canes, he surprisingly began dispersing them with a familiar glow to his face, almost like when he was reunited with Saliene.

"Uncle, I must admit that I'm confused. The humans can see you. what's up with that?"

Lucifer offered a small girl a sticky candy cane informing me, "Ever since you removed my horns, I've been becoming more comfortable with my looks and I just thought that doing this gives you so much joy. I just thought that I'd like to help you. Maybe see how it feels to walk a mile in your shoes. After all, I've filled the role of Satan, so I hope you don't mind if I tag along." Was this a test for me or Louie, I wondered.

My heart, elated as much as a 16-year-old boy losing his virginity I promised, "Uncle, any time you spend time with me, I'm honored and happy to get to spend time together."

The next few weeks soared by, Christmas came and went, and Uncle had a bounce in his step and a smile that just makes you want to smile too. New Jersey and you – perfect together!

"I want to thank you, Nephew. The last three weeks were so much fun. I can't thank you enough. I kind of hate to get back to the task at hand," he announced.

Before leaving, he strolled happily up to all the reindeer and gave them all a pat on the head and a carrot. The reindeer thought to themselves that it was hard to believe that he was the same guy who had been dealing in pain and hate for centuries. He then shook Louie's hand admitting, "My man, you have been wronged by me and I'm sorry. Well, back to work." Since he apologized to Louie for wronging him in the past, was Lucifer prepared to hand the torch to Louie in an effort of forgiveness?

In the following days, devastation, the likes of which man has never seen before, plagued the lands. Fire, earthquakes, cyclones, hurricanes, volcanic eruptions, freezing temperatures, blizzards, and lightning storms had taken their toll on modern man and killing someone to take what you need or just want became the law of the land. Man, unfortunately, had turned on himself. Billions upon billions were dead. Small gangs were formed and none of them trusted each other. The smarter ones hunkered down, others actively hunted out those they viewed as a threat. Me and Louie became tired of having to see man's true face. Louie had made sure I had not had to kill anyone, but he has laid a path of dead who had tried to stop us. We have once again returned to the forest where we recalled good times and bad. But were there more bad times to come? Would they be bad enough to cause a termination to our friendship? Only the loss of the torch and not becoming Satan could cause that.

In Satan We Trust

It's Not Always As It Seems

"Louie," I said, "My body aches all the time. what's going on? This body was supposed to maintain its condition all the time. Am I just so full of sorrow that I can't bare it any longer," I told him. This was the time, if any, for Louie to come clean to me. If it didn't happen then, perhaps it never would. Would he, indeed, tell me that he was going to be Satan?

Louie shuffled over to a fruit growing by my seat at the table and picked it. His eyes, filling with water, presented the edible delight it to me requesting, "Eat this!" He was lost in thought and started trembling. "It's almost time to take your place with your own kind," He announced.

Yawning I queried, "So, how does this work now? I don't go into another vessel, I just what, do the moth to a butterfly thing?"

Through the forest appeared Koda. Speaking, he asked, " 'Sup, grrruys?" I realized his last word was a combination of a growl and the word 'guys'. He's pretty cool that way.

"Koda, you sure are a site for sore eyes," I told him.

How's everyone," the might Koda asked while looking at me and then Louie.

"Wwwwaaiiitn." Replied Koda.

"Ok, we're ready, right Louie," I asked.

Louie cleared his throat stuttering, "Not just yet. I need more time."

Koda growled, "Timmme nnnowww."

I suggested, "Louie let's just go down now and we'll come back later."

Louie turned to me exclaiming, "You can't go. You have to leave that body here. Koda, you go back and tell them."

I interrupted, "No! I don't fucking care what they threaten to do to me."

The Mighty Hellhound's eyes glowed a deep, dark red color while screaming at the top of his canine lungs, "FFOOOOLLL!"

I jumped in between the two, like a boxing referee and demanded, "Koda, you go home. I will straighten out Louie."

Koda stared Louie down. It looked like a hand-wresting competition until I yelled, "KODA, I SAID GO. You're my friend and believe me you want to keep it that way. Now, go back to Hell and tell everyone to just be patient." With, that Koda turned and started on his journey home.

Louie, pointing to the table asked serenely, "Sean, can I speak with you?" This was it I decided. He was going to finally tell me he was the chosen one to become Satan, not me.

While resting at the table, I reached for two empty glasses and raised them up as high into the air as I could get them. Momentarily they filled with ice cold beer. "This seems like a conversation we are gonna need drinks for," I informed Louie.

"I've never heard you defy them before. What's wrong, my friend? Wait, you called me 'Sean'. You haven't used that name in quite some time," I stated. He *was* going to tell me after all and I'm surely glad I had a drink in my hand.

Setting my drink in front of me, I passed Louie one of the filled glasses of beer. Before he could totally reach his hand out in an effort to accept the drink, his hand, still trembling, finally gained the strength to take it. Chugging it down like a college fraternity brother, he admitted, "Sean, I've become attached to this guy right here. I mean we had a great time. Before, with all the other lives of yours, I was always around in some way or other and I've liked each one of them, but I've been with you as a friend and for once in my life I found someone who I have never doubted was a true friend. This is why Satan wants to save the human race and when you are dead, Satan may come back and never find someone like you. Then he will probably wipe out all human life on the planet." Confusion struck me once again as he was being evasive as to whom Satan would be.

Feeling like the wind had just been knocked out of me emotionally, I said, "Louie, I think you're a bit confused. I *am* Satan and I am Sean. Louie, shaking his head in disagreement disagreed, "Satan, I'm talking with Sean. See here's the problem with what your parents have done. Satan, I hope you will feel the same about me when you're born; but Sean is going to die. His soul will go to Hell and I hope you treat him like Sean has treated the souls in Hell. However; while in this body, I don't know exactly who Satan will turn out to be. You see, without his contribution, you share his heart but not his soul. The future is uncertain, but you have learned things from him. I just hope that you retain his compassion, my friend. Maybe I should have told you this sooner, so you could thank him, but your race feels superior to humans and they are of value. You just never gave this man a thought. Once you found out you were Satan, you just assumed you were you and let the memory of him fade even though he still is just as much Satan as Satan is Sean. Remember, it's not always as it seems. Sean's my friend and *you're* my master. Was he trying to convince me to stay as 'Sean'?

"Louie, it's me, Sean. I believe you are confusing the boy, but I think he will still be a good man. Put your fears to rest. I share so much more with Satan and he feels the same as I do especially towards you," I implored.

Louie, appearing relieved stated, "Sean, you're still young you don't have to die. The whole 60 60 60 deal doesn't have to come." He reached into his jacket and pulled out the jerky. You can still live forever." He wanted to be Satan. Of that, I was certain.

Rising from the table, like Lazarus did, and accepting the jerky from Louie, he admitted, "My dear friend, I must confess something to you. Last year when that hole opened in my chest and you became so very saddened, I did something that I told you I wouldn't do. I read your mind and I knew what they wanted you to do. I also had visions from the gift you gave me, and I believe I can help you." This vision I was speaking of was not the conversation vision. This was a totally different vision. I had forgotten about it until now.

Louie stood up stating, "Sean, I just cannot do it. You changed my life for the best. I just want my friend to live a long, healthy life. You can choose to change your destiny. As you say, 'things aren't always what they seem'. Whatever happened to you making your own destiny?"

"Louie, I know you care deeply for our friendship and you've taken chances that could severely cause you an eternity of misery, but I also understand the reason why. Satan assured me that your loyalty is admirable, and he won't let anyone punish you when we're done here," Sean exclaimed.

Louie, tears rolling down his face like a waterfall answered, "None of that matters. I still won't do it. I've watched all your other lives die, mostly by horrific means. I just think if they have any mercy, they could let you die peacefully instead of the way it has to be done to fill the silly 60 60 60 bullshit."

In Satan We Trust

I tried my best to ease poor Louie's pain saying, "Louie, I have been aware of how I was going to die or be born and I'm ok with it, please don't let me be the reason you don't finish your job."

Louie, sobbing uncontrollably by this time replied, "I refuse to do it! For once in my life, I want to do the right thing. I've found through you the real reward of doing that which is honorable. If I do this, I will for certain have a black soul and then all you've done for me will be lost. Dropping to his knees, he begged me, "Please, I've found peace. don't make me return to being an assassin. Without a soul, I felt like a man once again, a man of conviction."

"I need to ask you a question, Louie. As you know, they are all waiting for Satan to arrive and they have a schedule and they will stop at nothing to meet their deadline. Do you plan on taking on all of Hell to try to save me? And if I know my warriors, they will take you alive and force you to watch while someone kills me. I told you I would never lie to you. I would much rather have you do this than suffer. For me, it's going to happen one way or the other and as I say I've seen the end and you must do it," I explained.

Removing Cain's blade from where it was hidden in my attire, and pulling Louie to his feet, I placed the blade in his hand, looked him square in the eyes saying, "I love you, my friend." Was he going to plunge it into himself and become Satan or stab me, so I would finally take Satan's role? I had to keep my faith in him as a friend, the dearest friend I had ever had in all my lives. My bet was *I* would be Satan, but it's not always as it seems.

In the beginning it was like a tug-of-war or an arm-wrestling match, but I continued eye-to-eye contact with him. With the blade securely in his hands, I thrust his hands forward plunging the blade into my chest. As Louie's eyes widened and a brilliant white light poured out of my chest I continued, "I'm sorry, Louie. But it's the only way I could save you."

My mortal body hit the ground as Louie collapsed in a heap, crying out and he decided then and there that he would never leave that spot, as that was where his most egregious act was committed, and his soul died. Louie was, for the lack of better words, an emotional mess, like Billy Bibbit in *One Flew Over The Cukoo's Nest,* lying on the ground like a hunter's prized bear skin rug.

Poor Louie was just a shell of his former self from that time forward. He was last seen much later on a rock in the forest sitting crossed-legged, Indian style, reading the book titled *Catch 22* by Joseph Heller, longing for and missing his long-time friend. After all, Sean did suggest he read the book someday.

In Hell, through the molten lava arises an amber crystal form. Satan has arrived and as his eyes opened, a tiny tear streamed down his face and he says out, "LOUIE!"

Made in the USA
Middletown, DE
12 September 2019